CW00506908

First published 2014 by Jurassic London
SW8 1XN, Great Britain
www.jurassic-london.com

Cover shows *Resolution* by Howard Hardiman
www.howardhardiman.com

Artwork by Gary Northfield (www.garynorthfield.com), based on original imagery from the collection of the National Maritime Museum.

978-0-9928172-1-3 (Trade)
978-0-9928172-3-7 (eBook)

Printed and bound by Imprint Digital, Exeter, UK

eBook conversion by handebooks.co.uk

IRREGULARITY

art by
Gary Northfield &
the National Maritime Museum

cover by
Howard Hardiman

edited by
Jared Shurin

To failure

CONTENTS

IRREGULARITY

Excerpted from the "missing diary" of Augusta Noel, recently discovered in a cache of documents in Penwith. Reproduced by kind permission of Nicholas Harkaway.

MY MOTHER WAS ONE of those women of a type I have come to dislike intensely, who believe that everything in their mothers' days was better than it will be in their daughters', and she was constantly caught between the desire to commiserate with me for my lot and the overwhelming need to blame me for this fall. She could read, for example, but chose not to, lest her head fill with an unfashionable weight of ideas, and, in consequence, she opposed my going to university or indeed being educated in anything much beyond the management of a household and the aesthetics of the person. A well-bred girl should perhaps know about music and even play an instrument, but if so it should be one which did not expose the person to undue sensuality. This meant neither a stringed instrument where vibration may pass from the instrument's body – scandalously designed in a caricature of femininity and therefore somehow party to mysteries of sex I should absolutely not come to hear of, despite my possession in some measure of every feature thus described – to the flesh of the player; nor a woodwind instrument which might by excitation of the lips stimulate earthy passions. Brass, of course, was simply too manly and forceful for a young girl. The lesser harp, she averred, was ideal because the tone was delicate and flowery and the playing was a minor mortification, being uncomfortable to the back and shoulders and miserable for the soft skin of the fingers. The great harp was quite unacceptable, being a toy for courtesans and foreign adventuresses.

My father had entertained a string of such foreigners, each more glamorous and aristocratic than the last as his renown as a gentleman engineer increased, so one might suspect her of partisanship in this last, but in truth, I think she was glad when he removed himself to Tunis with a woman who optimistically claimed the title of princess from her minute fiefdom in Bohemia. It meant, at least, that she was free of his incessant explosions. The tinkle of glassware and the smell of burning did not sit well with her, no more than the stark, Newtonian understanding of nature which he applied not only to the world of inert objects but also to human beings. It was his conviction that people, like billiard balls, must first be impelled and will then move onwards until intercepted, and that any deviation must be due to a spin imparted at the outset of their journey. For my father, the world was a linear progression made up of linear progressions, so that the planet and the sun rolled through space, and on them we all rolled as well, along the cushions and across the felt, knocking into one another and producing the appearance of chance or choice. This, my mother said, was both offensive and ridiculous, and she would not have him tell me such things, nor any of his other modern notions, and now he was gone with his fancy woman and his vile, stinking chemistry, well, there at least was an end to it.

That he continued to govern my education, under laws of patriarchy which I myself subsequently worked to overthrow, was a conundrum for us both. He enabled my present intellectual breadth as surely as she would have prevented it had she had the means. To assert her right to make me in the image she desired, she must accept the arguments I advanced into the face of her stony disapproval. To bring me up short, in turn, as I railed at her, she needed only to observe that had she been properly enfranchised – very much against her better judgment – I most assuredly should not be. Thus we lived until her death in an analogue of that place posited by the French mathematician, Lagrange, where opposing forces cancel one another and the field of events, though in tension, acts as if it is uncontested.

For all that, this is not the story of my family arguments, but the story of how I came to know that the world is more strange than my father ever imagined or my mother ever acknowledged, and it begins with her death, which was abrupt but hardly unexpected.

She died on All Fool's Day, the first of April, a celebration she found entirely odious for its frivolity and for its lingering sense of licence and misrule. The annual upending of certainties and established orders which was traditional in the Middle Ages was to her a lower class amusement – it did not occur to her to search for irony in this perception – and as such was to be avoided and dismissed by anyone who perceived themselves as coming from quality. This it must be acknowledged she did, and we did, for generations back on either side, without any possibility of denay. I inherited her effects – my parents had no other children and my father would have insisted on an equitable disbursal of funds and objects even if it were otherwise, primogeniture being one of those customs he most considered wasteful. How many bad kings has England suffered, he wrote to me once from his Tunis palace, that had wise sisters or strong mothers?

Among these effects was an envelope addressed to me, made out in her somewhat flowery cursive script, within which was the singular and unanticipated instruction that I present myself at the town offices of a solicitor named M_____ and upon demand announce to him a succession of nonsensical words, which must be sung to an enclosed musical score. This I did, to the profound mutual embarrassment of myself and Mr. M_____, and he in consequence agreed that he had certain instructions in turn: that he must pass to me a key to a certain house, and bring me safely to the door. In anticipation of my arrival and my positive identification as my mother's daughter, he had taken the liberty of hiring two former army men who would perform that last office and remain at my disposal for the remainder of the day. In they came, Mr. Buck and Mr. Trimble, and a more unlikely brace of guardians you never saw: they had narrow, mistrustful eyes and huge-knuckled hands, and skin made rough and brown by time spent, M____ said, in the Afghan mountains. Neither man spoke, and I realised that here was a true challenge of my mettle. Today, for this brief time, I was their commander, a post other women had occupied in these last feverish years: Jane Digby had her Bedou and Sardarni Sada Kaur fought for her kingdom. I stiffened my spine and inspected them, without the vaguest notion of what to look for, but under this scrutiny they instinctively fell into a sort of parade rest, and when I turned to go their manner was crisper and more confindent than it had been a few moments before.

The cab ride from M____'s office to the house lasted no more than a quarter of an hour, but in that time my imaginations were remarkably lurid and bizarre. I imagined for the first moments that I had given myself into the grip of some remarkable religious conspiracy and should shortly be captured and taken by nuns to an out of the way place, and there live out my life at my mother's behest as a prisoner unless I should in some manner counterfeit the symptoms of redemption according to instructions she had given, and be released into the keeping of a suitably masterful – yet dispassionate – husband.

My next thought, at the extreme remove, was that she had for all of her life been the proprietress of a bordello – or more, a seraglio – so staggeringly licentious that only the most corrupt and the most powerful might enter. I pictured myself discovering that, far from having been against the act of sex on principle, my mother had been the greatest expert in the permutations and possibilities between human bodies in matters of pleasure and excess that the Empire possessed, and that my father had not left her in pursuit of greater eroticisms but lesser ones, or had gone off with her blessing to pursue his own mastery of the craft she had imparted to him. My experience in this regard being somewhat uncertain and hasty at best, I was concerned that I should be at a disadvantage vis à vis my employees. From this it followed that I might have to learn about and experience, for good and sufficient reasons of practical governance, all the most outré indecencies that man had devised. I found I did not entirely quail at this prospect.

In quick succession thereafter I imagined myself the heir to a lost kingdom, to a criminal organisation trading in opium, and to an alchemical order preserving the secrets of antiquity.

What never occurred to me for one moment was what I actually saw when I opened the door and stepped through the narrow opening, Mr. Buck and Mr. Trimble loitering in the street to see off any opportunistic thief.

It was a library.

I was seized immediately with a sense of weight, as if the presence of so many books created a concrete pressure on the mind as a concentration of gas does upon the inner workings of the ear. I felt that the thinking aspect of my self lay like a droplet upon a flat surface and the pressure must soon cause me to boil and become vapour, slowly dispersing in space. This feeling was so certain, so intimate, that it appeared to come from within my body. I stepped back and slammed the door.

The afterimage of thousands of books hung imprinted on my eyes. It did not matter to me if each and every one was full of provable falsehoods and stupidities: any text is an image of a mind, and any mind is worthy of attention. A book is a portrait not only of what it is about but also of its author: between the lines of text is the ghostly impression of a person. A library, by extension, is a mosaic describing its librarian. In this house was not only a gathering of educated thinkers preserved on paper but also the last residing flavour of my mother, and it was a flavour most covert, most occluded and concealed, that she had revealed to me only now that she was dead. I felt that for the first time in my adult experience we were about to have a real conversation.

The toughs were still behind me, taking some amusement from my actions. To men accustomed to standing down smugglers and thieves in the alleys of Cheapside and enforcing the collection of debts from drunken officers of the cavalry waving pistols in all directions, no doubt a house full of books is a slight enemy and one easily dispatched with matches. For a moment I thought to rebuke them, but then realised that it was obliquely a compliment: neither of them would mock a lady of quality, but both would feel free to find amusement in the folly of a superior officer. From which it followed, however, that I must find my courage or lose their respect. I drew breath and opened the door once more. The effect was no less astonishing the second time, but preparation was evidently some defense, as I was not blasted back over the threshold but found my feet, and was able to come into the room and stand at the centre, taking stock.

The walls were entirely covered up with shelves, and these were entirely full of a broad-ranging catalogue covering the latest work on the natural sciences and extensive political discourses and the arts. Burke was there, and Condorcet, and so too were Newton, Hooke, and Leibniz. There was no obvious logic to their arrangement: Milton rubbed shoulders with Euler, Lavoisier with Metastasio, and yet as the eye travelled around the room there was an appropriateness to the placements, a sense of journey and of balance. I felt that if I were to begin at any point in the maze I would find myself guided by implication or quotation to nearby texts and thence outwards in a webwork of reference, inspiration, inference and opposition. Likewise if I placed my hand upon a book I knew – there were few enough that I could claim to know well, but these were immediately apparent to me because the brain apprehends the names of things it understands more clearly than those it finds yet mystifying – I determined that behind my back I would find some inverted image either of the content or the character of the text. The disquisition on anamnesis in the *Meno*, which I had always taken as a literal argument on the topic of reincarnation, I now perceived in an instant, as I looked over one shoulder and glimpsed a beautiful edition of Voltaire's *Zadig*, to be a metaphorical rumination on the nature of argument and the governing principles of the human brain.

The tables, meanwhile, waiting placidly under the stacks of newer books, suggested threads and traditions of narrative or poetic style and schools of thought.

There was only one chair, and I sat in it, entirely bewildered. I could not begin to reconcile this trove with the woman I had known, and nor could I imagine when she might have come here. Had she, then, inherited it from someone and passed it on to me as she had found it? But no: there were recent writings here: the place was maintained. Was it some gift of my father's she had withheld? Had she for some reason purchased – with what money I could not imagine – the services of an archivist and scholar to assemble it for me? Was I standing in the shadow of a person hired to create a perfect Heaven for an inquiring mind, or some diabolical Hell where every track of understanding eventually petered out in disappointment and frustration? Could someone, working with these materials, reasonably expect to stifle or to drown the urge that was in me to learn and to understand? The more I looked around, the more I thought not, but the more I believed also that I was still looking only at the shell of the egg. I passed through the library, therefore, into the other rooms of the house, but they were quite bare, literally bare, with wooden boards and shuttered windows, as if awaiting more books or, perhaps, myself, to seek out what designs and furnishings I might desire.

And then, returning no wiser to a room constructed for the most part out of the assembled understandings of mankind, I saw the book I was looking for without really knowing that I was looking, the book whose existence was implied by the position of all the others, which must surely resolve the puzzle of the library.

It rested on the table nearest the door, and a glance at the other titles told me this was a place of triage and taxonomy, for here alone the serendipitous organisation of the rest was in abeyance. This table was a muddle of new arrivals, and the most motley of them all was a smooth, remarkably precise volume, most curious in appearance.

Unlike the books around it, this one was not bound between hard covers or kept loose-leaf in a box. It was instead protected by a varnished design printed or painted onto flexible card. The covering image was unconventional, an inward spiral in browns and greys which evoked a profound sense of foreignness, in the manner I have seen where an artist from Italy is asked to work in the style of the Dutch. The final product of such commissions is almost right, but the execution comes with all the wrong signals and habits as the technique of origin is entirely different, so that the whole belongs in neither country but rather in some space in between. So it was with this book. I knew at once that there was a mathematical underpinning to what I was seeing, and that was familiar, but the way in which the thing was presented was quite alien, deriving from a different sensibility that seemed to decry ornamentation and reach for purity of form. Of course it was itself an ornament. The paradox relieved my alarm somewhat: wherever this book came from, publishers were the same there as they are anywhere else.

The book was called "Irregularity".

I opened it at random, and I read the page you have just read, and as I read on I came to these words – these, which you are reading now - and when I reached what is printed after the word "possible" I was filled with a sense of wonder and alarm. The biological aspect of what I learned was remarkable but not metaphysically challenging. The implications of what I was presently experiencing were far more significant and seemed to require that I continue with great caution. I learned, then, that at some time in the future it would be possible to create a physical replica of myself, and that she would possess none of my memories, would not be me, but that she would - will, must, and in some way already does, as evidenced by this book – nonetheless feel a curiosity about who I must have been which could only be allayed by a direct communication from myself. I would be the template on which she was built, a living architectural design, and from that inception she must inevitably derive some sense of commonality and identity, and wish to know me, just as I instinctively reach out to her, my sister, my mirror.

Following after this understanding came the stark realisation that I must right at that moment codify and condense every speculation I had ever ventured about free will and determination into a single practical decision for myself. However tempting it might be to step around the notion of fate and prove by defaulting that I was not bound to write the passage appearing in this book, such an action might have consequences beyond the rhetorical demonstration of my own freedom to act. Might my desire to demonstrate independence – itself, after all, a consequence of my earlier life – cause a misfire in the Universe and the orderly flow of time and therefore destroy or fundamentally remake the causality in which I lived? Or would I simply demonstrate that the book did not apply to me, after all, and I was just a step along its road to that person, whoever she might be, whose life greatly resembled mine to this point but thereafter diverged?

It seemed to say the least hubristic to experiment, so I ceased reading the book, and began writing instead. Paper and pen were laid by in the desk. I have not tried to remember what was written, but am writing what occurs to me, so that this is a true statement of self and a document created by me in this moment and not copied out from the Universe's later recollection as an unauthored, orphaned anomaly. I will edit it tomorrow, and by then my recollection of what was written that I did read will have faded, so what I write will govern what appears in the text and not the other way about. I am not sure if this is more of a paradox or less, but I look forward to spending some time considering that matter after I have done this thing – very likely the rest of my life.

It did not strike me, as a practical matter, remarkable that my body might be replicated. Robert Hooke, whose writings rested on a shelf but a few feet away between the travels of Al-Masudi and Mary Wollstonecroft's wonderful *Vindication*, had identified the cell in 1665, and from such tiny beginnings it now appeared everyone must come. That a future medical science should learn how to grow a person entire from a single part did not seem so remarkable, as some amphibians may regrow a limb or a tree may be germinated from a cutting, and I was assured by the evidence in my hand that it must be so. To travel backwards in time and supply me with this book, I reasoned, must surely be a sufficiently onerous task that no one would set about it merely to play a trick upon a minor scholar, any more than one would build a city in order to have somewhere to keep one's hat.

Why anyone would bother with me, in particular, I did not know, unless of course it was the presence of this message itself, with the samples of bone and blood I have appended, preserved in various chemicals and sealed as best I can like an ancient reliquary and sent with the manuscript itself into the future by way of the firm of Mr. M____.

No, the biological business I am sure is commonplace, though I suspect it is hard work. What I cannot begin to comprehend is how this book comes to be here, in this library which I might myself have assembled, which so perfectly accords with who I am that I know instinctively where something will be found and even whether it is in the shelves at all. Mr. M____ informs me that there is money, too, for the maintenance of the place and the purchase of more books. I have had more shelves built. The new books, and those upon the tables in the first room, now reside in the next. It is all quite elegant, but quite impossible, and I am half of a mind to give up and blame it upon fairies, as Wessel did in his play. I say "half", but in that I do myself an injustice. It does not occur to me to propose so mythological an explanation. If I am sure of anything, it is that no thing is unknowable, it is merely not knowable yet.

And to you, my very far off, very loved, and no doubt very curious sister, made from my old dry bones, I can offer this: that my parents were both wrong, and so no doubt am I in all sorts of things, and so too will those earnest people be who are your parents and your guardians, and they will also be right in unexpected and unintended ways. They will keep secrets, too, lesser or greater. Perhaps they will tell you how all this came to be, or perhaps they will not know either, will wonder how I came to know about you, and the mystery will run on. Who was my mother? What else did she keep from me? Why did she not tell me until this late revelation? Through this library – which Mr. M______ assures me had been hers for decades – I know her more than I ever did before. It is lonely and sad, but it is also mysterious and impossible, and her life must somehow be folded in upon itself as this book is, and the Universe embraces that, contains it, and does not suffer by it.

And that is wonderful.

A GAME PROPOSITION

Rose Biggin

WELL, NOW.

There's a hostelry in Port Royal, or there was; little to no point in going there these days, unless you've a fondness for charred things. Were you to go there yourself you'd see some old posts and a plaque but once, oh *once*, once there were people and games and frolics and what fun we had – until there wasn't any more fun to be had, if you understand me, you pretty thing.

The little cherubs you see pouting away in the corners of the map, they were free to fly and they are still, if they want to; our wings though, they were clipped one night, clipped good and proper. I'm to tell you how it came to pass.

Can you picture a tavern? A bustling one. A hubbub of excesses, picture it for me now. With barrels and spillages and pistols cocked on whims and a violently low tolerance for lack of payment, whatever you're buying. Do you have it? No, no you can't quite picture it, not correctly, not yet. Mucky it about a bit. Add more dirt. This wasn't a high-end place, and it would never pretend to be one. And for Port Royal at this time, 'twas a piece of pride to be able to boast so. Vicars used to run away from Port Royal, hankies over their mouths. Fair enough. But this place? Some of the saltiest knave dogs that ever sailed the South Seas avoided this place.

And this place, this place, this was where we would attend. Me and my girls, my fellow ladies; and whatever picture of us you've got, you might as well mucky that up a fair bit too. We didn't stand on ceremony. We didn't stand at all, hardly. Well, we would if that's what was wanted. Nan in particular was a great one for doing it standing, or leaning up against walls. No-Conscience Nan would lean up against anything you wanted. Gravestones. Peg preferred to lie, but she'd sit at a push, or a pull. Jenny was for kneeling. And I – what was it that charming lad said of me –

"as common as a barber's chair: no sooner was one out, but another was in."

His ship sank on the way home.

Look, there were worse ways to earn five hundred pieces of eight, in those days. And we weren't even in it for those pieces. We were in it for what I'm to tell you about. We were in it for the fun that follows.

So picture it, this tavern in a part of Port Royal, just afore the turn of the seventeenth into eighteenth. And picture us four, the four of us. Strumpets wenches common whores all four. Having a veritable holiday.

I rolled the dice and turned over a card. "Full flush," I said, and Nan got a blush in her cheeks to match. And not much made old No-Conscience blush, so I knew I'd made a fair move.

"Aye," said she, "you've won that on a cheeky go, have you or have you not," and with reluctant fingers she pushed her counter back over the Caribbean swells. She'd wanted to go further.

"Two points forfeit," said Peg, "and I'll be having an easterly trade-wind as yet, come cyclone, come as not."

More picturing for you to do. A board, like as your trictrac or your backgammon. Overlay 'pon it a map of the world – all of it, the whole world, the most comprehensive cartography yet, says I – then overlay *that* with a grid, and counters, and wooden posts, and pegs, and cards, and dice. Do you see it? You haven't got it quite right, my friend, but hold on to what you do have. You shan't get closer. This was our game. I say was, because we don't play it any more.

"Three cards to you, Salt-Beef, and I'll be finishing a new round at whatever latitude!" Nan rolled the dice and cackled at the result. "A-ha! I'll place my prime counter facing westwards, methinks. More than a breeze rippling along that clime, then."

Now don't get ahead of yourselves; I see you thinking, I see you thinking that No-Conscience Nan was calling herself Nan for N for North, yes? True she liked to sit in the north-facing chair but we'd ne'er be so predictable. Although there were four of us, we couldn't be divided into north and east and south and west as easily as all that.

"Indeed, Nan," said Salt-Beef, "You're playing without mercy over that coast, no mistake of mine." She moved her own counter. "In fact, I'll take three score off the degree of tempest at that latitude, if you'll barter me for half a counter on the next turn-up of cards."

Nan grunted. "I'll consider it over a little," she said, as Jenny prepared to take her turn.

You'll know very well by now that there were four of us. We were well known in this tavern – although not for what we really were, of course. Only for what we seemed to be. Corsets and rouge and tankards of gunpowder rum – you can picture it sweet, it's all right, t'aint forbidden today – and my point is in this drinking place they all knew us by name. We hadn't started out with our nicknames. We were once Nan, Peg, Jenny and me. Now we were known as something much more salty around the mouth.

No-Conscience Nan, they called her.

And Salt-Beef Peg, who was there too, this night as every night.

And as for the third of us, she had earned her nickname proud: but you'd be a fool to ask Buttock-de-Clink Jenny anything if you weren't prepared to pay well for the answer.

And then there was myself. Four of us, and those were the names the folks of Port Royal called us. A joy for it. Four of us, as I say. Four of us were enough to play 'pon the whole world until this particular evening, darling.

"Three cards," said Jenny. "And I'll wager rapids along the Thames."

"Upstream?"

"Of course."

"Then – snap!" said Peg.

"Damn you through the blasted hemisphere," said Nan, who had to miss a go now.

Once a month we would meet, and you ought to know that we would meet when the Moon was full, so that she was at her strongest and able to take over the business of the tides for us. And we would retire to the back room of the place, this tavern, the one we called ours, and there would be no business today no matter who asked for us; and we got asked for by name oftentimes enough. On game night there would only be this. The board, the counters, the dice.

"I think old Salt-Beef's bluffing," said Jenny. "I'd move your counter up the next Tropic, Nan."

"I'd agree," said Nan, "apart from the way you're moving your own along the Great Dead. You can't fool me for a fool, and I'll take two of your precious Navy shipwrecks for that." High stakes, did we play for? None higher.

And now I'm to tell you, though I can't think you deserve it, but as I said before, I've got clipped wings now, and I'm to tell you about the last game we truly played.

Jenny was counting her cards. "I'm afore the equatorial, I believe, my sweets," she said, reaching to take up the dice. "And if I can square it with a circular, I'll take two wrecks off of the Madagascar coast."

"You bloody won't!" said Peg. "I'm to pass a current up along there and sink a frigate and if you go denying me that I'll pull your hair out."

"Listen here, you trollop," said Jenny, preparing to roll. "You counted nine other –"

Then a man's voice said, "How goes the game?" and Nan nearly fell off her chair.

We glared at the intruder; Jenny stood up to stare and I tell ye, my sweet, she could loom when she wanted.

Men weren't meant to come here. Once a month was the wenches' back room for games, and all the barkeeps knew that was sacred. We four looked to each other, deciding to try words a little afore commencing violence. "Get gone," said Jenny, and Peg she growled.

The man bowed, which was a gentlemanly enough act, but he didn't go like we were asking which marked him out as a rogue to me. Nan had got her composure back and was fiddling with her hair and, if I weren't mistaken, preparing to bat her eyelashes at him, No-Conscience to the end. I could see it myself, the man had dark hair that was pleasant enough, and knowledgeable eyes and a smile that was interesting. And that's as complimentary as can be got out of me. He wasn't swaying on his feet; nor, I noted, was his jerkin completely covered in a drunkard's dribble; and so it seemed he was, if not sober, surely able-brained enough to know what he was getting himself into. Well, by that I mean us as a quart of angry ladies; nothing else. Nothing *more.*

"Might I not join you, madams?" he said. Peg took her turn to stand up now. She'd turned a shade of red she had, my lady Salt-Beef, and she was cursing fit to make the northern breezes blush.

"We don't invite anyone to play with us," said Jenny, fierce old Buttock-de-Clink. "It's a game for four, with dire consequences. Get you out."

The man looked at our board, the pieces strewn about mid-game. "I'm new in Port Royal," he said. "I sail aboard the *Roebuck*. Before that I'm from London. From England." At our ignoring him he bloody well kept on, did he not know wiser? The next thing he said gave his wherefroms away even if he hadn't just told us: he was truly an Englishman no matter how far flung he would ever travel, for as a conversational gambit he disparaged his home weather. "Plenty worse than these climes, the weather in England. Damn rain and the drizzle."

That did it. We won't take comments about the weather, not on game night.

"Now look here," said No-Conscience Nan, screwing up a paper boat she'd been idly making out of an abandoned bible page, and in doing so damning a thousand sailors. "You whipsnap," she said, "I'd break you in half across my knees if I didn't think ye'd – "

"Confound you for a fool," said Salt-Beef Peg, "if you think ye'll be getting anywhere with us walking in here uninvited and for – "

"Blast you with a thousand blizzards!" said Buttock-de-Clink Jenny, and with a slam of her hand she trumped enough cards to make the rain fall even harder that autumn in his home city.

He took our anger, soaked it up. He bowed again, at me this time.

"My name is William Dampier," he said. "May I join your game?"

Looking backwise, at this point we might have made everything different, and all right for us; and the worse for you. But at the time there was something about his nerve that made me want to test it for a turn or two.

"Sit," I said. "Join us." The others looked at me, Nan starting to enjoy it, Peg not sure, Jenny fuming like a soggy bonfire. "It seems safe enough," I said, "to add a player for a single round." I placed a new counter on the board, near the mark that – how was he to know? – signified the *Roebuck*.

Peg saw. "That's a naughty tidal wave you're sending on, there!" she said.

"Don't tell him," I said. Peg shook her lovely locks; she wouldn't. Nan's eyes glinted.

"Tell me what?" he said.

"Tell you what," I said, "Let's talk stake. I'm telling Salt-Beef strumpet not to tell you I'm betting a wager on your very own *Roebuck*, so help me, but so help you more." Even Jenny smiled when she saw what I was about.

"Ah," he said, and I hoped to the great north trade-wind that he was beginning to get the weight of what was happening here. Nan whistled in appreciation – and somewhere, off the coast of the Galapagos, a butterfly shuddered at the change in the air and altered its course.

"What do you want to play for?" said Jenny. "We know who you are. You're an explorer? What's that to us, who've seen the world already? You hothead, layabout sailor, no-good-for-nothing-"

"You needn't bait him any more than we do by our existing here," I said.

I rolled, I moved the piece. Peg tapped her nails on the board. She had a splinter she was using for her place-marker; it was from the wreck of Sir Clowdisley's *Association*, the naughty girl. That boat was nothing but splinters now. She'd won it off a lucky throw months afore, landed not just that flagship but the *Romney* and the *Eagle* sunk down in the Scillies.

Now, I –

What's that, you say? The *Association* sunk in seventeen-oh-seven; and yet Dampier's map came out in sixteen-ninety-nine, and wasn't that when we got our wings clipped, so how could Peg be playing with a piece of driftwood before the ship had even got wrecked? Well, aye. You ask and I'll answer as straight as I can. It's most certainly true that we were put down in our power as the century turned. Dampier did what he done, no doubt of it; but to this day we've still got some strength in us, and some of our bets take a long while to pay off. Old Nan, she was playing with a piece of metal set to go down in northern waters many, many years ahead, in a freezing cold sea and with severe want of lifeboats; she was always a shrewd spreader of bets. I've still a hold of a piece of white plastic from a vessel that's yet to begin its time on the seabed. Now if you'll let me continue.

"Will you take a turn clockwise or widdershins?" I said. "I'm to play half-crosswise, old No-Conscience here goes whichever way suits her." Salt-Beef Peg in the meantime moved a small pawn across a continent of her choice; and rolled a dice to confirm the co-ordinates of her new cyclone.

I do hope you are paying attention to the rules, by the way.

I'll say this for our man William Dampier. We played rings around him, and at our every roll of the dice the currents and the tides and the winds played havoc with themselves over the open ocean, swooping around an erratic course like a child's spinning-top. But through it all he did seem to be trying his best. And also he kept on talking, the rat. Twas all small-talk – none smaller – until just before the seventh round.

"Tis a risky game for a man who travels the ocean," he said, "to seek new lands, and chart them. But a greater danger, as I see it, is to seek to know the course of the winds." His eyes twinkled at mine and I leaned forward to look into them more close-like. It was curious, what I saw.

I do hope you are paying attention to the rules.

Now I don't know where the man William Dampier got his information. Don't think us omniscient. We aren't. How he knew what we were, and, further to that, how he knew what our game was about, *truly* about, is a mystery to me.

My corset was heaving against the edge of the playing board – I'd pushed it there as a test – but Dampier's eyes didn't flicker there once; in point of fact, Dampier was smiling but not really at my body, nor even at my face. He was looking at the ravaging storms and the swirling currents that swelled beneath the façade of wench I went by in those days. Somehow, he knew me for what I really was. When he looked at me, he saw the winds.

It made me daring. "If only a man had arrows," I said, "to shew him a course along those general and coasting winds, for they're pernicious things indeed, or so I hear." *I'll punish you for knowing*, I thought; *and you can watch*. I dealt him a card and the final round was begun.

Dampier lost. Bored of tracking his personal travels, Buttock-de-Clink Jenny took a wider approach and sunk a naval brigade in a vicious typhoon that wasn't to strike for a century. No-Conscience Nan asserted it so Dampier's *Roebuck* wouldn't sink – she was too fond of his lovely dark hair for that, I could see her thinking it – but she did snarl his journeys enough that it would be a decade before he got home. Salt-Beef Peg whipped up some currents that would get him court-marshalled for cruelty. Twas he and I who were really at chess. I chased his play a whole three times around the world.

Seek to know the course of the winds, indeed. Nobody had known the course of us yet. So I shook his hand at the end of it all, and I told him thus; "the winds might not be forever at your back, sir, as the old blessing goes – but you've earned yourself a curious stare or two."

And then we four departed about our usual fair and foul business across Port Royal. Ah, what more to tell?

It was sixteen-ninety-nine when the Discourse was published, to great acclaim, of course, you'll know this; and a jack sailing into Port Royal brought the newly-published map into our company. Nan stole it from him during a tryst, brought it screaming to the rest of us.

A diary of journeys and travels, descriptions of fauna and beasts – not news to us, nothing of interest. No, 'twas one of the charts made us tremble:

A Discourse of Trade-Winds, Breezes, Storms, Tides and Currents

A map of the world. Much like our playing board without the grid and the counters. Without the cards and the cribbage sticks, without the dice. But with – oh, what the map did have. All demarcated, set down, drawn on, made official, there in permanent pen and ink and etching.

William Dampier, I thought. You absolute cock of a bugger.

"He's mapped us," said Jenny, in a tone that meant murdered us. It wasn't necessary to say so; we all knew. In truth we'd sensed it a long time afore Dampier's damned publication. Somehow, after the game he'd played with us, the game I now consider our last, our dice hadn't rolled the higher numbers, and our cards were dealt into bad hands, and our darts had missed their marks.

"Look there," said Jenny, pointing to the map's southern edge. In an illuminated strip writ to look like a scroll, Dampier's own spidery writing suggested that navigators "Note, that the *Arrows* among the *Lines* shew *Course* of those *General & Coasting* winds." I went to the board, none of my sisters stopped me, and I smashed the counters to pieces. Even as I did so, I knew I hadn't powers to sink. Not now.

Stupid myself, I thought. Fool of a – I'd let our vanity get ahead of us. We'd mocked him for daring to play us at currents and storms, and of course we were the better players and of course he hadn't won. But that had never been the intention. He'd seen us playing, and that was enough. The game – the true game, the game his challenge to us *represented* – *that* game had been lost as soon as I'd put the dice into his hands.

For a brief while we continued to meet, playing for matchsticks. But it wasn't the same now our power was pretence. Our monthly games fizzled out like damp dynamite to nothing. Like Dampier intended when he mapped us. We left Port Royal, one by one, not long after.

How do you map the winds? Did you think the answer was to play dice with them? Shipwrecks determined by chess? Cribbage for controlling currents, poker to pinpoint a tempest, trictrac for typhoons – backgammon, darts, beggar-thy-trade tides? That's how Dampier did it. He didn't have to win, you see. Not in those days. He only had to get a look at the board. Pay attention quietly, note what he saw, then go away and write it up with accuracy, vigour and vim. "A Discourse of Trade-winds", published sixteen-ninety-nine. To this day it makes my very breath itch. I'll give you a discourse of trade-winds, my darlings.

I am brought to my main purpose. I say it here. This is my reason for telling you, for finally getting it down into words, what Dampier did, truly *did*. I have told this story in order to announce that I, I, yes I indeed, I myself, the very I – I say that I challenge you – yes you, my dear of dears – I challenge you to a rematch.

I will play with any he, she or they who wishes to take me up on the game. There ought to be enough information in these preceding words for you to divine the rules; and this time, of course, the mere sight of play won't be enough. You will be required to win. Now, do not consider me unfair. In the case of your victory I promise you more knowledge, for there is much more you can know; there are many things that can yet be prevented. In return, we will play for double the stakes – I'll take it all away, I say, and everything will change.

If you don't turn up, I might play on my own and mess things about in any case. It's in your interest, then, yes? Wait until the moon is full, and find me.

THE SPIDERS OF STOCKHOLM

E. J. Swift

BEFORE THERE WERE THE SPIDERS there was the emptiness. The emptiness made its home in the space beneath Eva's bed, a narrow and dusty cavity but large enough to accommodate the body of a small, nimble girl. There were times when it was necessary to hide inside the emptiness. Times such as when Eva's mother could be heard roaming from room to room and weeping, a process which might go on for hours, the sound ebbing and falling like a music box which plays its course and is wound again.

Ever since the news of Eva's father, Eva's mother had divided her time between weeping and cursing Axel von Fersen. Without his Pomeranian ambitions, Eva's father would undoubtedly not have been posted to Straslund, nor killed there in such ignominious circumstances. Now they were alone in the world, and so was Sweden. At first Eva had cried too. It was expected. But a year had passed, and her life went on as it had. When she thought about her father she felt mostly a sense of bewilderment, that this man in his meticulous uniform – a man she had only limited memories of, whose military boots and epaulettes seemed ill-suited to his quiet, reserved demeanour and passion for butterfly collecting – had occupied a space and now was gone.

Like the emptiness, Captain Lindberg was an absence. A before. But he had always been an absence. In death, he had somehow become more prominent than in life. That was the confusing thing.

Eva liked to imagine herself in places where emptiness did not matter, where emptiness was in fact the norm. The sea, for example. Before last year, the sea had been a regular feature in the Lindberg household, a source of pride and delight, related as it was to the shininess of buttons and the deeds (noble, Eva's mother said) performed by Eva's father when he was not at home in Stockholm – which was most of the time. But the sea was no longer safe. The sea was an accomplice, the thing which, along with the Prussians, had snatched away Eva's father and committed his body to the deeps.

Eva did not realize the full repercussions of this taboo until it affected her daily expeditions. Birgitte always took her to the waterfront, where they would look at the sea and the seagulls and the great tall ships of the Swedish East India Company, and conjure up heroic acts enacted upon faraway seas. At least, Eva would think of heroic acts, and Birgitte would fuss, about her skirts, or her eating habits. Eva, although she loved Birgitte very much (perhaps even more than her mother, whose love was a perilous and unpredictable thing) would wish Birgitte a thousand miles away, while she remained free to scale rigging and spy though telescopes. On a good day, Birgitte permitted her to speak to the sailors and ask questions. Eva liked to know the words for all the different parts of the ship. *Topsail*, they told her, as she pointed. *Bowsprit. Foremast. Stern.* This was how their afternoons went.

Until after Captain Lindberg.

Suddenly, Eva and Birgitte were taking different routes – carefully engineered routes which avoided so much as a glimpse of the sea.

"What about the ships?" Eva asked, when it had become clear that their new regime was not an accident of time and Birgitte's bad memory, as Birgitte claimed. "When are we seeing the ships?"

Birgitte said they would not be going to the harbour any more.

"But why not?"

"Your mother doesn't like it."

The emptiness, Eva thought. It had expanded out of the house, seeping into the streets. She felt a tug of resentment towards her mother, whose indiscriminate weeping had the power to consume even the smallest of pleasures.

It took time to convince Birgitte that this was a secret they could keep between them. Even after she agreed, the maid did not look comfortable. Birgitte would huff and shiver and complain about the bitterness of the sea air, in an effort to move them on quickly. The gulls, she said, flew too low. They might swipe at Eva's hair, or drop something unmentionable upon her dress. There was a certain look when her eyes fell upon Eva, which Eva did not at first understand. Birgitte felt sorry for her.

The look shocked Eva; Birgitte was not meant to be sorry about anything. You don't have to be sad, she wanted to say. I don't miss Father. Her mother missed him, of course, but even this Eva struggled to comprehend. How could you miss a person who had never been present, the sudden permanence of whose absence was less of a surprise than an inevitable conclusion? But she knew that Birgitte would be horrified by this sentiment. Adults had ways of talking, roundabout ways which seemed to thrive by ignoring the exact matter of the conversation. So she said nothing. She looked at the ships and set her imagination loose upon the nearest one. All at once she found herself sailing to distant, undiscovered continents.

Eva had mentioned this sailing desire to Birgitte only once. The maid looked scandalized and said such notions were not suitable for a young lady.

There were many things, Eva was learning, which might not be spoken aloud. They lived in the emptiness, unstated, and so unfixed.

The first spider appeared with no warning. Eva woke, curled and cold one chill autumn morning, and there it was.

A large-bodied, lightly-furred one crouched in the corner of the ceiling. Her first instinct was to shout in fright, but before she could utter a word, the spider moved. Its motion was not fast and scuttling, as she expected. It was slow and careful and deliberate. As she watched, it released a single, shimmering thread of web. Eva was transfixed.

All through the morning – whilst Birgitte helped her to dress, the maid's fingers deftly working buttons and frills, whilst Eva's mother came to stand in the doorway and gaze at them and opened her mouth as if to say something and then did not, and went away, whilst Eva dutifully ate her breakfast, whilst Birgitte opened some books and asked questions about the Kings and Queens of Sweden without really expecting a response – Eva had one eye on the spider. There it was, moving delicately from strand to strand, expanding and perfecting its web.

And she knew the spider had one eye following her.

She sensed it.

When Eva and Birgitte returned from their afternoon walk the spider was gone. Eva waited impatiently for Birgitte to take her outdoor clothes, and as soon as Birgitte was in the next room she climbed onto the bed and peered up into the corner of the ceiling. A thread of web fluttered listlessly against the wall.

The disappointment was crushing.

It was clear what had happened. The housemaid had come to clean the room. Sweeping and dusting, poking into corners, she must have destroyed the web. Eva did not doubt that the spider had been killed.

It was stupid to cry, but she couldn't stop herself.

That night Eva had the most vivid dream of her life. A storm raged over the ocean, black and churning. Buffeted every which way by the winds was a ship, its sails torn to shreds, the crewmen running about the decks like ants as the ship rolled first to port, then to starboard, its masts almost touching the water with every violent list. As Eva watched (from a distance – she was flying, she thought) a bolt of lightning smote the ship and it exploded, masts splintering and toppling, bows wrenching apart. From its exposed interior streamed gold. Threads of gold, wriggling through the black sea. Veils of gold, settling upon the surface of the waves. Airborne gold rising in feathery plumes, scooped up by the many legs of spiders, who suspended their webs from the clouds to catch the gold, and devour it.

Eva.

Someone was calling her name.

Eva.

She opened her eyes and gasped. The spider was directly over her head, dangling from a slender thread. She could see the individual hairs on its segmented body and its many, twitching legs.

"Spider," she whispered.

The spider moved quickly then, scurrying up the thread, across the ceiling and down the wall too quickly for Eva to follow.

It was the same spider, she was certain of it. Somehow, it had survived.

The discovery filled her with delight, until Birgitte arrived. Her appearance presented a fresh dilemma. The spider would spin another web. That was what spiders did. The housemaid would return, the room would be cleaned, and the spider's home would be lost once more. Unless Eva could find a way to save it, the spider's fate remained uncertain.

An idea came to Eva. Over breakfast, she brushed some crumbs into a napkin, and when Birgitte's head was turned, shook the napkin quickly under the bed.

Eva's mother sidled around the door. At her breast she was wearing a pin given to her by Captain Lindberg. Her fingertips brushed over the surface of the pin in a constant repetitive gesture.

"Birgitte," she said. Although her eyes were on Eva. Such anxious eyes!

"Yes, Fru?"

Eva's mother looked confused and slid from the room. She moved like water, seeming to pour herself from perch to perch, never letting go one handhold until she had grasped the next. Birgitte closed the door. Her mouth set in a pinched expression which Eva knew meant trouble, curtailed walks or a sudden enthusiasm for embroidery, but today it did not matter. Today, she had a secret.

It was a fresh, damp day for their expedition. Birgitte said there had been a storm last night. Between the wind and the thunder, she had not slept a wink.

"A storm?" Eva was surprised. "I didn't hear it."

"Fröken must sleep like the dead," said Birgitte. "God rest their souls."

They were nearing the waterfront. Birgitte peered ahead.

"What's going on here, then?"

The harbour was all commotion. Too many people, decided Birgitte, and began to lead Eva away, but the girl tugged in the other direction, and between the two of them straining and the press of the crowds they found themselves moving closer to the harbour rather than further away.

Birgitte asked the questions. It was a ship, they were told. An East India ship, almost at the completion of its journey home, capsized in the night by the storm. Its cargo had been set upon by rogue vessels.

"Pirates?" asked Birgitte in a low voice, as though by shielding Eva from the word she could protect her from their very existence. Eva listened intently.

Pirates, yes, but everyone had prospered, beggars and thieves alike. The loot must be all over Stockholm.

Eva remembered the sinuous threads of gold from her dream and grew horribly afraid. What did it mean, that she had dreamed this thing? Who wanted her to know? Now the roles were reversed; it was Birgitte who was curious to see the damage, and Eva who wanted to leave, overcome by a sick, dread feeling in her stomach.

By the end of their walk, the feeling had shifted its shape, settling into something quite different. She had known about the ship, before anybody else in Stockholm. The spider had told her.

She knew it would be waiting. Crouched in the space under the bed, occupying the emptiness. The crumbs were still scattered across the floor – the housemaid had been too lazy to sweep under here, a fact Eva had been counting on. But the spider had not touched the crumbs.

It must have been waiting all day.

For her.

"Spider," Eva whispered. She rolled a crumb towards it, watching in fascination to see what it would do.

The spider inched forwards, leg by leg. It reached the bite of bread. One foot settled lightly upon the crumb, and Eva waited, breath caught in her throat. Then the leg withdrew. The spider retreated.

It was no good. This was the wrong food.

Eva felt the spider's disappointment as a physical presence, as if strands of its web had settled upon her hair, enclosing her head in its fine meshing. She understood that the spider had given her a gift, but she had not been able to reciprocate.

The next afternoon there was no expedition. Eva's mother had a visitor. Birgitte coaxed Eva into her best dress – one so tight around the chest she could barely breathe – and brushed her hair until Eva's scalp tingled. She could feel the tingling all the way down the stairs and into the guest room, where Eva's mother was perched on the edge of her chair and a gentleman was standing by the window, admiring the view. There was something odd about the scene.

"This is Herr Gustafsson, Eva," her mother said brightly. It was her hands. They were the source of the oddness. They were not twisting around one another, as they usually did. They lay calmly in her lap.

The gentleman turned.

"So this is the little one."

Unlike most of the (recently declining) visitors to the house, Herr Gustafsson was not wearing a military uniform, but he was smartly-dressed in the fashions Birgitte liked to admire around the wealthier parts of Stockholm. His powdered hair and heavy face gave him a serious, rather lugubrious look.

"Say hello, Eva."

"Hello, Herr Gustafsson."

She sensed her mother's approval, her burst of pleasure at this exchange, an introduction that was *going well*. She tried to ignore the itching of her scalp.

"Herr Gustafsson is a man of science," said her mother.

Eva stared at Herr Gustafsson with renewed interest.

Gustafsson coughed and said it was so. He was interested, he said, in the butterfly collection of the tragically late Captain Lindberg. He, Gustafsson, was working at the Royal Academy with a great man, Carolus Linneaus. Perhaps – there was a small chance, he thought – they would have heard of Linneaus?

"No," said Eva's mother. Then, perhaps fearing this could jeopardize the fragile success of the visit, added in a flood of anxiety, "But tell us of him!"

Encouraged, Gustafsson spoke at length. Linneaus was a great man, a great – he straightened his lapels, a little self-consciously – man of science. He was about to publish the tenth edition of his *Systema Naturae*, a revolutionary classification of the animal, plant, and mineral kingdoms, and there was much excitement amongst society members across Europe. Gustafsson was especially interested in the *insecta* class, and that was where the butterflies came in. He had hoped it might be possible to have a glimpse of Captain Lindberg's collection. He would be all discretion. Indeed, they would barely know he was here.

Eva's mother said that she was pleased that Captain Lindberg's collection was of such importance. She would be delighted to show Herr Gustafsson the butterflies. She rose from her seat, and Herr Gustafsson made as if to rise in response before noticing that he was already standing.

"Does the book have spiders?" asked Eva.

"Spiders?"

"Why do you mention spiders?" Eva's mother cried.

Herr Gustafsson said it was a reasonable question. In fact, spiders came under the same category as butterflies, although they were not his speciality, or even Linneaus's speciality. Spiders, he said, had been thoroughly examined by Carl Alexander Clerck in a publication just last year. Herr Gustafsson would go so far as to say it was the most comprehensive study of a single creature yet undertaken. Truly, they were living in an age of scientific discovery, and Sweden was its hub.

"But it's unusual, to find a little girl interested in spiders."

"Do you know what they eat?"

The gentleman said that spiders were hunters and used their webs to catch flies. They ate meat, "Just like you or I."

Eva could see her mother's mounting anxiety as she tried to steer a course between the pleasure of *going well*, Eva evidently having sparked the gentleman's interest, and the impropriety of her child, a female, wishing to discuss the habits of arachnids in the guest room. In a heroic effort to rescue the situation, the mother offered Herr Gustafsson tea. He refused at first, then seemed to realize his error, and said on second thoughts a cup of tea was exactly what he wished for.

"Did you know there are over sixty kinds of spiders in Sweden?"

Eva shook her head. She worried now that she had endangered the spider by mentioning it.

Eva's mother told Herr Gustafsson that Captain Lindberg had collected over a thousand samples of butterflies, and by some unseen cue, Birgitte appeared and escorted Eva from the room, to the relief of all.

That night when Eva checked under the bed, there was a second spider. This one was smaller-bodied, a mottled shade of brown. The black spider edged forward hopefully.

"Spider one and spider two," said Eva softly. "I will find you flies."

Eva.

Her dream was more of a nightmare, a ghastly vision of the Black Death sweeping across Stockholm, with children dropping dead house by house, mothers running screaming into the street, and a man with a cart piled high with bodies. The bodies were human, but they each had eight limbs.

In the morning, Birgitte told her that a terrible thing had happened. The Jensson's youngest boy had died in the night. A sudden fever. Birgitte said they should not speak of it in the presence of Eva's mother. Eva could hear, several rooms away, the rising tide of weeping, and thought that it was already too late.

Eva glanced under the bed. She knew she should be frightened, but her knowledge was exhilarating too.

The spiders had seized hold of the possibilities in the emptiness. They had the power to make things happen.

Every day a new spider arrived. Some were as small as Eva's fingernail, others as large as her hand. The spiders had specialisms. They told her about births and deaths, weddings and funerals, accidents and abrupt changes in fortune. Sometimes the events were small. Eva was able to help members of the household with mysteries they had thought unsolvable – such as the time Birgitte lost her hairpin, an heirloom that had belonged to her mother, and her grandmother before that. Where did you look? Eva asked, and instigated a second search during which she was able to recover the pin from the exact location revealed to her in the previous night's dream. Birgitte was delighted.

"You are a lucky child."

Eva woke each morning full of itchy anticipation, and could not rest until the truth of her dream had been revealed. Once or twice she could not resist baiting the maid.

"I have the strangest feeling, Birgitte. I have a feeling that an old lady died."

Birgitte choked and crossed herself.

But Eva had to be careful. The prophecies were a secret between herself and the spiders. It was a delicate balance.

In exchange for their omniscience, Eva had to feed the spiders. Flies were hard to find, until she learned to check the house before the housemaid had done her tasks. She found dead ones then, dried up on their backs around the edges of the rooms. She took to keeping a wooden box in her pocket and filled it with the fly carcasses. The spiders shared these offerings amongst themselves.

At night she brought her candle down to the floor and she lay on her stomach, marvelling at the work of the spinning spiders, the flame of her candle illuminating the intricate patterns of their mysterious creations. How did they do it? How did they know the exact length of the thread required, where to send it, how to attach it so that they might cling to any surface, however impossible?

"What will you tell me tonight, spiders?"

If she closed her eyes, she thought she heard their voices.

Eva Eva Eva Eva Eva.

Still she did not have names for them. She had thought of many, but none were suitable. Sometimes she thought she had hit upon exactly the right name for one of her collection, and went to sleep chanting it to herself, but come morning it would have vanished from her memory. They remained numerical: Spider One, Spider Two. Spider Three, the finder of lost things. The one who had made her lucky.

On his next visit Herr Gustafsson took Eva aside.

"There's something I want to tell you. But –" he hesitated. "Perhaps we might not mention it to your mother."

Eva said she could keep a secret, and Gustafsson said he did not doubt it. He had been, he said, to the Royal Swedish Academy of Sciences, to take a look at *Svenska Spindlar.* He had noted some facts which he hoped might interest Eva. Would she care to hear?

Eva would.

True spiders had not only eight legs, but also eight eyes, and two palps (the word Clerck used for arms, Gustafsson explained).

Every type of spider had a particular name. The first part of the name was always the same: *araneus.* The second part of the name defined the spider. As an example, the first spider to be described in Clerck's famous publication was labelled *araneus angulatus.*

Eva repeated it eagerly to herself. *Araneus angulatus.* At last, she was learning.

That night Eva did not dream. Her sleep was as blank as an unwritten letter. She woke in a state of panic, her nightgown damp and sticky with sweat. She tumbled from her bed and looked for the spiders. There they were, each spider crouched at the heart of its web, the webs set at angles to one another like a set of mirrors in a store. The webs emanated a soft, phosphorescent glow. Eva counted them quickly, terrified that one might have been lost.

"Spider one, spider two, spider three..."

They were all there.

"What did I do, spiders?"

They were offended, she thought. She had failed to ask about their names. The opportunity had been there, to describe them, and she hadn't taken it! After all, the spiders knew her name. She had profited by their gifts but she had not made enough effort to understand them.

Over the next few days Eva undertook a careful study of the spiders. She drew pictures, making sure to include the eight eyes, the little palps, as well as the markings on their backs. She hid the drawings under her pillow. Her dreams returned. Eva located the cook's missing delivery of sugar and warned her mother not to go out for tea until after two o'clock, because there was going to be a rainstorm. Her mother looked perplexed.

The spiders spun and seemed content.

Upon Herr Gustafsson's next visit (the butterfly collection appearing to be more extensive than either Eva's mother or Gustafsson himself had originally anticipated) Eva managed to smuggle the man of science one of her drawings.

"I would like to know the name of this spider."

Gustafsson promised he would investigate.

Eva overheard Birgitte say, when she did not think Eva was listening, that it would not be a surprise if Herr Gustafsson were to ask for the hand of Eva's mother in marriage.

Birgitte's acquaintance said it was for the best. Someone was needed to run the household. And then there was the child, without a father. But it was the same for many in Stockholm. The wars...

Birgitte sighed and nodded. The wars.

It never seemed to occur to anyone that Eva's father had not been there to be without. Had they forgotten about the emptiness, or had they never known it was there? The spiders offered greater company than any of the rare, stilted exchanges between Eva and Captain Lindberg. Eva could not bear to think of a time before the spiders.

Eva had to wait some days before the return of her drawing. Days which passed in a whir of impatience. She could hardly sleep, and her dreams were broken and restless, the spiders unable to speak to her with their usual fluency. They too, were waiting. She needed Gustafsson to return. What if Birgitte was wrong? What if he had finished with the butterflies, and there was no other reason for his visits? Eva could not let down her friends.

When he finally returned she submitted to Birgitte's ministrations in silence, surprising the maid into comment.

"See how nice your hair shines up when you don't wriggle so!"

Eva did not care about her hair. She wanted her drawing back.

She had to sit through her mother's insistent proffering of tea and cake before there was a chance to speak to Herr Gustafsson alone. He handed her the folded piece of paper with a private wink. In exchange, she presented him with her second study.

When she unfolded the paper, her hands were trembling so much she almost tore the drawing. A chance to redeem herself. She had waited so long for this!

Above her drawing of Spider One, Gustafsson had written two words in his ornate script.

Araneus diadematus.

"Araneus diadematus," Eva whispered. "Araneus diadematus."

A glow of pleasure warmed her body from head to toe. *Araneus diadematus.* She knew the name. She had succeeded. She rushed to tell the spiders the news.

Her dream was death. It was not bold and dramatic, the way the ship had burst in an explosion of gold. It was still and noiseless. There was a garden. At the end of the garden, a glut of blackberry bushes, and spread across the bushes, a vast web, as tall as Eva, as wide as a door. There was a spider at the centre of it, but as Eva approached, premonition sank her heart like a stone.

The spider was dead.

She woke sobbing, stricken with grief. Not wanting to see, but knowing she had no choice. For many minutes she lay in her bed, sensing the emptiness beneath her with a weight that had not been present for months. When she finally gathered the courage to crawl from the sheets and look at the space below, it was exactly as she had feared.

Araneus diadematus was dead in its web, legs curled in on its body as if in a hopeless defence against some unseen foe.

The others remained. She felt their eyes upon her, eight-fold. In accusation, they were one.

They knew what she had done. They had known it before she knew herself.

She prayed that Gustafsson would never return. She repeated the prayer to herself, over and over. *If he doesn't come back, the others are safe.* They still gave her dreams, as though they had no choice, in the way that they had no choice but to keep spinning their webs, ever thicker and closer in the space under the bed until there was barely room for Eva's hand. But Eva could take no pleasure in her foreknowledge, overshadowed as it was by the death of *diadematus*.

Autumn advanced again, and the waterways of Stockholm were thick with fallen leaves. Birgitte had no more talk of marriage. Eva dared to hope.

He won't come back. He won't.

If he doesn't come back, the others are safe.

"This was a good one!" said Gustafsson. He was delighted with himself, unable to conceal his enthusiasm. He had no idea of the horror his revelation had unleashed.

Eva held the paper tightly. She was resolved: she would not open it. If she did not open it, she would not see the name, and the spider would be safe. As soon as she had left the room she could destroy the drawing. Rip it to pieces. Set light to it with her candle. She would burn the evidence to ash.

Eva's mother was at the window, commenting on some calamity in the street below.

"Quick," whispered Gustafsson. "You can take a look now."

She shook her head. Gustafsson withdrew, clearly puzzled by her response. Then his face cleared.

"Of course, my writing. It's not very clear. I'd better read it for you. This one is *araneus quadratus*, the female variety, judging by–"

"No!"

Silence.

Eva had spoken loudly. She had shouted. Her mother turned, stared at her, shockwaves permeating the serenity of her face.

"What is the matter, Eva? What excuse do you have for such rudeness?"

Eva could not speak. The words stuck in her throat. She clamped her hands over her ears, trying to block the name from her memory.

I won't remember –

Dimly she was aware of speech from those around her.

I won't remember –

"So very, very sorry–"

"Please, it's of no consequence–"

"Birgitte!"

I won't –

The maid's hand was on her shoulder, steering her from the room, into the hallway, up the stairs.

"What's got into you then? Don't you push back, young lady!"

Eva resisted with all her remaining strength. She did not want to go upstairs. She did not want to go into her room. Tears streamed down her face as Birgitte propelled her firmly, inescapably upwards.

The housemaid was in her bedroom, cleaning. On the floor was a smear of bloody pulp.

Quadratus.

Eva screamed.

The housemaid had killed *quadratus*. Stamped on its small round body with her shoe. Birgitte and the maid did not understand. It was a spider, they said, over and over again. It's dead now. It can't hurt you. It's dead.

You don't have to be afraid.

The girl had been acting strangely all morning, said Birgitte. Perhaps she was getting sick. A sleep would calm her down.

The two of them pressed her into the bed, cocooning her in the sheets, bringing a hot brick to warm her feet. Birgitte prised the sweaty piece of paper from Eva's hand and unfolded it. A creeping numbness had overcome Eva's limbs, making her powerless to protest. Birgitte showed the drawing to the maid.

"How peculiar."

They tucked in her arms until only her head was visible above the covers.

"Get some sleep," Birgitte said. "And calm down. We can't have you disturbing your mother like that."

In the emptiness beneath the bed, she felt the presence of the remaining spiders. There was no spinning. Only a thick, collective stillness.

There were no more dreams. Eva did not expect it. She had betrayed them. She was not surprised when, over the next few weeks, the spiders began to disappear, leaving behind the dusty threads of their abandoned webs, sad grey constructions clinging on to the emptiness under the bed. One day the housemaid remembered to sweep there. And then the webs, too, were gone.

Years later, Eva Gustafsson-Lindberg attended a lecture at the headquarters of the Royal Swedish Academy of Sciences. The speaker was Carl Alexander Clerck, and the subject was *Svenska Spindlar.* But when the esteemed arachnologist held up specimens of the sixty-seven different varieties of spider, Eva closed her ears, not wanting to hear. Instead, she spoke softly to herself, in her head.

Spider one.
Spider two.
Spider three.
I will not forget you.

THE LAST ESCAPEMENT

James Smythe

I WANT MY MONEY! I shout these words at the council who decided these things, because the money is rightfully mine, and there are not many ways that I can subsist in this world without it. Because, what else is the driver? What else moves the world in the way that we likely expect? A deal, as I seem to repeatedly have to inform gentlemen, is a deal; and these are not men of their words, despite their protestations of the opposite. They say that they need more tests before releasing anything, because the device that I have built is untested, unverified. Tests! Does Harrison need tests? A man who is proven perhaps circumvents these things. For me, lost as I am, crawling from beneath his shadow... I am tested. I am pushed to my break. I stand before them with my sea-clock, and they all hide their smirks. I can see their lack of faith in me, in mine. I ask for a funding, as I have heard that Harrison received such a release. They refuse me. Their laughter is less than hidden this time.

Money is the perpetual hag that seems to outweigh all other of humanity's concerns! Forfend that we should think about the betterment of ourselves. (And still, the deep irony of it: I am working on this clock for a reward, because living is not enough; and the clock itself will enable the crossing of the oceans with something resembling expedience, thus furthering the income and profit from trade and such. If I were to stop and examine the reality of this, perhaps it would all begin to collapse under the weight of such flawed logics.)

I do not know how many times I am to try this: to create a time-keeping device that will hold its measure on a journey across the sea. Every day, the same thing: a task as simple as steadying a pendulum, the rock of left to right; of making it sturdy, able to take the yoke of a storm and hold it still. Time is regular, this is the crux of the problem, and when travelling the seas, time is lost. It evaporates, like salt-water from a deck – though time, of course, leaves no trace. It is such an intangible thing that we try to measure.

Attempting to recreate the effects of the water in my own home has proven impossible, so I have taken to a smaller boat, cast out into the waters around the coast. Storm-rain beats on the hull, and the boat rocks, and so I time it as best I can; two devices on the same boat, one a control for the other. My eldest, Yohann, works with me, of course: aiding me where he can. His understanding is perhaps more simplistic in its way, less inherently attuned to the workings of the clock, but regardless! So his hands are steady, and so his eyes are sound. Mine falter. It is a failing of humanity that we are so flawed, so designed to collapse. Most mechanisms grow stronger with age. They are redrafted and remade, and subsequent images feature fewer of the foibles of their earlier kin. We are not so lucky. Our bodies degenerate just as our fathers' did.

On the boat, we monitor the clocks constantly, almost to the detriment of our lives. Surely there will come a point where the waves rock us so hard that we capsize; and still, should we, my concern would be with the escapements on my clocks, and wondering whether they maintain their sureness even as they are tipped underneath the water that we are so desperate to tame.

I do not travel well, my gut-sickness attests to that. And would that we didn't lose time as we do! My plans, all of them, rendered so slyly null. Time is lost – as vapour trails, smoke, the wisps of dehydrated water.

There is nothing for it. I have come too far to be refused this now.

The device is nothing but excrement. Too much time has been lost. Even Harrison's earliest attempt at this held better. Still, I remind myself, he had practice, and funds. He was not working from the pittance that I am. I smash the clock onto the ground, and I watch the guts of it spill out, tumbling from the wooden skeleton that held them. I gather the wood: it can be used again, in part. When we first learned to harness the trees, we were masters of nature, I suspect. We bent and broke the world and we turned it into useable gain. We built ships, when we knew that wood would sustain such a thing; the float of them enabling the use of water in such a way that we were masters of another domain entirely. On and on, a cycle. Salt from the sea! That same salt that is left when the water is gone, and see how we use it! A preservative from nothing but dried-up spume.

My drawing board is full of attempted failures, that by my own measure would perhaps be classed as successes. A man lives by how he gauges his own success; and there I can see that I have lived well. So my best escapement failed. It was not exacting enough. I have to design another.

With clocks, there is an adherence to a rule of construction. That, as you force the casement to smaller and smaller sizes, so the internal organs – when time is so fluid, so full of life, how could one not think of it as something akin to a body, churning with blood and gusto? – must in turn become smaller. More compact, and therefore more delicate. My tools become subtler, forcing interactivity on a microscopic level. But, there's less chance of failure. The delicate nature of the device means that everything is somehow more exact. So I force it smaller. Smaller means that there is less chance of chaos's intervention.

How small can this go?

I commission new tools for this task. The sheer thought of it: that there are ever-decreasing sizes of devices for practitioners and designers to use to create objects of ever-decreasing size! So my tools are already small, practically minute; but they must be made smaller still. Does somebody build those tools for the tool-maker to build mine?

News comes from Harrison, and I destroy my design. He has abandoned clocks in favour of – and I can scarcely believe it, even as I think these words – a pocket watch. Mudge and his lever escapement – a joke, I felt, always a quip that would never work – have bested Harrison's attempts at the sea-clock. A pocket watch!

I am nothing if not adaptable. A clock to be held in the hand of a seaman; so small that it can be monitored constantly, should it need to be; and that will not fall, or be swayed by the movement of the boat upon waves, simply because it is anchored to a man himself. I have not seen it, of course, because such a thing will not travel, will not risk being taken into the hands of our rivals. (Such is the constant, unerring threat of war: we are terrified that a mastery of time might somehow allow an advantage to our foes. I would destroy my devices a hundred times over – even with the pain that such destruction wreaks upon my soul – before allowing a Spaniard, say, to take control of it.) I have heard a report, though, of its general size. It seems impossible.

It is obvious that my tools will not be up to this task, so I discard them. I commission more. This endeavour is too costly by far.

I build an hourglass to distract myself – the most basic of clocks, being so easy to force a constancy of time through it. Measurements, nothing more. I use gunpowder.

I am careful when grinding it, as the properties of such a thing are volatile; and I can only make it so small, so fine. It's incredible how little gunpowder is needed to flow for that single minute. Great dust that passes into nearly nothing.

The committee force me to seethe with their almost unbearable arrogance, but I grit my teeth – I think of my father, of his words to maintain that I should stay steadfast and staunch, even in the face of adversity (and what adversity this is!) – and I thank them for their kindly offer. They give me funding. Yohann says that this is reason for celebration, but what does he know? He brings the naivety of his youth to all of his opinions. Would that he could see past these.

But there is food, and tools, and materials. Gold is soft, and it's apparent that such softness is something that I can use. To embed the escapement inside the gold itself, carving out a space for it where it will not be able to move, seems sensible. There is no room for error.

The escapement will not fit; or, when I manage to make it fit, it does not work as I wanted. The device overspills with its insides, like the slopping of intestines from a slaughter; and when I attempt to wear it, to move around, it loses time even here. I stand in front of the clock that I have built for our home, and I wave my attempt at a pocket watch around, and I watch the seconds become lost.

It does not work, and I cannot see how to make it work.

Yohann tells me that we are nearly run out of money. I tell him to get out; that his inane bleating will not help me now. Harrison is there! He is at the forefront! He is breaking all that he knows in order to create – and, perhaps, that is what I have been missing. Innovation, rather than the invocation of the groundwork that others have laid. I am using their escapements, or variants of. I need my own. Something that I do not have, and I do not understand how to achieve. I feel pity for myself, and I hit my son, to force him to leave the house, and to leave me alone.

I am asleep when inspiration strikes me. She comes to me as what might be a woman, but could easily be a man. A creature; a spectre. So vague in my mind's eye that she is almost intangible, but then she strikes, and the knots and weeds in my thoughts are untangled. I am searching for something that is unfailingly reliant on that which we cannot change: gravity, the turn of the planet itself, regardless of where we stand upon it, reliant on a mechanism more complicated than my current devices, though yet also more simple.

And then, I see it. We are attempting to tame water; so, perhaps, water itself is the key? As it moves on the outside of the ship, so rocking the boat whereupon the clock itself will be forced to be, perhaps water itself is the key to balancing it? The liquid inside the mechanism, acting as a stabiliser? I see cogs and gears, the teeth of the thing inside the liquid. A new escapement; true inspiration.

When I wake, I am coated in sweat. A fever has set in, but I know that this fever is, itself, a gift. Inside my mind, the escapement begins to work.

I work quickly. I carve the sections I will need, using the smallest tools that I have. It does not matter for this stage if they are perfect. I reuse materials, ideas. I have to do this quickly. God knows that Harrison will be working fast;

and our other competitors (though I see them as nothing more than chaff, if I am honest with myself).

I construct a box – airtight, I ensure – and then I flood the mechanism. The water engulfs the escapement, filling the holes between the teeth of the cogs. As it turns – as the mechanics work, the piston arm forcing the wheels to turn – it is sluggish. I adjust the measurements. Still, sluggish. Still, it's not correct; but it feels like I am advancing.

She is white and pale, my muse; like, I think, the froth on the surface of the waves.

I am stricken. Yohann is strict with me, forcing me to take to my bed, telling me that nothing should rouse me. Under no conditions am I to work, these are his instructions. But, of course, how can I stop? Can an artist cease creating, even as his hands cannot hold the brush? As a writer cannot grasp the pen? Even in disability, their minds are as they were. Their minds work as a machine of their own, unbeholden to ailment and misery; and so, too, does mine. Tick, tick, tick, it goes; the ever whirring machine of a clock.

I manage to wrench myself to the workshop, but I cannot focus. My eyes wander into a fog that I would swear did not exist outside of their periphery in the moment before it overtakes me, and I am forced to grip the table. I drop my tiny tools to the floor, and I scurry for them. They are too delicate to risk being trodden on. Should the plan for this new escapement work – and I am sure that it will, as my mind is full of waves, of the flow of the tides, of the rocking back and forth, the motion of the seas that it will one day service – I will need them. Expediency is of the utmost import from this stage. I say this to Yohann, and he urges me to my bed again. He cleans me before my night of fitful sleep: waking, sleeping, urinating. Never still for more than minutes at a time.

As it comes light, I am overcome with a cough that is so strong that it feels as though I might lose my insides to it. I lurch to the edge of the bed, and I spit the waste to the bowl of my own piss, murky in the waters. It is only when I push back the curtain that I see the blood pooling inside there, swirling into and clouding the water; and how it settles, heavy at the base. These two fluids, so lost together.

The feeling of being well again – of my health being fully returned, my vitality come back to me (even as I feared, though I would not admit it, that death was coming for me, finally; having outlived my purpose, failed in my task, my one role) – cannot be underestimated. Even as I run a fever – as Yohann insists on my perpetual sickness – I know that I am well. My body will not fail me. The fury with which I am able to resume my activities is astonishing, and I find myself in the workshop for a day and more in one solitary stretch, relying on my son to bring me food and drink. Without him, I suspect that I would barely have breathed!

More word from London: that Harrison's watch (to watch something suggests that it never boils, so cocksure in naming convention is the assumption!) is fiercely mechanical, unlike anything that I have created. Across the seas, they are all calling him a genius. He constructs his own tools, go the rumours; and he has built the device from nothingness, from the ether. Of course, it is hewn of metals; of course it has an origin, a place of birth.

But as I work, something strikes me: that it is hard to compete. It is hard to imagine how I might, given the skills at his disposal. Harrison has money, and a reputation; I am alone. (Yohann reminds me that I am not; that I have his assistance. Of course, he is insane. What he offers is peripheral.) This is my task to bear, my shoulders heavy with their own skin and bone.

I take a boat into the rivers. A small tug, destined for nothing more than trawling the river-beds, but still it manages what I want. There is a storm, perfect for my cause; and the waves caused from the tide's swollen ache replicate what I need. I clutch my own watch to my chest to keep it as steady as possible, and I watch as this new escapement – the Drowned Escapement, I have termed it – attempts to maintain the time. Stable, stable, I try to hold it. My arms shake with the excitement, but they are nothing compared to the ebb of the boat herself.

When we return, we have lost nine seconds. Over the time that we have travelled, this is unacceptable, wholly and totally unacceptable. Those are nine seconds that we will never get back, and I must. I must.

The principle is fine. Yohann says that I am not thinking properly; that my ailments (the sickness that I suffered) has somehow cheated my mind from my usual ways of logic. I am, he tells me, in his sternest tone, not clear-headed.

I have banned him from the workshop.

Because the joy of a clock, really, is that nobody knows how it works. For the moments where it is keeping time, maintaining its steady beating rhythm, the means by which it achieves that rhythm are closer to magic. When it is shut – and I know, there is a fashion for the glass frontis piece, which I shall ignore duly – there is a mystery to what occurs inside. Nobody knows what makes the time be stuck to. Time, that constant that we have invented ourselves – broken down, to fractions and fragments –

adhered to with some curious notion that we, humans, can decide how it works.

The principle, as I say, is fine. But something is askew. Water has its own tide, but perhaps the tide inside the clock needs to be more than the tide outside. It needs to be heavier.

Oil does not work As a fuel, it cannot be beaten, but it does not mix as well as I might want it to. Instead it settles quickly, and the mechanism is left in the water itself. The escapement, I nurture. I give it a coating, to ensure that it does not rust; and I smooth the edges, to expedite the ease with which the gears will shift when submerged. But still it does not perform as I would have it.

At night, I stare into my bedpan; and then, from those bloody depths, inspiration arises.

The butcher sells bags of the stuff at prices that seems almost scandalous for what would otherwise be waste. It is either bagged or tossed to the gutters! Still, this is what I must pay: for the blood of an ox (such as I am assured it was), there is a margin. Good blood, he tells me. His accent is not local; more, some lilting thing that rises and falls as he stumbles over the words. I would sooner not pay him, but I do not have it in me to kill an animal myself. (Yohann, when I tell him the plan, shouts. He tells me that I am gone insane; that I am no better than those scurvied wastrels eating the flesh of rats on the streets.)

I mix the blood with the water and I pour it into the casing, and I wait. Everything turns. More tests need to be conducted, that much is apparent; but it needs to have more water. It must be thicker, I think, even if only slightly. I watch the gears move, and the blood disperses, the water a thin pink; and then, as the gears stop, when I let the mechanism cease movement, I watch it settle in a cloud at the bottom, pulsing almost; my life, as something akin to a jellyfish on the bottom of the ocean.

The muse: she clicks her tongue in perfect rhythm, because this is how she comes to me. She touches my palm, and I understand her. It is more than blood: it needs more to it. It needs life. What has come from the cow is dead and cold, but I am the creator; I understand the weight that is needed.

And we understand that we are the sum of ourselves. My blood, my design, my time: all of these things working together, in one beautiful unity. She touches my forehead. I am asleep and awake at the same time, and she is the silk of my curtains and my bedsheets and even of skin; the thinnest skin that has ever existed.

I slice my hand open with my letter-opening blade, and the cut is sharp and straight: a line that breaks the skin but does no real harm. I do not think that I would even feel it were I not looking at the wound as I exact it. That blood runs out, down my fingers and into the box. I cannot tell if this is what was needed, but so it flows down. It ceases after a while – barely a percentage of the clock's water itself, but still, it is there. Plumes of it; as a fungus. I shake the clock and listen to the dulled tick coming through the water, and I look at my hand, which has stopped bleeding; and then I put pressure on the wound, because there is more in there. I know that there is.

I buy a medical journal, because my hand can only take so much, and I need to know where the blood in the body comes at its thickest. The concept of this seems so logical to me, now, that I can scarcely believe that I didn't see it before. To take the body – such a perfect device of itself, and practically a clock, so permanent and constant is the rhythmic beating of the heart – and to somehow infuse my escapement with it! But the body has so many types of blood. I remember, years and years ago, cutting my foot when I trod on glass. The blood from there ran so weakly, but was almost ceaseless; every time I applied pressure, so it began again. But then, from inside me, the blood that I coughed up when I was lying in my bed, that was thick. It coagulated. Surely that is what I need?

The journal speaks of devices used to drain blood in order to balance the humours. I am a man of science, I have to admit; my own dealings with such vague ancient ideas are long ignored. The body is a machine, of type, and it balances itself. But perhaps the tools used on the body in such instances might be useful to me?

I send Yohann out to find me something that I can use. I am not feeling as though I should leave the house today; my limbs shake slightly too much, and my hand is greyer than I would like to admit, underneath the bandages.

The drainage device is terrifying to look at. A clamp, two arms of metal, with protrusions that slide into the skin around the thigh, it reminds me of nothing less than an animal trap, left on the floor of the woods for unsuspecting rabbits or deer. And here I am, willingly putting myself to its jaws.

The thing straps to my thigh. I sit in the chair in the workroom, trousers pulled to my ankles. My legs look dirty, I think, but that will not stem the blood when it comes. It is attached with leather belts that tighten to a point of near-pain in themselves, and the flesh underneath them swells with the redness of my trapped blood.

On the top of the device, a lever, which I am to pull. This will lower the spikes into the skin; and, from there, the blood will drip down – or run, I am not entirely sure of the pace at which it will attempt to evacuate my body – so I have placed a bowl beneath, empty, ready for capturing. I must expedite transporting the blood to the clock, I think, because I am not sure how long life remains inside it. Is it while it is still warm? Does that make sense?

I am not sure that I can do this, because it is one thing to be harmed, and yet another to harm yourself so willingly. In the name of invention, of course. That is what I say to myself. I do this in the name of invention.

And I question, when I pull the lever, and the spikes slip into my skin and my muscle, and the blood pours, if I have entirely thought this through.

She comes to me while I lie unconscious in the workshop, and she rouses me. She tells me, her fingers the essence of cold, that I am to wake up. She leaves trails of black on my cheeks, and she dances her fingers in the blood as it runs from my thigh, and she tells me that I am doing as I should. That a clock, I am to remember, is only as rhythmic as the rhythm with which it is constructed. She says, You put your soul into these things. Her voice is a echo through a drunken mind. She says, You are doing good work. Soon, eternity will be yours. She leaves me then, and I question eternity; because, if it never ends, what need have you for maintaining an awareness of the time in which you have endured it?

The leather bracers holding the device in place have slackened, because my leg is thinner than it was. When I am fully awake – the grogginess will not leave, but I have worked in states far worse than this – I dip my finger into the bowl (tainting it, I am sure, but still this is my flesh going into it, which makes me feel that the purity of the thing is intact) and it is still warm. I remove the device from my leg. The spikes are so thin for so much blood! It flows again, when they leave my limb, and I attempt to stem this. I have got enough, I am sure.

I stand, leaning on the table. My one leg trembles as though I were older than I am, but I am able. I heave the bowl from the floor and empty the contents into the clock. It threatens to drown the escapement, but does not. So much blood! How much can the human body hold, I wonder. I add water, because surely that is the crux of this? The blood and the water, mixed together. Through this, miracles are achieved.

The mixture is thick. The escapement turns, and the blood-water churns. Fluidity, lubrication. The teeth of the gears click into place, silent inside this fluid. It works.

I send Yohann – who despairs, and sobs, even as I press the coins into his hand – to book me another boat. This must be tested in the wild.

Two seconds! A journey of near ceaseless sickness from my part, so choppy and unbridled were the waters, and only two seconds were lost!

Yohann tells me that I should inform the society. They will want to know about this, and test it themselves. He says that he will take it to London. I am too sickly to go, he says. Too old. I tell him that my muse favours not the age of the man that she inspires, and he laughs. There is no muse, he says. There is science, of course.

His answer to everything. But I agree. Maybe sending him across the continent in my stead is better.

There is still work to be done.

I wave Yohann off. I have taken to using a stick, because I siphoned more from my leg to make the second version of the watch for him: this time, smaller, far far smaller. It has not been tested in the wild, but the principles behind it are the same. There is no reason to suspect that it will not fulfil the task. If it can be as steady as it ought, the prize funds will be mine, and I can retire.

But then, when I sleep – and my sleep is always fitful, a perpetual stream of visions of boats and seas and the arms of the watch face winding their way to some hateful, inevitable finality – she visits me again. She climbs inside me and inspires me. My task is not done. Imagine: two seconds! The tick is so constant and stable as to be close to infallible. But – but! – it could be closer. It could lose no time at all.

The four humours: blood, phlegm, yellow bile, black bile. They are what, remedial science assumes, forms the balance of the human body. So, logic dictates, that if I am to search for balance – for a form of ballast, almost – using those things would only assist me?

I build another watch. Smaller, still. Smaller and smaller I carve the escapement. No longer the drowned escapement, but this one the living escapement: created from that which once was. I turn to the journals, to see the easiest ways to extract the bile that I crave; and I let my mouth fill with the waters of my throat, hawking up from as deep as I can muster to spit into the bowl. The blood can come last for this, I think.

I cough, because I am being so tough on my own throat, but that's when the phlegm is best extracted. In the water, it congeals.

Mercury is the best method for black bile extraction, say the journals, so I take balls into my system. I have never felt such agony inside me! The tug and gnaw of them as I attempt to process them is violent. I lie on the floor of the workshop and I cradle myself. Would that Yohann were only here to see this! To see the endeavours that I am undertaking in the name of this most dedicated science! He would surely know that this was only logical and right, because even as I question it – and I pray for darkness, for the cold hand of she who visits me, who cradles me and speaks to me in her tongues of another life past this, and of all that I can achieve – I start to exhume the blackness from my body, letting it torrent into my cupped hands, overspilling into the bowl with the phlegm.

Of course, it is not pure black. There is blood in there, as viscous as any I have ever seen. The bowl is full of a grey. I keep it warm, to protect the life that flows in there. In the morning, I feel better. Weak, still, but I find that the concoction has grown darker and thicker.

It is time for the yellow bile.

Hateful vomit! I lurch and quake to expel it, having taken in berries from the garden that I know to have the desired effect. Yohann, when he was a child, consumed them, and we spent days worrying for his safety. Now, I am in control, and this was the route of most ease. It is not the first vomits that I am interested in, of course, because that contains the little food that I have eaten; but what comes after, as my body purges.

Yellow into the mixture, but it does not change the colour. The thickness is alarming; but, I know, it needs the blood to achieve completion.

My other thigh is unmarked as yet, but then the spikes do their worst. I do not sleep this time, and yet still somehow she visits me. As my head lolls and I force my eyes to stay open, I see her. She creeps through the room, then wraps herself around my legs, underneath them; and she drinks from the bowl, lapping at it as though she were feline. It is nearly enough, she says. She says, I can taste your life, and it goes. Tick, tick, tick.

The blood into the bowl, and it is complete. And then, into the watch. The escapement turns. It turns, still, and I know, without needing to test it, that it will not lose any time. It will be perfect.

I do not eat, because I do not want to take my eyes from this new creation. She sits with me the whole time, stroking my hair. Her cold hands soothe my brow. For days all of my clocks are as they were, and then, after one final sleep, that changes. My new watch has stopped. The mixture is too thick, I consider; but then, it worked before. It turned. The pieces are degrading, I realise! Because they are not designed for the acids of the bile, perhaps? Because the coagulation of the blood is not conducive to their turning?

The materials are too weak, she whispers. There must be something else. There simply must be.

The escapement is of piston arms, and then gears of teeth. Replication is the way to creation; this we have known since we left the Garden, since our broods were born of our loins in facsimiles of our own images. This needs more of me, I know. That is what she has told me, though not in so many words.

My teeth are loose, those that are left. I have twelve, which is enough. Two are abandoned, as they snap when I am prising them loose. The miniature tools that I had commissioned are, it transpires, the perfect size for the leverage required. I slide them into my gums and out they come. A collection: and my gums are so smooth. This blood runs thick in my mouth, and I ensure that I do not waste it.

My most prominent bone is the ankle. And how round it is! How smooth, how apparent that it must be something that I can utilise in my clock! The shape of it is already perfect.

I have a saw for metals that will find easier movement through the bone. And curious, when one considers that metals and ores degrade under the strain imposed by the body's workings, where bone – so soft and malleable, of all materials – is able to somehow withstand them!

It was to be expected that I would no longer be able to walk; or, perhaps more accurately, to bear any weight on the leg from whence I took the bone. It will heal, of that I have no doubt; and, until then, I have the workshop. This is, she tells me, all that I need. No sense in moving from room to room, attempting a sense of normality, when what has happened is so far beyond normal to me. This is inspiration! It is the very depths of what I have been attempting to achieve!

The bone of my ankle-ball, shaven down and sliced, forms the three gears. Along the crest of that bone's curve, so the gears become smaller still. They are, I discover, small enough to fit inside the casement that I have created for my watch! So small, and perfectly so. For the teeth of the gears, I have carved slices from my own detrenched molars, and these I have affixed in perfect symmetry. The space with which there is for them to lock between each other (thus forcing the turning of each subsequent gear) is slight, to be sure, but the mechanism works perfectly. Teeth slot together in a mouth, that is apparent – they grow and manipulate to form those slots – so why should the same not be true of this watch that I am building?

She asks me if I am hungry, which I am not. Not that I know. She tells me, should I need it, that there is sustenance. The bucket; it cannot all fill the watch.

Yohann is not yet returned home. Ha! What he would say, could he see my work! Bone and teeth and blood and bile and bile and phlegm: so the body is complete, transported. And see how this will work!

She asks me where I thought, before this, that inspiration came from. She is my muse, and I know this; so I blame her. She takes this as a compliment. Here I am, weak and inspired.

She says, Give me your all. She pushes her fingers down my throat, and I gag on her nutrients. There is more, she says. More of you.

She shows me the pipes, from a douche. Simple as anything I have ever seen. I bore holes into the wood of the watch casing, and repeat my earlier sicknesses, for the biles. They drip from the escapement. I seal the box, and I attach the pipes, which are of a thick rubber, slightly worn but intact.

She helps steady my hand, for the knife. No, not a knife; a scalpel. I use this to carve notches and whittle the insides of these machines; and how easily it slides into my skin, at my wrist. Quick, quick, the pipe goes in. It fills with blood. I have put a leather strap from the trap onto it, and I fasten it to my wrist, feeding the pipe inside me. The blood flows, a constant supply. Out of me and into it. Watch it. Squeeze the pipe; and how warm it feels.

Harrison! Constrained by what he thinks he knows! What wonders could I have showed him, would that he had only been interested?

She tells me that I have done it: a perfect escapement. It will never cease while I watch it; while I breathe.

The watch does not stop while she – I cannot be sure that she is even human, now – stands behind me, proud of my work. She strokes my hair. I have not put a hole into the clock, for the blood to leave; to come back to me, where my body might recycle it.

I have done only half of this. There is more, but I am weak.

I watch the watch and shut my eyes. Thud, tick, tock; behind my eyes, the seconds go.

The minutes.

The watch stops. Oh never. Oh, never.

THE ASSASSINATION *of* ISAAC NEWTON *by* THE COWARD ROBERT BOYLE

Adam Roberts

"YOU WILL EXCUSE ME if I remark," said Boyle, "how strongly I am struck by your resemblance to *Brian May*."

"I do not know the gentleman," said Newton, attempting again to rise from his chair, but of course again failing so to do.

"Of course not. My own acquaintanceship with him was but brief. We discussed the New Astronomy!" Boyle shook his wigless head. "The *new* astronomy. And is novelty the salience? When God made Adam and Eve, he made them perfect. Subsequent novelty in the generation of their offspring has produced only chromatic *dissonance* of skin and society! Of *cutis* and culture! Novelty must connote decadence, surely, or entropy is nothing?"

Isaac noticed that, as he became agitated, Boyle's Irish accent became more pronounced. "You promised me, sir," he reminded him, "an explanation for my foul murder."

"So I did," agreed Boyle. "And you shall have it! If only you may *comprehend* it."

"I have not," Newton said, pulling first his right hand and then his left against their respective chains to test the tensile strength of the links, "as yet encountered any *marked* problems in the realm of comprehension, sir."

"Of course not!" Boyle. "Oh but my admiration for your genius *is* sincere. Or for what your genius will surely accomplish!"

"One does not usually express admiration for a fellow Christian, sir," Newton noted with asperity, "by murdering him."

At this, Boyle laughed. His large and labile mouth opened wide enough to display the hump of his tongue. Laughing stretched his already long and narrow face longer still, emphasising his equinity. Even his laughter sounded like whinnying. "It is, *eheu*! on account of your very genius. Believe me, my friend, when I tell you the reason you will agree with me that it *must be done*. See! Plato!" He pointed with his gun at the monumental statue of the philosopher, away to Newton's left. "*He* knew the truth."

"I know of no passage in Plato condoning assassination," Newton observed.

Boyle opened his eyes very wide. "I might clip off your ears with a knife, sir, as I saw in a play upon my travels. As –" And when Boyle sang, his voice was revealed as a surprisingly pleasant thing:

Rustics to the left o' me, jesters to the right o' me, and I hither

Confin'd in the midden with thou! Confin'd in the midden with thou!

"...but I shall not," Boyle concluded, looking suddenly very sorry for himself, "so disfigure you by *cropping* your ear. It is enough that I must murder you, here, under the shadow of Plato. Plato, who knows the reason."

"While I, being a lesser philosopher, do not," Newton reminded him.

"Such composure in the face of imminent personal extinction!" Boyle said. "May I, Mr Newton, ask your age?"

"I shall be twenty next week," Newton replied. "I must in turn press a question upon you."

"About the statues?"

Newton looked about him. The two men were in a cavernous space: forty foot from floor to shadowy ceiling. High windows emitted bright but wintry light. A walkway ran about the walls a little space beneath these, thirty feet up; and all along the wall were many paintings hung, as paintings are, higgled and piggled. But it was not the paintings that caught the eye; it was the many sculptures. Newton had an eye that could assimilate the exact number

I am struck by your resemblance to Brian May

of objects in a crowd of objects, and he saw that there were forty two stone figures, from child-sized satyrs blowing on pan-pipes, to Hercules wielding a club the size of a pillar, and trailing behind him a lion-skin large as a barge's sail. The statues filled the room, as if frozen in mid-bustle as mythological giants crowded about to eavesdrop of the conversation of the two men.

"No," Isaac said. "Not about the statues. About the reason you seek to murder me, sir, and so imperil your own immortal soul."

"The statues," said Boyle, pacing along the centre of the room, "are mostly classical. Here, though –" (he reached the far end of the small space available for pacing) "here – Cain slays Abel." And indeed, behind a row of putti, was the double-figure statue, Abel turning a terrified white face back over his shoulder at his white brother, whose blank expression and cataract-eyes seemed to regard the cudgel he was in the very act of bringing down on his victim's cranium with a purely disinterested objectivity. "Does this answer your question?"

"It does not."

Boyle gathered his greatcoat about him, and strolled down the space towards the door. He sloped his gun over his shoulder like a sentry. "Here," he said, pointing to another double-figure statue—this one of Apollo seizing Achilles by the hair. The god, slender and almost womanly beside the dune-bulging muscles of the warrior, held the Achaean back by the left hand. In his right hand was a golden rod. "This," Boyle said, urgently, "this is a better visual rebus for what I must do. I seize with my hand and hold back the too impetuous onward rush of..." He span about, and aimed the long-barrelled pistol at Newton's chest.

"I, an Achilles?"

"An Achilles of the *mind*, sir! It is said by many that one cannot kill an idea. And yet I must kill yours!"

"Is that spear made of gold, actual gold?" Newton asked. For even in extremis, his curiosity could not be quenched.

"Indeed! *Solidi auri*. And above, do you see?" There was a platform of some manner behind the first row of statues, upon which the rear row of marble was raised up the better to display them. "Atalanta plucking the golden apple from the dust!" The statue was of a maiden in chaste tunic gazing at her own hand, in which a yellow sphere rested. Behind her, Hippomenes –who had strewn the golden apples on the ground during their footrace, in order to distract her and so win the race himself – could be seen only from behind, leaning forward as if putting on a spurt of speed. He was the only statue in the space not to one degree or another looking down upon the two human actors.

"I was younger than you are now, sir," Boyle said, walking back towards the chair in which Newton sat, chained. "When I undertook a grand tour, my travels. These statues –" He gestured with his gun.

"Collected on your travels?"

"I did not travel to Europe, though people believed the Continent my destination. I travelled... much *further* than the Continent."

"Cathay?" Newton inquired, drily. "The Americas?"

Boyle ignored this. "I returned rich in gold and rich in knowledge. *Divites in auro et dives in scientia*. It has permitted me to indulge a passion for sculpture, bought from merchants who trade in the artefacts of the ancients. Property, such as this. But!" He ran, sprinting suddenly – the suddenness of the motion making Newton's heart jump – to the door. Beside the entrance, tucked under a colossal sculpture of Triumphant Achilles dragging Hector's lifeless body in front of the Gates of Troy, was a small cabinet. Boyle put his pistol down, opened the cabinet, and brought forth a stack of books: two folio, two quarto, one octavo. These he ported back over to his prisoner. "Knowledge! How little people are surprised that the son of an Irish escheator whose only boyish passion was alchemy – alchemy – alchemy – should travel to Europe, meet Galileo himself, and return a *genius* whose insights into the modern world are unsurpassed by any? Would *remain* unsurpassed, indeed, until you yourself should... but, see." He held up *New Experiments Physico-Mechanicall, Touching the Spring of the Air, and its Effects*. Then he tossed the heavy volume to the ground. Newton flinched as its spine split on impact. *The Sceptical Chymist: or Chymico-Physical Doubts & Paradoxes* was treated the same way, and then he let all the books but the smallest fall. "Here! See here –"

"I am enchained, sir," said Newton, with dignity, "and therefore unable to peruse the book."

Boyle laughed again, his whinnying snigger. He held the volume before Newton's face, opened it: *T Lucretii Cari. Liber Septem.*

"There are but six books of Lucretius, Mr Boyle," Newton objected.

"Exactly!" cried Boyle. He began pacing in a circle, reading aloud the Latin hexameters:

Scientia multae mansiones sunt in domo, atque qui
habitant in eo quidem variis causis et illuc perduxerit.
Secundum scientiam prae gaudio per plures
potentiae intellectivae, quae risum maxime propria
scientia et experientia satis hendrerit gloriam quaerere:
multi sunt qui fecerunt opera inventa sunt in domo
cerebro propter hoc super altare pure utilitatis causa.

"The versification," Newton said, "might be smoother."

"I have yet to reach the crucial part," Boyle replied. "Listen," he said:

Sequitur ex speciali theoria relativitione
illius molis et virtutis, sed ambo sunt idem diversis
manifestationes—aliquanto ignota pro mediocris
conceptione mentis einsteinii. Praeterea, erit
E aequalis est mc^2*, in quo vis ponatur massae*
per quadratum velocitatis lucis praebuit illa
parva mole vertat in longissime vim et contra.

"I find the reasoning ingermane, the specifics obtuse," said Isaac. "For what item of nomenclature doth the 'E' stand? And the other letters?"

Grinning, Boyle hurled the book with great force. It bounced off the knee of Athena, and fell to the ground, its pages flapping with a noise like pigeonwings. "We took this text from a New Astronomer, a Swiss, a famous *man*" he snarled. "In that country to which I travelled. And it was bethought a scheme *worthy* of our attention to render his words into Latin, print them up as by Lucretius, and deposit copies in libraries such that we, or our fathers, or our grandfathers might encounter them. Only why? Only to prompt the science of *our* day to develop with more rapidity and purpose! To obviate certain... difficulties in that far place into which I went. And I concurred! Fool that I was, for it seemed to me worthwhile; and why else had they helped me thither? And yet, what *became* of this scheme? Nothing! Our fathers, and our grandfathers, ignored the wisdom, nonwithstanding the eminent Roman's name attached to them."

Outside one of the windows a pigeon fluttered, scrabbling shadow briefly over the glass and then departing.

If one listened carefully, the sounds of an ordinary London day could be heard.

"*Which* country did you visit, sir?" Newton asked.

"I have another souvenir of my time there," Boyle remarked, his face brightening. "I have it about me somewhere." As he searched his pockets, he added, mumblingly. "E is energia. M, massus. As for the small cursive of the letter 'c', in epistula *celeritas* significat *lumen*."

"No man knows the precise value of such celerity!" Newton exclaimed, crossly. He had managed, without being observed by Boyle, to use his thumbnail to gouge a crescent-moon sliver from the nail of his forefinger. He was attempting, again without being observed, to manipulate this into the keyhole of the lock of his handcuff.

"Here it is!" Boyle pulled out a small piece of paper, a chit or note of some kind. The paper was green. "A portrait, printed upon paper," he announced. "Of whom? Guess!"

"Though I *am* young, sir," said Newton, "but yet am I not a *child*, to play such foolish games."

"Why then!" And Boyle danced – actually danced, with ponderous ridiculousness, upon his two clomping booted feet, and waved the piece of paper before Isaac, who caught the merest glimpse of the words ONE POUND – before Boyle tossed the scrap over his shoulder. It fluttered in a long arc down and a little way up, paused, fell back down in a lower arc, rose a little and finally fell all the way to the ground, at the feet of the gigantic statue of Plato.

"I have never seen so poor a forgery of a *pound* note, sir," remarked Isaac.

"Indeed!" cooed Boyle. "Ah! Ah! And *as* for the Lucretius, it has altered nothing. Depositing it in a dozen librariae, from thirteenth of centuries to the now? I said to them: Lucretius? Rather let us forge Plato! If *Plato* had spoken the verbum verum einsteinii the world would have listened! But" (this last, a glumly expressed *post scriptum*) "I fancy their Greek was not *lively* enough for the task."

"If they are the ones whose Latin you read aloud," Newton said, "I am surprised not at all. Are these the people who have suborned you to murder, sir? What, then, is *their* motivation?"

"*They* want you dead, sir? No sir! That is the *last* thing they want! It is I, and I alone, who accept the heavy burden of murdering my *fratris in scientia*. I alone! And the motivations belong to me, and to none other." In a moment, Boyle was at his side, and a knife was in his hand. Newton tried to flinch away, but his restraints made it impossible. Boyle had, evidently, taken one of his volatile swings of mood. "My reasons are my reasons."

"And they are?"

"Because," Boyle replied, his face suddenly glum, "because I am a coward." And at this he put his face in his hands and began to weep, noisily and copiously. Newton found the spectacle both distasteful and undignified. He looked away.

Shortly, recovering his composure, Boyle found a chair from somewhere in amongst the jumble of colossal statuary, and placed it six yards before Newton. He lay the pistol in his lap and sat in silence for a while. "Cowardice taketh many forms," he observed. "And before my – travels – I *was* an enthusiast for the New Astronomy. And now that New Astronomy itself renders me a coward!"

"I do not understand," Newton noted.

"The country into which I travelled was a place where the New Astronomy was king. They all believed it. Earth is found to move, and is no more the centre of the Universe. Stars are not fixed, but swim in the ethereal spaces. Comets are mounted above the planets! The sun is lost – for it is but a light made of the conjunction of many shining bodies together, no greater and in truth yea smaller than the other stars, yet only closer-by. The sun himself revealeth himself spotty, and subject to the mortality of all decayable things, to grow and eventually to die in a colour of blood and obesity of size? Is *this* the light God Himself made, the greater light to rule the day, at the beginning of all things? But the Bible saieth, *Their line is gone out through all the earth, and their words to the end of the world. In them hath he set a tabernacle for the sun.* Thus, I have seen the Sciences by the diverse motions of this globe of the brain of man become mere opinion, yet not error, but truth itself, that leave the imagination in a thousand labyrinths! What is all we know compared with what we know not? This, it is, Isaac, that maketh me a coward."

"Truth and God are coeval," Newton insisted, with the stiff ingenuousness of youth. "The one cannot lead a true soul away from the other."

"You mean by that," snarled Boyle, his lachrymous spirit instantly burned up in another of his sudden furies, "that I am no true soul! But I say to you Newton, it is the *truth* in my soul that pushes me on to your death! I stood in my new land, and learned what I could. I knew already that the universe was immensely larger than what was believed before the German Copernicus wrote his book. Oh, but I knew not the verity of it! Larger is a word that approacheth not even unto adequacy. The cosmos is so *much* the huger, and la vicissitude et la variété des choses en l'universe surpasses the *capacity* of the human mind to apprehend. This it is maketh me a coward, Sir. I do confess it. I looked through the optical and other devices of that place, and what I saw of their universe overwhelmed me. The perspective was total, and it produced in my soul a vortex of terror." His irascibility seemed to have melted back into self-pity. Truly, Isaac thought, and he tried for the seventh time to work his sliver of fingernail around the inner-latch of his handcuff-lock, such that he caught it again between thumb and finger, and made a hoop that might pull the pin free. For the seventh time the end of the tiny nail-strip slipped from his hold.

"What of it, sir?" replied Newton, with disdain. "Is it not truth?"

"It is truth! That is what so cowers my spirit. But I discovered something even the inhabitants of this other land did not know. I discovered that Ptolemy's model of the cosmos was true, also."

Newton snorted disdain from his nostril.

"You dismiss it, Brian?" said Boyle. "I mean, Isaac?"

"I have read Copernicus, and Kepler, sir. I have read Galileo, and seen the astronomical figures recorded therein. Did you not say *you* had met Galileo?"

"Galileo?" repeated Boyle, quizzically.

"Galileo!"

"Gallieo?"

Boyle's obtuseness was infuriating. "Galileo's *figures*."

"Oh!" Boyle sang out, as if seeing for the first time. "Magnifico! *Fine* observational data. But is the data enough? Must not data be interpreted? And how do we interpret? According to the idea. I confess, I am but a poor boy. Nobody loves me – born into a Waterford family. Yet even I can see, the idea *governs* the figures. In the days before Copernicus, natural philosophers looked to the heavens and saw – Ptolemy's cosmos. Earth at the centre; the astral bodies in crystal spheres all rotating one about the other, as the skins of an onion do. And in the other layers, the circle of the fixed stars; and outside that the primum mobile, that imparts motion to all the others."

Newton had had enough of listening to this nonsense. He shook himself as hard as he could; but his chains remained tight. "Will you let me go?" he demanded.

"Base miller!" cried Boyle. There was a pause. Then, recovering his self-control, Boyle added quietly. "Cannot let *you* go."

"Your wits have been poisoned by your travels. Ptolemy's system is an exploded relic of a time before accurate observation and natural philosophy unperverted by the Catholic Church was able to ascertain the true structure of the cosmos. I myself have begun calculations designed to establish..."

"I know," Boyle interrupted him. "What you will go on to establish. I have looked through the devices at the cosmos *your* ideas determine. And the fact is: just that I prefer to live in a smaller cosmos. Not pinchingly so! I would not be bounded in a nutshell and count myself kind of infinite space – oh no! I *like* grandeur. I like sublimity! Look around," and he gestured with one outstretched arm at the gigantic statuary with which they were surrounded. "I like to be surrounded by plastic art that dwarfs me! No egoismus, I! I have returned from my travels very rich and I have used my money to buy mansions, and to fill them with gigantic statuary! Every week new pieces come into my storerooms – this very space, here in Soho. And every month or so I have the pieces that most touch my fancy moved out to one or other of my houses. It gives me an enormous sense of well being, to stand among them. *But* – and this is my point: but it is one thing to be a human dwarfed by Ptolemy's cosmos – for that, though immense, is immense on a human scale. It is another to be dwarfed by the cosmos the New Astronomy perceives. That shrinks the human soul to a dot upon a dot, the merest *festucam*, a speck beneath the threshold of even divine cognizance. That is what makes me a coward."

"You would return to live in Ptolemy's solar system?" Newton mocked. "Why not yearn to live in Thomas More's Utopic realm? Or in Nephelokokkygia?"

"Those places were not real!" Boyle insisted. "Where the solar system *is*."

"Ptolemy's solar system was not real," Newton retorted. "Thanks to the spyglasses of Copernicus, Kepler and your magnifico Galileo have we come to understood that."

"And I say differently. I say – Ptolemy's cosmos was true; and Copernicus's cosmos is true. Smell out the difference between the former and the latter?"

"They cannot both be true," Newton insisted.

"Why may they not?"

"Because the observable data fit *not* the cosmos as hypothesied by Ptolemy," Newton insisted, growing heated. This, whatever other nonsense Boyle might indulge in, *this* matter touched his own intellectual propriety.

"In what ways do they not fit?" Boyle asked, simpering.

"Must we rehearse this, sir? In many ways. For example, the retrogression of planetary bodies as they are observed to pass across the sky."

"True," conceded Boyle. "But might there be another explanation for such retrograde motion?"

"You advert to the theories of Tycho Brahe?"

"Not I! I have been given access to knowledge Brahe lacked. The seventh book of Lucretius contained all the needful pointers, yet none have pursued them. But *I* know. Were the Ptolemaic system true, what might its dimensions be?"

"Were a unicorn real," Newton returned, "how long might its horn be?"

Boyle smiled and tut-tutted. "Consider if the inconsistencies in the Ptolemaic system be explicable in terms of science yet to be developed? Science that postdates anno domini 1631? Consider: the system in toto consisteth of nine spheres: Moon, Mercury, Venus, Sun, Mars, Iuppiter, Saturn, the stellatum, wherein are located the fixed stars, and beyond it the Primum Mobile. If the space between spheres be fifty millions of miles, which accordeth with the telescopic data, then the radius of the primum mobile would be four hundred and fifty millions of miles. Such a sphere would inscribe a circumference of two thousand eight hundred millions of miles – a distance it must perforce travel in one day. It moveth, then, at a velocity of thirty three thousand miles per second. I, happening to know the speed of light itself, know thereby that the primum mobile approacheth that luminal speed, by a fraction larger than a third. And at such speeds, as the science that lies beyond Brahe's ken assures us, relativistic effects begin to distort spacetime."

"Quoth what?" Newton exclaimed, disbelievingly.

"*Temporis spatio vel spatii tempore,*" Boyle replied. "For they are indissoluble. And such distortions, including vortices of gyrotopic interference set in place, much as standing waves in a spiral motion, would impart retrogressive swirls to the motion of the inner spheres. If Kepler had known the natural philosophy I now know, he would have understood enough to explain such variables as appeared to misfit Ptolemy's model. Relativistic effects in the primum mobile! Dark matter and graviton eddying."

"So ye deny the New Astronomy? Ye think it untrue?"

"It is as true as the Old Astronomy! Copernicus's system is as true as Ptolemy's. Or, it becometh true, as we collect more data. The New Astronomers in that land I visited take it as axiomatic, and are right to. They plan and execute passage from world to world by magic chariots, and in so traveling they find the cosmos just as Copernicus said. But had we undertaken such voyages in the thirteenth-century, we would have found the cosmos just as Ptolemy said!"

"Impossible," Newton insisted. "The logical law of non-contradiction is such that it be impossible *both* versions of the world are true."

"Yet both are, at different times. Different ideas seize the collective minds of men, and each idea determines which universe we inhabit. For as Plato says, the only true reality is ideational; material bodies are but shadows of strong ideas. And if we change material bodies by sculpting or assembling them, do they not change? And what if we change the ideas that underlie material bodies? Would the change not be grander and more universal?"

"A man may change his idea," Newton pointed out, "from one day to another, and nothing changes about the world."

"A man, surely. But all men? What if every man in the world changed his idea. What would come to the world from that? Some ideas are stronger than others. And once they take root in the collective consciousness, and granted only they do not flatly contradict the physical reality of the cosmos, why then they change that cosmos. And your ideas, dear Brian, are such ideas. That forged pound note shows it."

"You seek to kill me," Newton said, "for that you are a coward, and on account of a forged pound note that I did not forge?"

"I assassinate you," said Boyle, his face now grim, as he picked up his pistol and aimed it at Newton's chest, "because, with you dead, the ideas sufficient to bring Copernicus's cosmos into full non-Heisenberg life will never be. And so I can continue living in the more amenable cosmos of Ptolemy. I know the wrong I do. But those I met on my travels taught me that millions might die, if only the idea they fight for be pure enough, and so be accounted heroes and the war just. Millions upon millions of that place had been murdered to uphold lesser ideas than yours, Brian! Democratic anarchy was one. The wrongness of one tyrant and the rightness of another."

Boyle stood up quickly, quacking the chair back, and extended his right arm, with the pistol at the end of it. The click of Boyle's finger tripping the flint. The quieter click as Newton, with perseverance and luck, at last managed to unhook the inner-mechanism of his hand-cuffs. But too late!

The report of the pistol was a deafening thing, and Isaac clenched his eyes by reflex. When he oped them again, Boyle was standing, smoke cloaking him in slow-turning rags. The ball had missed its target. Even though fired at such close quarter. Newton threw his arms back and snapped the handcuffs free. He barely had time to register the look of surprise on Boyle's face as he jumped forward, shouldering into the other man's stomach. Boyle staggered, but did not tumble.

Newton ran straight for the door, but his feet tried to betray him. His left ankle jellied and he staggered left against the base of the Plato statue. There was a second deafening retort, and a keening *ping!* and the reek of gunpowder.

"Harder to aim than I fancied, sir!" hooted Boyle, behind him.

I know the wrong I do

Newton reasoned: the fellow cannot keep missing for ever. So he hurled himself at the door. But it was massy oak, threaded with metal, and locked – locked! Newton turn to see Boyle re-loading his pistol, thought of rushing him to snatch the key. He took a step forward, but the firearm was ready and aimed.

"Stand still!" cried Boyle, as Newton ducked to the side and in amongst the statuary.

He was breathing hard, and his left ankle hurt. He sidled behind the chunky, columnar legs of Athena, almost tripping over a reclining figure of, perhaps, a Fallen Trojan Warrior, holding a gold-bladed sword.

"Vitam quaeritis inter mortuos *statuas*!" Boyle called out. "Yet can I see your motion." But he did not discharge his weapon, husbanding his chance.

There was a form of broad shelf behind the first row of figures, six feet high and broader than that at the top – the statuary placed upon it towered over the massive personages at the front. Newton scrambled up, thinking of the high windows and wondering at his chances. The pistol fired again, and a hail of marble chips rained down. Now! Newton stood, clambered awkwardly up an albino stone Laocoön being throttled by a golden serpent. But the windows were still out of his reach, and, looking over his shoulder as he stretched up, he saw Boyle aiming his weapon. He ducked back down, and took cover behind the Trojan priest's petrified death-throes.

"Come out," Boyle called, impatiently. "Come out! Would you condemn our descendants to live in a universe that ignoreth them, to which they are less than nothing? Would you curse our children's children to dwell in a heartless cosmos of implacable infinitude? Would you have them fleas, sir, or angels? I can bring the latter about; you will doom us to the former. Come out, and we can return humanity to the proportionate cosmos of Ptolemy."

Newton breathed as quietly as he could, and pondered his options.

"Then," said Boyle, "I must come up and get you." He stepped in between the marble figures. Newton listened, picking out the sounds of Boyle's breathing, and the noise of his footfall. His life depended upon it!

"I can see you," called Boyle, sounding close.

Newton leapt, and felt his head jar painfully against something – Boyle's chin. The pistol discharged again and Isaac sensed sharp heat near his stomach. But no pain; the ball had not burst through his skin. The two men tumbled back, falling hard against the erect legs of Odysseus. Boyle was gasping, and flailing with his free hand. A blow caught Newton on the side of the head, and a second blow, but he pressed himself harder against his assailant. Newton's right hand fell upon the other's key-ring, and with a leaping heart he yanked it from the assassin's belt.

"You are on fire," Boyle cried out, in what sounded like a delighted voice.

It was true. Newton darted behind Laocoön, and wriggled through the three Graces, but his coat was smoking and little flames were wriggling like worms at the fabric. It took a moment to pat out the miniature conflagration. Looking back, Boyle could be glimpsed between the marble limbs, recharging his weapon.

Isaac looked to the door. It would take a moment to operate the lock; and he must give his assailant as little by way of a target as possible. He squeezed through the upper level of statues. Boyle called out: "stand clear Isaac, I see you not." His own heart pummelled his ribs. But he had the key!

Hippomene and Atalanta was the final statue; after Atalanta was only wall. Newton gathered himself, readying a leap down, and wondering which of the two keys on the iron ring would open the lock. The odds, he thought, were half-upon-half. "Lord God," he prayed quietly. "If it be thy will I survive this lunatic assault, then guide my hand to the right key –"

Looking back he saw, with a horrible clutching sensation in his throat, that Boyle had a clear shot. No time to wait. Newton leapt down, heard Boyle sing out "oh!" in disappointment, or elation. He landed on his bad ankle, staggered, and got to the door. The key went in, and a rough twist turned it. The mechanism slid free. The words of thanks to God were on Newton's lips, and he was speaking aloud, but his prayer was drowned out by the sound of the pistol discharging a fourth time.

Boyle's bullet flew wide. Newton was opening the door. The marble wrist of Atalanta disaggregated in a burst of marble chips, hurtling apart from the point of contact. The apple, sculpted at immense expense from solid gold, shot free, propelled along a shallow arc, striking Newton (he was opening the door) upon the side of his head. The force of the impact was determined by the mass of the object (which was considerable) multiplied by the velocity. It struck Isaac from the left. The momentum of the object was transferred to the skull of Newton, where it cracked the cranial bones along three distinct lines of fracture, and jarred the jelly of brain tissue within. If this latter collision had not been enough to kill the man, the swelling and tissue trauma of the blow would soon have done so. Newton fell right, and was dead before his body landed on the dusty floor.

Up on the shelf, surrounded by the figures from a once-exploded mythology, Boyle sat down. He placed the pistol, hot from use, beside him. His heart was racing. He sighed; which is to say, by instinctively pressing down with his diaphragm he reduced the pressure of the gases occupying his thoracic cavity, which in turn set up an imbalance with the surrounding atmosphere, thereby drawing more air into the lungs. Then, by reversing this physiological process, he utilised the fact that the pressure of a gas tends to increase as the volume decreases, he breathed out.

"At last," he said, to nobody in particular. The wind blew a sharp bang against the windows, and Boyle leapt up. "Anyway!" he exclaimed, jollily. "The wind blows."

ANIMALIA PARADOXA

Henrietta Rose-Innes

Île-de-France, 1792

"IN CAP D'AFRIQUE," I tell Michel, "the cattle are more beautiful than the French varieties. Great spreading horns. Red or grey, or speckled."

Michel grunts. He watches me with suspicion as I rearrange the bones on the long table in the Countess's orangery.

Through the glass doors and the dome above me, I can see bats flitting in the evening sky. A few lamps burn in the upper rooms of the chateau across the terrace. The Countess is no longer here. After the recent troubles in Paris, she left with her retinue for the countryside, perhaps even for another country. I did not speak with her before she departed. Perhaps I am simply shunned. Perhaps she is seeing other suitors, charlatans selling her the usual curiosities: misshapen bears, dull tableaux of common birds, amusing scenes of mice and foxes.

It is a cool autumn evening, but inside the orangery the weather is warm, even tropical. For a moment the expanse of glass makes me feel observed, as if I am placed here for display.

Michel is very slow, and has no sympathy for the material. He is an old village soul, accustomed to the creatures of the old world. He knows how they are put together: four feet, two horns, milk below.

"This cannot be just one animal," he says. He is laying out the long-bones, and indeed there seem to be too many of them, and oddly sized. Everything is in a sorry state. Some of the more delicate items have crumbled to dust in the sea-chests.

"Linnaeus himself does not account for all the creatures of the world," I tell him. "Not of Africa."

Michel shrugs, and lets a femur clatter to the table. "Monsieur," he says. "I am leaving now. You should go too: it is not safe."

But I cannot go, of course I cannot, not when I am so close. Late at night in the lamplit orangery I work on, fitting femur to radius, long bones to small. Boldness, I think, boldness and vision are needed here. But the bones will not do my bidding. They do not match up. They do not create a possible animal.

The streaks of light fade from the sky; it is that slow cooling of the day, so different to nightfall in southern climes.

I miss the boy's quick hands, quick eyes.

I remember the shape of his head. Jacques, Jakkals. He was a thin child, dressed in nothing but ragged sailor's trousers, held up by twine and rolled to the knee. Hard-soled feet, skin tight over ribs and shoulder-blades. All of him shades of earth and ochre, but flashed with white, like the belly of a springbok as it leaps away. Ostrich-eggshell beads at his neck, teeth like Sèvres porcelain. And that round head, close-shorn. One could imagine the bone beneath. When I first saw him, tagging behind as our party struck north from the Cape, I thought: there are men in France who would like that cranium in their collection. A pretty piece to cup in the palm.

Shadows gutter on the ceiling as the last of the lamp-oil runs out. Outside I see points of light and at first I think they are stars, burning low to the ground: the sky turned upside down. But no. They are flames, moving up the hill from the village, torches lighting faces in the crowd. The voices build.

The last time I saw Jacques his skull was crushed on one side, the front teeth gone, face caked with blood and dust.

I imagine he was buried with the usual native rites. Sitting upright, as I have heard it is done, in the old hide blanket, with nothing to mark the place but a small pile of stones. The vitreous black stones you find there in the north, in that dry country.

Cape of Good Hope

Venter was a chancer from the start. I met him on the church square; he was selling skins and ivory. With what was left of the Countess's money, I was procuring oxen, muskets, what men I could afford.

"I hear you're coming north," he said, his face shadowed by a leather brim. "I hear you're looking for animals."

"Special animals," I nodded. "Rare ones." I had been in the Cape a month by then, and my own rough Dutch was improving.

"Visit with us," he said. "We have a hell of an animal for you."

"Ah. And what kind might that be?"

I was not overly excited. Already I had received several offers of specimens. There had been enough European adventurers in these parts for the locals to imagine they knew what we sought. On the docks, a hunter had thrust a brace of speckled fowl at me, their bodies stinking in the heat. In a tavern, a wrinkled prospector had produced a pink crystal, its facets glinting in the candlelight. But the Countess wished for something she had not seen before. The foot of a rhinoceros, a pretty shell – these would not be enough. One of the slave-dealers had promised more exotic sights, native girls with curious anatomies, but this, too, I had refused. I was looking for something spectacular, something to cause a sensation; but not of that kind.

"It's big," said Venter.

"Like an elephant? An ostrich?" I said. "Perhaps a whale?"

"All of those things," he said, and tilted his head so that his pale eyes caught the sun, colour piercing the hues of hide and roughspun cloth. He was a handsome man, tall and with a strong jaw under his yellow beard, grown very full as is the habit of the farmers here. "It's all of those things, God help us."

I tried not to smile at his ignorance. "Come now, it must be one thing or the other. Fish or fowl."

He shrugged. "It flies, it runs. Here," he said, leaning forward and pulling off his hat. A waft of sweat, a herbal tang, the coppery hair compressed in a ring. "That is its skin."

I did not wish to touch the greasy hat, but he pushed it into my hands, pointing at the hide band. Spotted, greyish yellow. It might have been hyena fur, or harbour rat for all I knew.

"Keep it." He spat his tobacco into the dust. "You are welcome on my land. Ask for Venter. Up north the people know me."

It took me several weeks to gather what I needed for the expedition: oxen, two wagons, a donkey, the firelocks, the powder and lead. I could not afford slaves in the end, but employed ten bearers of the race they call here Hottentotten. The arsenical paste for the preservation of the specimens I had brought with me on the ship from France. My collecting trunk, which fitted perfectly into the back of the larger wagon, was a gift from the Countess, made by her own cabinet-maker, and had her initials inlaid in brass on the lid. Inside were dozens of ingenious drawers and racks for glass jars and flasks. I had also with me my fine brass compass – although the little hinged sundial did not work as it should, down in the south – and my most prized possession: my copy of *Systema Naturae*.

The donkey I disliked. It looked exactly like any donkey in any part of France, and was every bit as doltish and mutinous. But the oxen were splendid animals. I was glad to see the mountain growing smaller over their lurching shoulders as our party took the coastal track to the north. Happy to be away from that town, with its hot winds, its slave-drivers from every filthy corner of the world, its rumours of plague and war.

We turned inland. Game was plentiful and we did not lack for meat. It lifted my heart, to be out on those grasslands, with no sounds but the steady hoofbeats of the oxen, the wagons' creak and the good-humoured talk of the men in a language I did not know. Clucks and kisses in it, impossible for my mouth to shape. At times people appeared out of the bush to meet us on the road, and spoke to the men in their own tongue, perhaps asking news of the Cape. As we travelled further north, the land became dryer, flatter, broken by pans of salty mud cracked in honeycomb patterns and pink with roosting flamingos; elsewhere by tumbled piles of glassy black and olive rock. It was wild country. I had high hopes of finding some striped or spotted beast for my lady yet. Indeed, one night we heard a throaty rumble from beyond the firelight. Lion, the men whispered. But it did not approach.

The bearers were easy company. The boy, in particular, was useful; he brought back small animals and interesting pebbles, bird's-nests, snakeskins. As we travelled, he was constantly darting into gullies or turning over stones to gather up a feather, a piece of wool, a beetle carapace. Nothing extraordinary, but I saw that he understood my purpose. When we board-mounted a little bat, he very neatly fanned the wing for me to tap the brass tacks in, without needing instruction. It was hard to tell his age, seventeen or twelve, he was so thin. I think he ate better with me than he ever had in the town. Where he came from, I was not sure. He was not one I hired myself, but seemed to have come along with the older men. Jakkals, they called him. Though that was not his true name, I think. I started to call him Jacques, privately, when we worked on the specimens together. A sentimental impulse: it was the name of my own little boy, lost now these twenty years. With the men I called him Boy.

Some days into our journey, we were passed by a group of riders, also heading north. The commando, as such posses are called, were after a baster gang: thieves and runaways, they said, causing havoc on the farms. A rough bunch themselves, these vigilantes, guns slung across their backs. They peered at our party with suspicion. It was not usual to a see a solitary white gentleman in those parts, certainly not a Frenchman. I mustered my best kitchen Dutch to persuade them on their way.

The commando disturbed my men. After the riders left, kicking up dust to the horizon, they murmured uneasily to each other.

Later, I asked the men about Venter's beast, and handed the hat around the fire. They went silent. Between puffs on their long clay pipes, they said the name of the animal. *Gumma, gauma, gomerah.* Rasped in the back of the throat, in a way I am incapable of reproducing.

"So it is real?"

Hums of assent.

"What does it look like?"

"It has wings, very long." One man held out his arms. "Black feathers."

"And a head like a lizard, with lion's teeth."

"Very dangerous."

"It can eat forty, fifty sheep."

The oldest of the men, a dignified greybeard to whom the others deferred, pushed tobacco into the bowl of his pipe and said in his cracked voice: "It will look at you. It has the eyes of a man."

I smiled, to show I did not mind, that they made fun of me in this manner.

The hat was passed to the boy. He did not usually speak in front of the older men, but now he touched the hatband with the tips of his fingers. "Ghimmra." He said the name differently, with an altered emphasis, and when they heard him the others grunted and nodded approvingly.

"I know this," said the boy. "It is from my place. I am from that place."

Yes, I thought, that may well be. He has the look of a Bushman child. I wondered how he had come to be in the town.

The quiet authority in his voice, and the gravity of all the men, made me think that perhaps there was truth in Venter's story. This was, after all, a new world. Things were different here. Animals may yet exist of which Linnaeus had no knowledge, I mused. Look at the wonders they have found in New Holland: beasts with both fur and eggs.

The commando was already encamped when we got to Venter's homestead. Not much of a farm at all, just a poor dry tract of stones and sand and a mud cottage. No wife, no children. Some way behind the hovel was a domed skin hut where Venter, it seemed, kept a native woman. The riders were gathered at a fire on the packed earth before the house, drinking brandy; the woman brought them a new cask when the old ran dry. My men made camp some distance away, but I accepted a dram of the harsh white liquor and talked for a while with Venter and his companions.

"So, Mijnheer," I said to Venter, "where do you keep this animal you speak of? This – is it right? Geema, geemera."

He looked at me a little oddly then. "Where did you learn this name?"

I smiled. "I am a naturalist, my friend. My task is to learn these things."

"Come," he said, quite drunk already and putting an arm around my neck. "I will show you the proof of it."

Venter drew me warmly into his tiny house. There was almost no furniture in the single room, just a chair and a bed covered in skins. On top of a wooden trunk sat a weighty old Bible. He set this aside and opened the lid of the chest, then proceeded to bring his precious items out into the lamplight, one by one.

I very nearly laughed out loud. Nothing but ratty pelts and dried-out bones, drawn from a dozen different carcasses. He held up the butchered wing of vulture, then what seemed to be the skull of a large bovid. Of some interest, but nothing extraordinary. At least he had not gone to the trouble of stitching it all together into a single beast, as I have seen done in fairground wonder-shows. I would not have been surprised if the man drew out a fish-skin or a bolt of flowered cotton and tried to tell me it was the hide of some fearsome predator.

"Sjeemera," he said. His way of saying the word was different, more sibilant.

I smiled and thanked him and said that this was all most interesting, and that I would be glad to inspect his collection more carefully in the daylight. So as not to offend him, I picked out one or two small items – a few dark quills, a shed snake-skin. If I wanted the bones, he intimated, I would have to pay. I quickly made my goodnights.

I left the fire and the drinking, choosing rather to lie in my own tent, close to the soft snorting and warmth of the oxen. Still, I could hear the men of the commando talking and laughing late into the night.

Jacques, who slept at my feet inside the tent, spoke into the dark: "The animal, Mijnheer."

"Yes?"

"I can take you to its place. I know where is its cave."

I was silent for moment. "Is it near? Can we walk?"

"No. It is still a day from here. We must take the wagons. We should go tomorrow, early."

"How do you know?"

"This is my place. My people are here."

That night there was a great storm, wind lashing the tent, the oxen bellowing. Something shrieked like a child in the trees down near the river. Later, we heard the calls of some large animal – but with a yelping, yawning quality, quite unlike a lion's.

I covered my head with an oily sheepskin kaross and thought of France, the motionless winter trees, the pale light touching the branches as delicately as gilt on the curlicues of the Countess's cabinet of marvels.

In her reception room, I had balanced on the spindliest of chairs as she showed me her celebrated collection: birds' nests, curious stones and the skeletons of small animals, arranged in the specially built case of glass and wood all lacquered white. Light spattered off the touches of gold leaf, off the sunburst wings of the suspended hummingbirds. A thoroughly unsystematic approach, I noted, *Mammalia* mixed in with *Aves* mixed in with *Fossilia*.

"Is it not pretty?" she asked.

"Indeed, very pretty," I agreed. High in her powdered hair, among the silken bows, another iridescent hummingbird was pinned. The blue flattered her eyes.

She noticed my gaze and touched the stiff little bird. "From India," she said. "Do they have such things in Afrique?"

"If so, I shall endeavour to discover them, Madame."

"Hm. I think not," she said. "From Afrique I want something... magnificent. A new kind of elephant?"

"Perhaps something not quite so large..."

"A tiger!"

"I believe they lack the striped kind there. I will try for spots."

"Oh but I like the stripes. In the Jardin du Roi they have a leaping tiger, suspended in the air. It is quite wonderful. See what you can do."

"Madame."

That had been months before, but it felt like a hundred years. My mission now seemed laughable. How could the Countess have thought that a spun-sugar cabinet might contain any part of this elemental land? In my half-asleep state, it came to me that I had done things altogether back to front. All her pretty shells and pebbles... I should have put them in my pockets, brought them with me on the ship and set them free, here in this world of ancient stones and long horizons.

In the blue dawn, the oxen stood shifting and blowing steam. The men packed the wagons quickly and quietly. It seemed important to leave before the commando stirred from their drunken sleep, although no doubt that would break all this country's laws of hospitality. The armed company had made us nervous, and even the oxen seemed to tread softly for fear of breaking the chill and fragile silence. I was pleased when the little grey house dipped out of sight as the ground rose, as earlier I had been pleased to leave the town behind. As I had been glad to leave France, too, if I were honest, the dark wave sinking the shore in our wake. Always onwards, to new things. Away from old sadness. New wonders, I told myself.

We found ourselves creaking up the start of a long mountain pass marked by stones. As the wagons ascended and the broad, brightening plain fell away below us, so too my spirits lifted. The track was edged with tiny white and yellow flowers. I thought about collecting them to press, but I did not want to halt our progress. And *Regnum Vegetabile* had never delighted me quite like *Regnum Animale*.

At length we came out onto the neck of the pass, where Jacques indicated we should outspan. Above us was a rough tower of boulders.

"Here," said Jacques, and started up the scree. He went lightly, leaping barefoot from rock to rock. I struggled behind, sweat soaking my linen shirt. My face was flaming, even shaded by Venter's odorous hat.

In the shade beneath the rocks, the sand was cool. I took a moment to catch my breath. Jacques was crouched close to the base of a boulder, peering at something. At first I could not make it out, but then I saw: an image painted on the stone, about two hands tall. An upright red body with a long pale face like a deer's or a hare's, but the finely muscled legs of a running man. Tiny white dots on the torso.

Despite my flush, I felt myself grow cold. "Is this what you have brought me to see, this... hocus pocus?"

He patted the floor of the cave. Was he smiling? The white sand was scuffed with a multitude of indistinct tracks, including our own. "Here," he said. "Here is where it puts its eggs."

"But this is no real beast," I said, angry. I felt more deceived by this primitive display than by Venter's skulduggery. "This is nonsense, Jacques! Why do you wish to trick me too?"

He did not answer. Instead he squatted and pushed his fingers into the sand, digging away several inches. Under the top layer the soil became damper, darker. A smooth white curve emerged. For a moment I thought it was a human skull rising from the ground. But he shovelled his hands down around it and, after some heaving, forced a gigantic egg to rise from the ground. It was bigger than his head, much bigger than an ostrich egg. When I bent to help him raise it, I felt its weight. It was smooth and cool to the touch, and very heavy, as if full of molten metal. I took my water-skin and poured a little out; washed free of sand, the egg glowed like a great pearl, with a bluish cast.

"What is it, Jacques? What kind of bird?"

He spoke quickly, tongue clicking.

"What? I cannot understand."

He sighed and closed his eyes and his arms floated upwards. Then his head jerked back as if in a fit, ribs jutting tautly. I stopped forward in alarm, then realised: it was a pantomime. This was for me, so I could see the nature of the animal. His hands flapped and slapped his sides. Feet scuffed the sand, tracing a circle. He bowed his neck and kicked at the ground, arms out like wings, then opened his mouth very wide and groaned. Teeth like the white quartz in the rocks, not porcelain at all. Teeth bared as if in pain.

"That's enough."

At once he stood quite still, as if I had slapped him.

I ran my hands over the slick surface of the egg. "Tell me truthfully, now. Is this creature real?"

The boy nodded, although his eyes were cool.

"Then find me one. Find me one to shoot for my Countess. I have not time for make-believe."

I wrapped the egg in a piece of oilcloth and put it into my leather bag. Its weight hung awkwardly off my shoulder. As we walked back down the scree slope, I saw below me the two small wagons, the men lounging in the shade. It occurred to me for the first time that they might easily drive off without me, as I had heard happen to other adventurers. Once this thought had struck, it became harder to look away. I felt I needed to pin the men in place with my eyes. I thought of their uneasiness these last days, their murmurings to each other. The boy, I thought; they would not leave the boy behind. But perhaps the boy plans to flee, too. This is where he comes from, these hills.

The men greeted me civilly, but distrust had entered my heart. I sensed their alertness when they saw I carried a prize. The old man came up to me quite boldly, reaching out a hand as if to touch my bag, but I turned away from him, holding it closed.

I laid it next to my camp bed, where I curled up almost immediately, exhausted from the climb. Falling into slumber beneath the odorous kaross, I felt, for the first time on this journey, a longing for home, for walls around me, for the close skies and low ceilings and mossy damp enclosures of the old country. Rather than this bleak kingdom of stones, this *Regnum Lapideum*, roamed by unnameable animals.

The bright sky woke me like a slap. Blue, so blue, it filled my eyes to the edges and beyond. I lay staring up at it for some minutes before I realised what it meant. The tent was gone.

They had taken the horse, the oxen, the wagons, the muskets and ammunition. And Jacques, Jakkals, the boy: gone too.

Leaving me what? The donkey, presumably out of some chivalrous impulse: I could ride it in shame back to Venter's. The egg: it perched on the sand, balanced on one end. They had not wished to take it with them. And my collecting trunk. It stood askew on the ground, spilling its drawers into the sand, preserving fluid leaking from a corner. Its tiny compartments lay open to the sky, its intricate systems mocked by the boundless land. Carefully, I slid the drawers home, checking for broken jars and vials. Of course I could not move it on my own.

At my feet, the dry mud was cracked into hexagons, marked only by the points where the tent-pegs had been sunk, the impress of the cooking pots, the cold firepit and the long churned wake of the oxen. I put on Venter's hat with its fancy band and stood in the small puddle of my own shade.

I would have stayed there perhaps indefinitely, staring at the donkey staring at me, if there had not come some time later – I cannot say how long – the reports of many hooves on the dry earth. It was Venter and the riders. They slowed as they came alongside, and the man nodded a greeting. He seemed amused, hair glinting in the sun as he doffed his new hat. The others barely looked at me; they preferred to read the story directly from the earth. It was not a difficult tale.

The men wheeled their horses around me and took off to the north, faster now, chased by their shadows. That was what the commando was there to do, after all: pursue miscreants, thieves, absconders.

I followed on foot to the top of the pass, where the land fell away. I saw where the wagon wheels had gouged a track, a steep descent back and forth to the plain far below. It was even vaster than the one we had crossed the day before, pale yellow like a scarred old lion-skin, sparsely veined where darker bush marked the watercourses. Far off were flecks of white and gold: a herd of springboks. Their heads were raised at identical angles to watch the slowly fleeing wagons, which churned in their wake a creamy plume of dust that hung in the air like blood in water. They were heading for a line of bluish hills. They did not seem to have gone very far, although the distances were so great it was hard to judge.

Directly below me, more dust rose, marking the far faster progress of the commando. The riders had reached the bottom of the pass and were striking out across the plain. As the two trails converged, I realised that, despite my losses, it was the wagons I was urging on. But the riders were remorseless. A few minutes later, I heard the dull concussion of the first shots. In the long-echoing stillness of the desert air, the buck leaped into the air and away, hanging for a moment on each bound like low-flying birds.

I turned away and walked back to the immobile donkey. I stared up at the blue sky, letting Venter's hat fall from my head. Very high up, a great bird was wheeling, but I could not make out its markings. I could not identify it at all.

In the evening, they found me waiting back at the house. Venter let the boy's body tumble from the back of the horse onto the ground. So light it barely stirred the dust. So bloodied that at first I thought an animal had slain him. But then I saw his head. Musket-ball, I thought. I'd seen that kind of wound many years ago, a boy myself, in the Spanish wars.

"We lost the others in the hills," Venter said, shouldering past me into the house. The stench of powder and sweat and blood. "God damn it. Brandy."

Outside in the raw sun, I saw the kitchen woman come, not with brandy but with an old kaross in her hands, dark and creased as a tobacco leaf. She knelt to fold it around the boy's body, tucking it close with tense thrusts that made the muscles stand on her lean arms. At the last, he looked like a seed in a pod, a bat wrapped in its wings for the night.

South Atlantic Ocean

Already on the ship I could tell the specimens were rotting, that my techniques for preservation had failed in some or all of them. Perhaps the dank air in the hold had affected the formula, or seawater breached the wax seals. Not trusting the seamen with the delicate objects, I had chosen to keep them in the cabin with me, and lay on my trunks like a dragon on its hoard. I found it kept the seasickness at bay, despite the smells of meat and arsenic, to press my cheek to the cool wood. I dreamed the sea-chest beneath me was a coffin lid, with beneath it Jacques' face, lips drawn back from broken teeth. But Jacques was buried under stones, hands clutched around his ankles. Far from the sea.

The trunks were my fortune. I'd bartered every other thing I owned to get that damned boer to haul me and my cases and jars back to the Cape with its hellish summer winds. With every mile my monies bled away. The oxen, the guns and the wagons, the servants... all those seemed now like outrageous riches, as opulent as the Countess's silver dinner service.

I'd even sold Venter my precious *Systema*. He had put it next the Bible on his chest carved of yellow wood. I doubt very much the man could read either book. But it comforted me that Linnaeus's pages were not blowing through the veld, catching on thorns, being used to light pipes around campfires. At the last, the scoundrel pressed his collection of pelts and bones upon me; that at least was something.

Neuroptera, Minerœ, Muraena, I breathed through my nausea. I glimpsed through the blue porthole a long head turned towards me, obscured by the slow flap of a leathery wing, riding the hot wind from the Cape. At other times it followed beneath the ship. Once, in the early morning, I heard a deep boom shiver through the body of the vessel and I knew: it was pounding its head against the keel.

But when I went on board later that day, the men explained: "Cannonballs. Did you not realise? But we are safe now, by God's grace."

Corsairs. I laughed, and the sailors looked at me strangely.

In my notebook I tried to scratch a sketch of the creature I saw in my dreams, its serpent neck, its gaping jaws. *Amphibia, Vermes, Hydra.* The words were fading from my mind. The pen skittered away from me, the inkpot spilled.

In the third week at sea, the captain, a melancholy Swede, red-eyed, came down to complain of the smell, and insisted that the skins be turfed over the side. I was too sick to resist. Each drawer of my wooden cabinet was filled with corruption and shame: all lost, all for nothing.

But still I had the bones, and the egg in its wool-packed box. If I pulled aside the wool and laid my finger on the shell, I fancied I could feel some movement, a flip or shift in the sac of fluid within. Could it be alive? One storm-rocked night it escaped its nest and rolled elliptically across the deck. I scrambled after it, trapping it with my body.

At times I thought: this will be the making of me. It will be a sensation.

At other times I thought: it is my ruination.

Île-de-France

I have abandoned the bones. All I have left is the bluish egg, heavy as a cannonball. It was cool when we found it, but here in the orangery I can feel it has gained warmth, like a quickening thing. Palms pressed to its curve, I close my eyes; the last thing I see in the gloom is the egg's pale glow, like seashells, like bone, like quartz. I try to remember the shape of the painted creature on the rock, those many months ago. The red flanks, the calves and thighs, the long muzzle. The sheen of the wet rock behind it. A wonder.

Outside, shouts and the sound of breaking glass. The windows of the chateau. I think of the famous white cabinet, rocking on its ball-and-claws. The mob is coming closer, *Vive la Révolution*, and now the egg trembles against me as if in answer to that roar. Flames on my eyelids, an orange campfire light.

Breaking glass again, and closer, and all around. A wrench inside the shell. A black blast, a roar of heat: shards of glass strike me and as I topple back I feel the great egg crack in my arms, and something blood-hot and wet and writhing clambers from my grasp. As the walls of the orangery shatter around me, the newborn opens its wings.

When I wake I am on my back, staring up at the dark sky. The dome is broken. The chateau burns, and orange-lit smoke obscures the stars. It is too late for fear.

High above, the great forms hangs with wings outspread. Lizard-jawed, fish-scaled, coal-feathered, impossible. It pulls back its neck and screams. I cry out: something wordless, for it has no names that I can say.

It hears.

Looping its serpentine body, it turns and drops towards me. A hot rush of wind, and for a moment I see its giant eye.

It is a human eye, and every other kind besides. It is like no living thing, and yet contains all living things. It is animal and mineral and angel, and every being yet to be invented, all creatures of the coming age.

It rises up again, on wings of smoke and fire.

FOOTPRINT

Archie Black

Despite the continued (and, frankly, baffling) popularity of *Cathedral of Death*, the 1977 Hammer Horror gorefest which is a staple of sleepovers and midnight cinema showings, few people are aware that the film was itself based on a true story. Well, a "true" story – the largely–forgotten nineteenth century antiquarian Simon Laverman's reproduction of what he claimed was the diary of one J. L. Frontis, an engineer involved in the reconstruction of London following the Great Fire of 1666 – specifically, rebuilding St Paul's Cathedral. Frontis, if the diary is to be believed, was deeply involved in the development of Christopher Wren's masterpiece.

The facts are these: a cathedral dedicated to St Paul the Apostle has stood at the top of ancient London's highest point, Ludgate Hill, since the early seventh century. The first St Paul's was destroyed by fire in 962; the second (by the same means) in 1087. Work on the cathedral that would precede Wren's building, generally referred to as Old St Paul's, began in that same year. Like so many of the great building projects during this period of history, took decades; following yet another disruption by fire in 1136, the cathedral was not consecrated until 1240. The Great Fire, which raged for close to four days in late 1666, consumed upwards of 90% of the homes within London's ancient Roman walls, as well as eighty-seven churches... and Old St Paul's.

A few more details bear noting: the first St Paul's was constructed over the ruins of at least one and probably several pre-Norman religious buildings including, at least, the Roman cathedral of London and a Roman temple to Dis Pater (who may have originally been a Celtic god). The footprint – that is, the plan of the building as laid across the ground – does not exactly match the footprints of Old St Paul's or the earlier buildings, which were aligned upon an exact east/west axis. Rather, the footprint of Wren's St Paul's is rotated by a few degrees to the south-east. Wren claimed that this slight alteration aligned the cathedral so that it faced the sunrise of the Easter Sunday of 1670, the year that construction began.

One of the most famous stories about St Paul's cathedral concerns a stone Christopher Wren found, a fragment of an ancient monument bearing a single Latin word: *resurgam*, "I will rise again." Wren used it to mark the central point in the new cathedral, to give his engineers a precise spot from which to measure.

Wren's St Paul's has never caught fire.

Simon Laverman (1814 – 1878) published the *Diary* in 1852, and it experienced a brief period of vogue until the Great Gold Robbery of 1855 overtook the public consciousness. Edited versions began appearing about ten years later, first in volumes devoted to the Great Fire and later in collections of ghost stories, for which the Victorians had a passion. You're probably already familiar with *Diary*, though you may not remember it – *Diary*, presented as entirely fictional, has been a staple of middle-grade textbooks in some form or another for at least fifty years and, as we know, Hammer's *Cathedral of Deat*h is based very, (very) loosely upon it.

It is very likely, however, that you have never read the piece in its entirety. I loved the story as a kid and (of course) I'm a huge fan of the film. When, while on holiday in Yorkshire at the end of 2012, I found an old copy of *Diary* in a collection of ghost stories, my curiosity was piqued. Who was J. L. Frontis, who was S. Laverman, and when was the story actually written - if it even was a story? The harder I worked to discover the truth about the story, the more questions I raised. It took me more than a year to track down a first edition from 1852; even the hallowed

British Library has no copy that hails from earlier than 1863.

I am no historian, so it is not my place to speculate about the authenticity of Laverman's work. Certainly his introduction, also reproduced below, suggests a man with an ideological axe to grind. Not to mention the style in which the diary is written, which is, even to my untrained eye, *significantly* more nineteenth century than seventeenth. Laverman's disgust with the seventeenth century's intellectual preoccupation with reason and order, at what he considered the expense of the human soul, is obvious and, not to put to fine a point upon it, pretty suspicious. Also suspicious: his claims to have destroyed the original diary itself because, among other reasons, its author was the kind of guy who wrote down his dirty thoughts about the ladies. Laverman, he claims on his own behalf, was forced to destroy the diary to ensure that no sensitive soul might ever learn the corrupting truth that men think about sex a lot.

What is important for our purposes is that the original 1852 publication is being reproduced here, complete and unedited, for the first time in close to two centuries. Despite Laverman's insistence that Frontis' seventeenth century spelling and punctuation be retained, which I personally consider part of his effort to establish the authenticity of a subpar forgery rather than a considered academic decision, I have taken the liberty of modernising the text for the sake of today's reading public, who may not have the patience for Frontis', shall we say, "experimental" writing style. (Fifteen different spellings of "appearance" being, perhaps, a bit much for the casual reader.) Again, it goes without saying that the authenticity of Laverman's document and claims are questionable; Laverman is not the first antiquarian who claimed to have discovered a valuable historical document and then destroyed it in a bid to preserve its integrity. But the story itself, as well as the story *surrounding* the story, remains a compelling one, and so I am proud to present *The Diary of J. L. Frontis*, unedited and unaltered, for the first time since its publication in 1852.

Archie Black

London

2014

✠

First I must set the stage. Surely I may pass over the history of the Great Fire of London, the details of which are known to every child – of the bakery fire that began early on September 2nd, 1666, on Pudding Lane and, four days later, extinguished itself against Pie Corner; the fire which destroyed 70,000 houses and laid waste to the greatest city in the world. Perhaps less well known today are the glut of extraordinary city plans that were presented to Charles II in the wake of the destruction, many suggesting the rebuilding of the metropol according to the clockwork imaginings of that century's finest minds – everyone from Sir Christopher Wren to John Evlyn to James Hooke, and multitudinous others, all of whom wished to see the cramped twists and turns of the medieval city widened and straightened and regularised, as the minds of that century wished to widen and straighten and regularise all human endeavour, with no thought to the variegations and variety of the human spirit, much less its ingenuity. With no regard for the pneuma of London's ancient history did they plan the wholesale destruction of the human traces of the city's past: the winding lanes; the tumble of buildings, each individual in its noble architecture, its indomitable spirit.

The sainted Wren had been contracted to save Old St Paul's, which was following the conflagration a ruinous pile, its proud spire the victim of a lightning strike a century before; its exquisite nave become little better than a covered market, where children threw stones at jackdaws with little regard for the sacred space within which they gamed; the churchyard buildings torn down for scrap, or inhabited by dissident preachers and booksellers. Inigo Jones oversaw an attempted restoration beginning in 1620, but the political upheavals of the 1640s brought an end to the project and the great cathedral fell once again into disrepair. Following the Restoration, Wren was brought in to complete the work of his predecessor, he decried man's monument to God as "wanting in accuracy" and advocated its wholesale destruction. When, quite rightly, the outcry of the inhabitants of England and the rest of the world became to great to bear, Wren capitulated and agreed to restore the cathedral according to Jones' model.

We certainly cannot lay the blame for the Great Fire of London at Sir Christopher Wren's feet! Nevertheless, it goes entirely without saying that he benefited mightily from London's tragedy, no more so than in being given permission to carry through his plans to rebuild St Paul's. Upon discovering that the damage was too extensive for even the great Wren to repair, the plan to restore Old St Paul's was abandoned and the new cathedral was built upon the footprint of the cathedral before it, and likewise the cathedral before that, and the temples that preceded even that to a numinous prehistory shrouded from us by the mists of time, all erected along the same axis of east to west, and all exactly upon the footprint of the house of God that preceded it. So was Wren's St Paul's wrought, from the crypt to the lantern, wholly anew, but with one slight, and puzzling, alteration; the plan of the new cathedral was placed not along the true line that runs from east to west, as all previous structures had been, but instead rotated several degrees along the axis of north and south.

Although the change has been commonly attributed to Wren's desire to prove his mathematical and astronomical genius by predicting the exact point at which the sun would rise on a given day in a given year, yet another attempt by the process-minded men of the Age of Reason to exert dominion over the mysteries of Creation, this *Diary* evidences that the change was the suggestion of one J. L. Frontis, a minor surveyor on the project, whose work in excavating the remains of the crypt of Old St Paul's, as diligently recorded in his *Diary*, formed the basis of his recommendation to destroy the old structure and begin anew, and almost certainly contributed to his mental deterioration.

My discovery of this *Diary* stands as testament to the enduring spirit of those same mysteries of Creation hitherto referenced; for here we have, at long last, an alternate and truthfully more satisfying – albeit unsettling – explanation to account for this irregular act by Sir Christopher Wren, the seventeenth century's most regular mind.

Little is known of J. L. Frontis, the engineer whose excerpted diary this essay introduces. Of his birth and childhood we have no information; the name James Lighthorpe Frontis appears on the rolls no earlier than 1663. Where there can be no doubt is that one James Frontis was involved in Wren's cathedral project, following the Great Fire of London, for years; his information remains complete in the surviving records and accords to the text below.

Less certain, however, is his fate; James Frontis' name vanishes from the primary sources in 1674. No explanation is ever produced,by the official sources, but that fact is not necessarily significant in and of itself; a hundred possibilities suggest themselves. Frontis may have met with an accident, may have been required of necessity to quit his position to care for his ailing wife, or may simply have left the project altogether; such behaviour was not uncommon in this period of upheaval.

What is certain is that one Jas Frontyce was admitted to Bethlehem hospital in 1675. Better known now as Bedlam, Bethlehem was one of the most famous lunatic asylums in all of history. The first reference to "Frontyce, the Mystic of Bedlam" appears in print in 1677, in the correspondence of Lady Fitzwinter; by 1683 "The Mystic" was well established in the Bedlam and appears in the hospital's catalogue, which advertised to interested viewers during this barbaric period that "he may be visited on Tuesdays between 9 and noon, to expound upon the pagan gods of the old city and their multitudinous airs and eccentricities to the delight of all ages".

I discovered this curious little document in one of the grimmer bookstores off Fleet Street; a slender volume bound in decaying paperboard, I am ashamed to say the *Diary* was being advertised for its prurient content, although the purveyor, being familiar with my antiquarian interests, particularly relating to the Great Fire, heeded its value as an historical document and recommended it to me. I blush to recall the more lubricious entries that made up so much of the *Diary's* content; so many compositions of such a crude and off-putting nature did it contain that I was forced to destroy it after replicating what few entries held any historical value, for fear that the unexpurgated whole might fall into the hands of those delicate creatures for whom such admissions must, by nature, be abhorrent. Despite the wholly incalculable value of retaining such a document for the historical record – in the author's own hand, the ink still strong, marks of his quill impressed deeply into the aged paper – for posterity, I could not in good conscience allow the Diary to survive whole and true. Better that it haunt only my dreams, than risk its infection to spread to even one other.

There can be no doubt that James Lighthorpe Frontis was mad; this *Diary* stands testament to his descent into lunacy. Whether that James Lighthorpe Frontis was the same Jas Frontyce as was admitted to Bethlehem and became known as "Frontyce the Mystic" will almost surely never be positively ascertained. All I can do is recommend this curious document to your interest, and recommend that you draw your own conclusions upon the evidence as presented.

S. Laverman

London

1852

✤

2 June 1667
Following a long day amongst the ruins I required air; even now we turn up ashes from the fire in dark pockets, and beneath the great heat-cracked stones; we step into the darkness and suddenly black clouds arise to choke us. So many of these did we find today, despite how many times we have sent the boys down to sweep the ruins, I cannot number them in my memory.

Through the twilight I wandered the streets. Much of the rubble has cleared away months before, and new houses built, and yet amidst it all a few old houses still stand; was it Nature, capricious as a girl, or our all-seeing God, that saw fit to destroy entire streets, save a single humble dwelling here and there? I strive to find these structures and talk to those who inhabit them; I wish to discover the reason their homes were spared and they are willing to talk to me for the price of a mug of ale, sometimes less.

Tonight I found two ancient men, brothers, their bodies decayed but their minds fresh and sharp, who lived on Honey Lane, hard by the Church of All Hallows, which was destroyed in the fire. Yet their hovel, from which they sold thread and buttons and some herbs for poultices, was spared. I spent several hours with them in their lodgings, which were appalling, and how many things we discussed. The brothers claimed to have lived on Honey Street for forty years or more, though neither could count beyond ten they made repeated reference to having opened their shop during the early reign of Charles I which was, I admit, fascinating; imagine having been present for *his* coronation parade and *his* execution! Though these men made no such claim to the latter, they did demonstrate that remarkable facility for memory that is so common amongst the uneducated classes, repeating what can only have been verbatim the recollections of another who did see the unfortunate monarch lose his head – a local boy who climbed to the top of the Banqueting House to watch the festivities.

These humble men have the city in their blood, their souls; they wept at the recollection of fleeing the fire with what few meagre possessions they could collect in the dead of night and returning, weeks later, certain to find everything gone – their lives laid to waste, their shop and livelihood vanished forever beneath the dust and ashes. And yet, in His infinite wisdom, God saw fit to spare them. The elder recalled, with tears streaming down his face, kicking aside timbers that still smoked, embers that yet glowed with life on either side of their little home, hoping to save it from the risk of a further conflagration. Now, as the city slowly begins to rebuild, they remain, yet selling their thread and their buttons.

Why did you return, I asked, and why do you stay? How could they not, where they had known everything, they told me. The fields where the refugees have fled stink with effluence, the piteous screams of the children who know nothing but want and chill. Dreadful as is the state of the street where they have long lived, still it is preferable to the alternative; of shuddering in shacks built from half-burnt timbers and broken bricks, of hay and old clothes.

Finally I asked, as I always do: and what of the cathedral?

Ah, they said, God saw fit to spare us, but not the cathedral. They said their own father told them of the lightning strike and the fire that caused the spire to collapse and burn, and his father before him of the fires that raged through the cathedral year on year. They themselves spoke of the trade that was wont to occur in the nave, the zealous men who preached blasphemy in the transept. Perhaps, they said, perhaps God has passed judgement upon St

Paul's and the vices of Ludgate Hill. Perhaps the cathedral should not be rebuilt but left to crumble, testament to the vices of man and the judgement of God.

7 June 1667

Extraordinary discovery in the crypts today; a monument from Elizabeth's reign, a carven man, nearly whole and unharmed by the fire or subsequent exposure. Nor the looting which I am appalled to note continues, despite our constant presence on Ludgate Hill.

I was engaged in outlining the easternmost wall of the apse when I discovered the monument; he with his starched collar and pantaloons, missing only his nose: and that may have been the work of vandals a century before! Blackened but uncracked he lay, considering the afterlife, his hands forever folded upon his chest in the attitude of prayer. Constantly am I astounded by the power of the fire; when every time I find a new stone cracked down the centre and I know it owes its wounds to a heat so intense only hellfire could outmatch it, and yet, here a simple carving that withstood even that. I felt in that moment of discovery God's grace alight upon my shoulders and the shoulders of all around me; truly we do His work in rebuilding our monuments to Him.

And yet, I find I cannot forget the warnings of those ancient brothers in Honey Street. Perhaps this monument is not evidence that God favours our great project, but an accident, an oversight.

A warning.

I am troubled tonight, and sleep eludes me.

15 June 1667

One of the stonemasons, uncovered a most curious artefact early this morning, in the churchyard, a stone covered in curious markings. W grew very excited and had it carried to his house to consider it at his leisure. He later came away to tell us the carvings were the writing of our Anglo-Saxon ancestors, those who lived here after Rome fell and before the conquest: the Dark Ages of Man, so called.

I neglected to mention that I had found a similarly carven stone in the north-eastern wall of the crypt beneath the apse weeks ago, though mine is much smaller, and likely more recent, for the carvings were in Latin. It must be a fragment of a monument, though the work is surprisingly crude. I could only make out one word: *resurgemus*. We shall rise again. A fitting epitaph for the cathedral, truly! We are told to report any such discoveries immediately but many of us do not, especially if they are small; I carried my stone away to show Mary; such curiosities and my stories of them do enliven her long days abed. Let W keep his large stone and all the glory of it. He does not know all the secrets the cathedral bears, nor does he need to.

15 *July* 1667

An accident; the scaffolding in the crypt beneath the apse collapsed towards the end of the day and a man was pulled from the rubble with his leg broken. He had been knocked insensible by the fall and woke screaming of rats, though I saw none; nay, I have never seen one amongst the ruin.

Another sleepless night; though I dropped off, I dreamt of children slinging stones at birds and woke with a jolt, and sleep proved again elusive. I arose and walked to Pudding Lane where the conflagration had its origin; many houses there are now rebuilt and I smelled good clean cooking smoke lingering in the air from the evening's banked fires. But I was not soothed; through the streets remain dark corners, gaping black basements and piles of rubble where the stink of that earlier fire clings on.

How desperately we have tried to brush it all away in the three years since it settled into the city's grooves and gaps; how singularly we have failed.

The land at Fish Hill at the bottom of Pudding Lane has been cleared and W is considering plans to erect a Monument to the Fire. I am not involved in the Monument and know little of it, only that W is bedevilled with indecision as to the design and structure as he wishes to construct too many things at once: a monument; as well as an observatory from which the curious may overlook London's rebirth, a hundred feet in the sky; and some manner of astronomical tower also, by which he means to impress H and L and a host of others of his knowledgeable Society. Perhaps he should contain himself and build a monument to God alone.

Tonight, though, the site was silent and empty but for the rats that survive everywhere and everything: the Plague, the fire. Blasphemous thoughts filled my mind as I wandered amongst the empty streets: how many of *their* kind did God spare, compared to man; how quickly do *they* refound their society and return to the city their ancestors have lived in as long as ours – while we are crippled with indecision, prey to too many ideas, unable or unwilling to grant that God may have a plan for us that our own pitiful dreams cannot and should not supersede.

The rats have returned to the city; for them it is the same as it ever was.

The rats who are to be found everywhere but among the ruins of St Paul's.

2 *August* 1667

I have asked at St Paul's whether any man has seen rats, or evidence of them, among the ruins, but no one has observed so much as a harvest mouse. I then asked whether they did not find this absence queer, but some said they wondered whether the smoke and ash kept the rats away, and others merely that it was evidence that the site is a holy place and God has seen fit to ban vermin from it.

22 *August* 1667

No discovery this time but a sighting. Instead a stonemason rushed from where the north aisle still stands, in part, crying that he had seen a monk appear from nowhere and then stride across the nave to vanish into a wall. This story, naturally enough, occasioned much excitement and work was halted for an hour or more while men scrambled about the wall where the spirit was said to have disappeared. I made a study of it myself, for as it happened I could hear the hue and cry even in the crypt beneath the apse where I find myself ever more drawn. Perhaps I hope for another curious find to pair with my carven rock, although what of the crypt in this part of the cathedral that can be cleared has been already. W visits daily to inspect our progress and I see him shaking his head as he draws his fingers along the soot-blackened stones. I begin to wonder whether the damage is too extensive to repair, for after three years' effort we are yet regularly plagued by accidents and the walls seem to crumble at the lightest touch.

The days are become shorter but the growing darkness still does not ease my sleeplessness. I fall asleep easily enough but my dreams, my dreams: I pull the stone I gave Mary from the north-eastern wall and a sea of rats come tumbling out; they overwhelm me, filling the darkness of the crypt with their dreadful presence until, in a blaze of unholy light, I wake, screaming.

I have taken to sleeping apart from Mary so that I do not disturb her.

23 August 1667

Three men failed to appear when the bell was rung this morning and I believe I am to blame, at least in part. It is no unusual thing for labourers to appear and disappear without notice, and at first I thought nothing of it. Toward the end of the day, however, I overheard two men discussing the three who had not returned to the cathedral; they spoke in hushed tones but I was seated nearby, and they did not see me. They were men I had asked previously about the rats; after I had raised the issue with them they had asked others and the word spread; no one had seen a rat on the church grounds in all our time here. The three men who left and never returned, so I overheard, were amongst those asked, and, being of some vile pagan superstition, they announced their belief that the cathedral is cursed – although for my part I should think an absence of rats a blessing!

And yet I turn the many incidences of fire that have plagued this edifice, and those before it, over and over in my mind: some house of worship has existed atop this hill for millennia, and each one has been met with ruin. I have begun to come to the cathedral grounds at night, when I cannot sleep; the nights are longer now and very dark. The night watchman allows me, for I am willing to make his rounds in his place, while I puzzle over the questions that plague me. Perhaps my nightly perambulations will uncover some secret that will set my soul at ease.

9 September 1667

I sleep very little now yet I am not tired; I work during the day with feverish energy and at night I walk and walk and walk. Dear Mary sleeps most of the day now, so she does not miss me – though I wish I had recourse once more to her sensible and well-ordered mind. The others at the cathedral leave me to my work and speak to me little; we all prefer it that way.

27 *September* 1667

The cathedral will not sustain a cat. I brought one two nights ago during another of my perambulations – a great tom with a white streak down its nose. I set it beside the north-eastern wall in the crypt and it bristled and hissed, backing away from the stones, staring wild-eyed in every direction before streaking off. Today a wall beneath the south transept crumbled and the labourers shouted out, for they had discovered a cat's carcass therein, much aged and dried out. We all went to examine the object and it could not have been my cat, which was alive and well but a day earlier, whereas this animal must have been dead for decades. But how did such a small thing, dry and brittle as last year's leaves, survive the fire, which burned so strong to crack even great stones? And was it merely my sleepless imagining that saw the same white blaze upon this animal's face as was on the one I carried hither? Was it covered in tiny bites? Was it merely the contraction of muscles following death that pulled the creature's face into that grimace of fear?

The animal was shown to W, of course, and then tossed into a pile of rubble; I intend to return tonight and bury it. Or burn it.

17 *October*

I have slept better since the discovery of the cat, but now Mary is restive, and speaks to me of her dreams. Rats, she says, her eyes red-rimmed and feverish, hundreds upon hundreds come bubbling up from the ground beneath the unburnt cathedral atop Ludgate Hill (she has never seen it since its ruin) and swarm in all directions down into the city, overcoming all in their path, eating and eating until there is nothing left... with hellish speed they overtake the city until the streets are flooded as though the river had risen, but it is rats, rats, rats. I have taken to reassuring her that there are no rats at St Paul's, and do not tell her of my own dream, the same every night now; it is terrible enough that I fear sleep even as I crave it...

I walk up Ludgate Hill to St Paul's; in my dream it is not a ruin, but whole and complete, even including the spire no man has seen in living memory: it is a moonless night and the city is dark, and I approach the west facade which is not as it was before the fire, following Jones' restoration of three decades previous, but older, crumbling, magnificent; the great cathedral of an ancienter city than ours. As I draw near penitents emerge from the building in two long, silent rows; they are draped in pale shrouds from head to toe and their gait is smooth and regular; they pass me by so silently I cannot hear so much as the rustle of the fabric that covers them, the whisper of their footsteps upon the earth. I enter the cathedral as they leave, and it is lit by an unearthly glow, as moonlight, though there is no moon; I see that it is the stones themselves, glowing; I wish to cross myself but my arms are heavy and my hands are still of their own accord. I am drawn with sure steps through the nave and through the quire until I reach the apse and then my hands are freed; I reach up and touch a stone and it depresses to reveal a hidden staircase; I descend and I am in the crypt, but it is not the crypt as I have known; the ceiling is held aloft by fluted pillars; the floor is not our solid flagstones but tiny coloured tiles, a mosaic as I have seen in Bath; even in the cold light I could glimpse terrible shapes amongst them; snakes and dogs and rats and pagan gods... The crypt too glows with an unearthly light, here even brighter than before, the stones blazing so they seem afire.

There, at the easternmost point along the crypt wall, I see it: my stone, the one I carried away for Mary all those months ago, set low in the wall. I kneel before it and pull it away, and discover it is concealing a hole the size of my fist, and even the pagan light that fills the cathedral cannot penetrate the darkness beyond. Yet I am compelled, I am driven to reach my hand inside and I, horror of horrors! I feel something within, small and furred, and I snatch my hand back but not before a sharp pain overcomes me; I withdraw my hand and I am bleeding as though bitten; and then, dear sweet God in Heaven, a rat huge and black, with eyes as yellow as the sun, and then a second and a third, tumble forth as water from a spring, and more behind them, and more behind *them*, and I scramble back but I fall and I am overwhelmed as a flood of rats boils forth and over me and out, up every flight of stairs, even climbing the columns and the monuments, blocking out even that unholy light, and I –

1 *November*

Neither of us has slept in weeks and Mary is as ill as I have ever seen her, starting at every noise, her eyes wild and staring, her thin hands clutching and clutching. I have made a decision. Tonight I shall replace the stone where I found it. There is no moon tonight and I fear the realisation of my terrible dream even as I know, I know, I know it cannot come to pass; the old cathedral is ruined, the Romans are dust and ashes; my God is the one true God, pater noster, qui es in caelis, sanctificetur nomen tuum, adveniat regnum tuum. Fiat voluntas tua, sicut in caelo et in terra. Resergemus resergemus resergemus.

4 *November*

Of what happened on the night I shall never speak nor write, but I replaced the stone. This morning I returned to Ludgate Hill, as I knew I must, though the idea filled me with icy dread, and I spoke with W, to tell him that the north-eastern wall of the crypt is unsound; that he must not rebuild the old cathedral; that he must pull it down and begin anew somewhere else, for Ludgate Hill is cursed, cursed; he laughed in my face and pulled me down into the crypt and then, oh God forgive us, *he found the stone*. He held it aloft and called out to the others, who dropped their tools and rushed to our side, and he said as I once did: *resurgemus*, we will rise again, a fitting epitaph! For there must be a cathedral here, atop Ludgate Hill; as there always has been, so there always will be.

And as he spoke a great rumbling began and the ground shook and the wall before which we stood, that cursed north-eastern wall, began to crack; great rents appeared across the faces of the stones still black from the fire even as we stood there aghast and then, as one, we turned and ran. Dust poured from the ruin and the sound, the sound was as thunder, as we – master and men alike – hurtled down the hill, but the cursed ruin did not fall.

Later W insisted we return to survey the damage; I was certain no power could compel me thither but W took me by the arm and said in a low voice that no man knew the eastern crypt better than I; that my services were invaluable and must be made use of; and I in my vanity allowed myself to be seduced, compelled to return once more. There was very little destruction, in truth, though we were horrified to find that the north-eastern wall had collapsed entirely and beyond – it was only the two of us who saw what lay beyond, a great cavern, so dark and deep light could only penetrate a few feet into it, and neither of us were willing to step therein, for we could discern what carpeted the ground: a sea of tiny white bones, the mortal remains of more rats than a man could count in a lifetime, stretching as far as the eye could see, cold as moonlight in that unholy darkness.

W stood silent and pallid for some moments and then turned to me. We must never let anyone know of this, he said. I must trust you to rebuild this wall, to make it ten feet thick, or twenty. I will tender my report that the cathedral must be rebuilt somewhere else. If I am not allowed – and I may not be, for there must be a cathedral here, there always has been – if I am not, I will engineer a method to keep this... this *abomination* forever buried.

2 *June* 1671

The plan of the new cathedral was laid out in completely today; it sits over much of the footprint of the old cathedral but turned several degrees along the axis of north and south, to bury for ever that blasphemous spot deep underground, beyond the old north-east wall. I alone have overseen the filling of that gaping hole that W and I once stood before in silent horror; I alone have transported cartloads of waste within and packed it solid, that it may support the structure that W will build atop it. And I alone will sleep knowing that the sea of bones can never again be reached by man, nor will the unholy flood that threatens London from within ever rise up to overwhelm us. And in my dreams, from now until the day God sees fit to receive me, I shall hear the sound of a thousand tiny claws scrabbling over bones, the music which day in and day out, filled my ears as I was about my task. There, in the darkness no light could ever reach, the rats waited and watched. May they wait until Judgement Day.

St Paul's will rise again, and us with it, and what secrets holds shall be contained beneath sixty-five thousand tonnes of clean white Portland stone. Pater noster, qui es in caelis, sanctificetur nomen tuum, resurgemus.

THE VOYAGE OF THE BASSET

Claire North

IT WAS IMPRESSED UPON ME, when agreeing to this expedition, that secrecy was essential. I have abided by this request but, as a scholar of the natural sciences, I consider it a poor practice of my craft not to set here down some observations upon the voyage of the *Basset*, that future generations may, when this secret is no longer sacred, come to share in our ventures.

I was only recently returned to England's shores from my voyage with H.M.S. *Beagle*, and had little thought of venturing to sea again, when the commissioners came. At first I was reluctant to even hear their proposition, considering that the work I had to do in documenting my experiences at sea and far-off land a far greater matter than any affair of state.

"But Mr Darwin!" they implored, "Can you not see the urgency? When Her Majesty is crowned it is an event which will define the nation! The eyes both of her citizens and of foreign powers – some still hostile to the Empire – will be upon us!"

I muttered some indignant noise as to the effect that it seemed unlikely, England's situation being what it is, that some few hours of pomp on Her Majesty's behalf could yet determine the fate of a nation.

"My good sir," retorted Mr. Fellows, a portly fellow of squeaking voice and flushing cheeks, "all the kings and queens of Europe will attend this coronation, the greatest statesmen of our age! The Emperor of the Chinese, the Moguls of India, Sultans and Khans, Rajas and Tsars pay her homage. Were the event to be anything but a triumph, I do not see how we could hold our heads up high in society."

There, I divined, was the heart of the matter; for these gentlemen were civil servants, tasked to ensuring a spectacular celebration for our Queen. They couched their actions within the language of mighty events and vital diplomacy, yet family men still they remained and I could not but feel that it was a question of their salaries and position at work which dogged them, more than any visiting dignitary.

"Be that as it may!" I exclaimed, "I hardly see how I, a mere naturalist, can be of any assistance to you."

"Mr Darwin, you are recommended by both Captain Fitzroy and the Reverend Henslow as the *only* man!"

This bold claim I met with some doubt, despite the naming of several men to whom I am indebted, but they then pursued the matter with words most unexpected to my ears. "We have a scheme – indeed, such a scheme! – that will guarantee the most magnificent celebration for Her Majesty's coronation, and you are essential. What, sir," asked Mr Fellows, "Do you know of the *lycaenidae?*"

Some four months later, in March 1838, I stood upon the wharves of Portsmouth harbour, in the thick oilskins that were the only thing for travel at sea, and wondered quite how I had agreed to be at this point. My patriotism, though no lesser than any servant of Her Majesty, was not my primary motive, for all of Mr Fellow's chatter – rather the mission at hand, the experiment and its consequences – that I could not permit to pass me by.

So on that cold spring morning, with wind from the north east and the sloops skimming across the sea, barely touching water, I set sail with perhaps the most unusual task I have ever enacted, upon the H.M.S. *Basset*.

Some basic observations on the H.M.S. *Basset*.

Though not quite so old as the *Beagle*, she had not seen a full refit for some time, which matter told in her creaking decks, her salt-scratched mast, her leaky cabins, and her six guns which, even to my landlubber eye, I perceived to be short-range and outmoded. The few men who tended these weapons took on double, triple roles across the ship of carpenter, cook, reefman and bosun, and looked askance at the guns like men trying to remember a stranger's name. Her commander – one Captain Worth – was a young man recently raised up from Lieutenant, though his youth was well measured by his confidence and a rolling kind of wit that had no qualms at mocking the maturity of his own position.

"Well, Mr Darwin," said he as I supervised the loading of my cargo beneath his decks, "if I get bitten in the night be sure I shall bite back hard, and you the man I bite."

At first I took these words to be sincere, and as we rocked back in the harbour I scurried around my crates, examining every side to ensure that they were tight, and hoping that the fleas and rats which infest every aging brig would not be mistook for my charge and care.

"The French will have some ado about us," he added that even as we took the tide past the Sound and out on to whiter waters. "I have no doubt we'll have to gut every man they send and scupper their timbers to the bottom before this business is done."

So horrified was I at this suggestion that I think I quite lost my colour, for he, examining my face, suddenly burst out laughing and, with a slap of his hand against my back and a shaking of his head exclaimed, "A jest, Mr Darwin, a jest! I had thought a man of your experience would know the sailor's wit!"

Yet though the Captain made light of the matter, news had already reached the ship that his jest could prove more earnest than we looked for. A French frigate called the *Ste Guilliame*, armed with intelligence passed to it by certain elements of the Americans, had been sighted sailing up the English Channel with orders – so the rumour went – to observe and, where at all possible, disrupt our mission. That such an act could occur at times of peace seemed to me barbarous but, as Captain Worth pointed out in one of his quieter moments, "When a ship vanishes in the middle of the Atlantic, Mr Darwin, who's to say if it was God or powder that took her? And though our purpose is science in the service of our nation, yet its implications, as I understand it, could be of great significance to us all."

Thus it was a quieter ship than the *Beagle* which caught the winds into the Atlantic.

An enumeration of my cargo.

Nearly all of the vessel's hold was given over to my mission, which was indeed the ship's mission, and that space which was not taken by victuals was rather consumed by my apparatus.

These contained, but were not confined to, five very large crates – large enough to berth five men in each by hammocks suspended across the walls, so the sailors grumbled – within which were the precious goods of my enterprise as five swelling mounds of earth, pebble and sand which were shaped to form the colony, or heap, of some approximately three hundred thousand ants mainly of the *formica fusca* species. The number needs must be approximate as the few months I had to prepare for the voyage was little suitable to counting each individual member of the heap, which must also have varied by temperature, humidity and the violent motion of the sea as the nest was transported to the cargo hold of the Basset.

Needless to say, keeping these creatures within their crates while ensuring a suitable supply of food, air and moisture was a considerable challenge and I believe I saw more of the inside of the holds in the weeks we were at sea than I had observed in nearly five years living within the *Beagle*. At night, dreaming of ants crawling across me, I would wake – only to recall that my skin manifested an anxiety, rather than an escape of my charges.

Yet if the ants were a continual worry to me, within the crates was a far greater and more delicate matter, for there the larvae of the *lycaenidae* were growing to maturity, nurtured in perfect symbiosis by the ants that tended them, for the primary form of this creature, as it grows and feeds, will upon the stimulation by the ant's antennae produce the sweetest of the honeydews, which is to the ant great nectar; and yet which creature will also, by its relation with the ant, force the ant to regurgitate some of its own food, which then may be digested. Thus the internal process of one creature feeds the other, whose internal processes feed the feeder, and nature finds its path to sustain itself and grow, a system working in perfect harmony, one part upon the other. Truly, if it were not to the heavens and the turning of the stars above that men look for God, I say that you shall see His mighty work in the humble and almighty ant.

Thus, my days so preoccupied with my symbiotic charges, thoughts of the French and their expedition to disrupt us quite fled my mind. Even Captain Worth – ever watchful beneath his wit – seemed largely to neglect the threat, declaring that in the ocean it was still accounted good fortune to find the shores of America when you looked for them, and that to find one frigate within all this mass of cloud and water would be a triumph indeed.

It fell, alas, to me, to undermine this confidence when, one sea-tossed night I sat with the captain in his cabin, taking turns to catch the pitcher of port which was sliding across the table between us with each shaking of the ship, when Captain Worth exclaimed,

"How did you come to conceive of this idea at all, Mr Darwin?"

"It was not my idea at all; I was merely judged suitable to tend to its execution."

"Then whose idea was it, for pity's sake?" he exclaimed, saving his glass from a tumble as the whole vessel seemed to jump and fall again with the pounding of the seas.

"I believe that a good many natural philosophers and mathematicians, who specialise in examining the motion of the skies, have developed the ideas behind this voyage. Though in truth, first credit for the notion – albeit not the execution – must go to our fellow sailors of the East, who it is said often times sacrifice to fanciful dragons and spirits to grant them good fortune and auspicious skies."

"Fairy tales!" he exclaimed. "I trust we are not sailing to test a superstition?"

"Supposition, perhaps," I replied, "Though an experiment which yields no results is arguably as important as that which confirms your hypothesis. My primary concern with this exploit is how to monitor its results, for in truth, even should our cargo survive to our destination – which is the challenge for which I was called upon to serve – the number of variables in what we are attempting to achieve are near incalculable. Even calculating the co-ordinates to which we are destined to go, and the volume of cargo which we must release to produce the desired effect, is itself a triumph."

"You are saying our position was deduced mathematically?"

"Quite so; it would not be valid any other way."

For a while Captain Worth was silent, drawing his lower lip in and out with a slight sucking breath, in a manner that put me in mind of an old man unsure of a new set of teeth. At last he said, "Then you consider it possible that the French might also have performed such a calculation, and concluded the destination to which we are bound?"

In truth, I hadn't considered it at all, but the matter now being set before me, I was forced to concede that yes, it was not, in theory, impossible, once they knew of the task we were set. Any mathematician armed with the same basic assumptions could, if they knew the purpose of our voyage, deduce its method – and so I told the Captain.

"But still to reach the coordinates; to be there on time – that is a nautical challenge, is it not, as well as a mathematical one? Already I am seeing large numbers of the ants die back; the implication can only be that the larvae are reaching their maturity."

"What if they reach maturity too soon – if your charge is ready before we arrive at our destination?"

"Then we will not succeed with the experiment," I replied, and now there was no humour in either of us. "The life cycle of these creatures is not long, and I do not have supplies to feed them above another seven days."

Captain Worth considered this, then laughing said, "Perhaps we should unleash your cargo now, Mr Darwin, see if they cannot give us a fair wind for the rest of the voyage! Then again, were there to be hurricanes in London I have no doubt you or I would receive the blame, merited or not. Perhaps therefore in good naval order we should simply stick to the orders given, and not pause to question them."

So we continued, servants to the wind that carried us, since – for now – no urgency could command the heavens to bend to our will. Every day I spent in the cargo hold, I observed the growing number of creatures dying, both ants and larvae beneath my care, and though I had calculated for such odds, the sight of it chilled me. I knew that this was a perfect balance of nature that I had brought with me from England, of larvae feeding ant and ant feeding larvae, yet it could not last for ever stripped from its natural environment, and death is a part of the course of life as ever birth is, and no less essential.

These reflections in me, growing the more philosophical as I witnessed my cargo being whittled away, induced a kind of lethargy so that, when the word came down of a sail sighted on the horizon, I found neither the surge of excitement nor the start of fear within me that sailors on a lonely voyage so often experience at the sight of another of their kin.

Indeed, going up onto deck, I could not spot the vessel at all, until the First Lieutenant gave me his spy-glass and, looking to the south, I caught a glimmer of what looked for all the world like the ridged limbs of a frightened *phasmida*, and which sharper eyes informed me was not merely a frigate, but a race-built frigate of an American design, now common to warships of a certain age upon these oceans. Of colours, neither I nor the Captain could make them out at this distance but as we continued on, I felt a stillness settle over the deck that did not reassure.

For two hours we held our course, and the ship, rather than gaining, seemed to hover like the blackness of distant falling rain upon the horizon, sometimes so far off that we thought it had fled; sometimes rising up across the grey seas from a temporary occlusion behind the running waves. At last, some two hours in, the Captain lifted the glass to his eye, then lowered it, then raised it again, and on now lowering it one more time turned to the wheel and gave orders to change our course and run full speed before the wind.

This order was immediately obeyed, and now all thoughts of my ants departed and I stood upon the deck and murmured in the Lieutenant's ear, "Has he seen her colours?"

"I don't know rightly what the Captain has seen," he replied softly back, lest his voice disturb the now stern concentration on the deck, "But if he bids us run before the wind, then run we shall, and let the Devil come."

Indeed, it seemed that our turning from our course was the signal that the other vessel had needed to confirm her own actions, for she too raised full sail and set to behind us, growing now in the horizon from a tiny dot to a rounder protrusion. She was still too far off for me to perceive her colours with my naked eye, but close enough that the Lieutenant turned to me and said the words we had waited for;

"She flies no colours."

"So she might not be French?"

"A ship which flies no colours has no good intent, regardless of her port."

"Can she catch us?"

He had clearly spent too much time in Captain Worth's company, for as junior officers often do, he had taken upon him the senior's mannerisms, drawing in his nether lip before murmuring, "She's newer than us, and built to run, which gives her an edge. But she's heavier too. We've seen port these last few weeks and had our keel stripped of all that might encumber her, so, lest she catches us in the next few hours, I'd say we have a chance of slipping from her right enough."

"Why the next few hours?"

"The sun will set soon," he answered. "Then it's God's will what happens."

Thus reassured – or perhaps not assured at all – I found that I had nothing to do but wait. To calm my mind – for no man for whom it is not his business can look at a shadow in his wake for more than a few hours and in any way feel productive – I went back to my ants and my larvae and, peeping open the lid on the foremost crate, was almost immediately startled by a flutter of blue in the dark.

My cargo was coming to its maturity, and now – with only three days to go until the fateful day of Her Majesty's coronation, and two days to complete our experiment – it was down to the seamanship of Captain Worth in finding our destination and getting us there whole, and I could do no more.

By the time the sun was beginning to set, the ship that pursued us was near enough in range that I fancied I could see the shapes of people scurrying across its deck. Looking back at them from the stern of the *Basset*, I wondered if they knew the full scale of the experiment we had been sent to conduct. Most assuredly, to those civil servants who had first enlisted me to it, their purpose was diplomatic, designed to secure the coronation of the Queen against a threat I considered trivial at best. But for men of learning, men who study the wonder of God's creation and within it see the masterwork of what He has wrought, our enterprise was no less than wonderful, and it seemed to me that every man of scholarship, every man of imagination, regardless of his language or place of birth, should in it find something extraordinary. This thought made me sadder almost than the fear of the guns, slowly coming into range as we headed towards the night.

The night, when it came, came fast, as it seems night always does across a great ocean, a darkness that descends between the blinking of this eye and the next. The order was whispered through the ship; no light, no lamps, no noise, and at that whispering every lantern was extinguished and no more was whispered at all, except for some turnings of the wheel and the slow creaking of the sails.

The game now was of guesswork and hope. Could our pursuer – whoever he was – follow us in this dark? Or could we execute some devilish cunning plan, as Captain Worth's tight-lipped confidence seemed to suggest, and slip past him and back on to our intended course?

I thought again of the mathematics that had created our destination, and wondered if the Frenchmen knew of them. If so, escape would be impossible, and we would have no choice but to fight, the enemy knowing our every move before we made it.

"You can do nothing here," whispered the Lieutenant in my ears. "Check on your cargo."

"Sir," I replied, "If I check on my cargo one more time I do not think there will be any of it left for me to observe."

"Then sleep."

"Can you?" I asked, and he had the sense to render me no flippant answer.

If night had come fast, dawn came faster, and I stood upon the deck not knowing where we were and, in my fitful state, beginning not to care, so long as we were near somewhere safe.

Of the ship that had followed us, there was no sign, and when the lookout confirmed an empty horizon, a cheer went through our crew, and all sails were raised to take us back to our intended course.

"A day – a day at most, Charles," promised Captain Worth, seeing my poor efforts not to fret. "We shall reach our target soon."

I believe that exhaustion compelled my body to sleep, though my mind would have none of it, for I was woken at a hot, late hour of the sunset by a scrawny boy, who summoned me to the deck with the Captain's compliments. Climbing upwards I found the wind had dropped to near nothing, and we were making way with the limpest of sails.

Stood upon the prow, Captain Worth beckoned me close, and passing the glass into my hand pointed towards the horizon and said, "Do you see it now?"

I looked, and beheld a small island of basalt rock, barely a comma upon the unending page of the ocean, a little protrusion that reminded me of those desolate lands where nought but fungus and tawny shrub grew in the side of the cliff, and where yet on these meagre pickings survived many birds adapted to nest in crevices, and insects to feed off of the birds, and more fungus which fed off the rotting bodies of the insects, life thus finding its way in even these most desolate of places.

"Are you ready for your experiment, Mr Darwin?" asked the Captain. "It is twenty-nine hours, by my calculation, until the Queen is crowned; will this be sufficient?"

"Most sufficient, if the scholars are to be believed," I replied, near to both laughter and tears with the relief of it. "The effect of our actions will travel far faster than the news of our success."

"Then, Charles, you may as well begin, for we shall set every man to the longboat and have no other thought save the prize."

So began flurry and fluster, as a great many men began to heave my crates up from the hold. Indeed, in all my time tending to them on the voyage, I thought I had prevented not a single insect from breaching those wooden walls; yet as we pulled them free we found several hundred ants which had somehow crawled through the base of the crates and settled down to die on the decks of the cargo hold. How many more, I wondered, had ventured out and lived? Perhaps Captain Worth would be bitten after all.

Our third crate was up on deck, and the wind was picking up strongly, taking us towards our target, when the cry came down, a sail, a sail to the west.

At once all eyes turned in that direction and even I, now used now to the sight, could tell upon looking through the glass that it was our old friend the unmarked vessel bearing down on us once again.

"What would you have me do?" asked Captain Worth. "I cannot fight her for sure, but I can run. If we run, though, we will not come any closer to your island, for I will not hazard my ship in a chase past those rocks, not even for Her Majesty. Are we near enough now for your experiment to bear fruit?"

I considered the grave decision the Captain laid before me, as well as the vessel approaching, and said, "My task was to tend this cargo, and I have done it; yours was to take us here, and you have done it. If that vessel seeks to prevent us from seeing our mission through, why then we as surely defeat them in the completion of our task as if we had taken to them with cannon. We have come this far, and whether our enemy will give us opportunity to go any further is doubtful. I would choose therefore rather to die succeeding in this mission than be run down like an animal far from success; I say let us get it done."

At this, the Captain smiled his great smile, and gave order to head faster for the shore and bring those crates up on deck, and I do not think he turned back to look at the pursing vessel at all.

I have, in poor scholarly form, and for the sake of my own interests, neglected to fully elaborate on the interests of the men who first engaged me upon this voyage. Let me then return you to some four months previous, to Mr Fellows sat inside my parlour, imploring me to consider the *lycaenidae*, and the question of Queen Victoria's Coronation.

And the mission – the great matter of state upon which our fortunes all turned, for which an exploit of scientific urgency was required? Why, how it shames me to confess it, but Mr Fellow's chiefest concern was:

"Rain," he exclaimed. "This country is blighted by the most irregular weather. George the Third had to change wigs seven times when he was crowned. Seven! It was a most disgraceful and inauspicious beginning to his reign. George the First had mud, they said, up to his thighs and left dirty footprints all the way up the aisle to the Confessor's Throne. Queen Anne's gout was antagonised by a particularly violent downpour; William of Orange barely made it to his crowning the streets were so bad, Charles the First..."

"You are concerned about bad weather on the Queen's coronation?"

"Concerned!" blurted the round civil servant. "It is more than concerning! It is a matter of the utmost social and diplomatic import! In China they throw mountains of silver into the sea to ensure hospitable conditions merely for sporting events! We would never go so far – not even for Her Majesty – the Treasury would never

Our wind made of a thousand, thousand wings.

have it – but thankfully we have far more sophisticated methods of affecting our environment. No, Mr Darwin, what we propose is not some fanciful ritual, but an effort to change the weather though a seeding, you might say, of the sky. A disturbance planted in one corner of the Earth may, as it flowers and grows, trigger an event in another place! A child sneezing by a certain tree in Tibet may produce three months of rain in Yorkshire, the heavens being so connected! Our scholars, through the most exacting mathematics, ensure us by these means the most marvellous weather for Her Majesty's installation as has ever graced the British throne. Which returns me to my original question, Mr Darwin: what do you know of the *lycaenidae*?"

What do I know of the *lycaenidae*?

I have observed that the species is common the world over, and notable for their delicate wings and recurring patterns of blues and coppers. The male has smaller forelegs than the female, though may sometimes manifest a metallic gloss to their skin. Delicately sized, yet some possess a spot at the tail which, to a predator, may appear to be the head of the beast, rather than the rear, and thus acts as a subtle yet elegant defence mechanism in the wild. The larvae are small, frequently flat, and can secret a substance which both attracts, and subdues ants, with which they share a mutually beneficial, some might say co-morphic, relationship. These are merely some generic facts that one may garner from a simple textbook, or even quiet observation of a busy English garden on a summer's evening.

What more may I say?

I may say that, twenty two hours before Her Majesty, Queen Victoria, was to be crowned Queen and Empress, a small, little-noted ship of the British Navy pulled to off an entirely unregarded island of the South Atlantic, and, in defiance of the brigandly vessel that pursued it, set to about a remarkable experiment. Her sailors hauled up to the deck five great crates, within which the balance of nature had been for so many weeks, and against so many odds, most carefully maintained, the *Basset* pulled back her sails that there might only be an expanse of sky overhead. With a *hey-ho* and a *heave-to,* they toppled the lids of those wooden prisons and relased their cargo.

From the larvae still unhatched in Portsmouth, a glorious transformation had occurred. Upwards and upwards they rose, every colour I had imagined, cobalt blue and azure green, wings of white cotton laced with violent, golden shimmers against the sun, copper blazon and red stripe, deepest black and yellow flare; upwards and upwards they rose, giddy to be freed into the sky, silver-veined and orange-breasted, dull maroon and brilliant violet, they danced around each other in a spiral, feeling their way towards the heavens; our weather-seeding project, our artificial wind, our wind made of a thousand, thousand wings which beat against the seas and the sky, and which wind would grow as they spread outwards, would twist and turn against the natural course of the world and break against another wind, and another again, until the clouds above rushed and twisted upon themselves like they too were caught in the rising dance. Before this sight, even our pursuers seemed to stall, for the winds turned against them and not a man, I think, thought himself of cannon, so mightily the sea rocked and the skies turned.

And those clouds that twisted overhead, would pull in cold air, whose absence would pull in more, and where now heat had been, heat was not, and rain would fall and water would rise and all things would be transformed –

just for a while, for a little, little while – and in England, in sunny, glorious England where my garden grows rich and the fruit hangs heavy upon the tree, for one day where the skies might yet have fallen, not a cloud would stain the sky, and the only wind would be as gentle as the beating of a butterfly's wing.

THE HEART OF ARIS KINDT

Richard de Nooy

"WHO STITCHED HIM UP, SIR?"

"The preparator. He was at work when I came in."

"But we ..."

"They took the heart, Ferdinand, and the rest of his innards."

"What?"

"There will be no incision in our painting."

"But that's preposterous, sir!"

"Tulp's letter is on the table."

The young apprentice removes his cloak and rubs his hands until they squeak and tingle. January's stinging chill draws deeper into his bones as he circles the naked cadaver of Aris Kindt. The callous morning light falling from the high windows of the Theatrum Anatomicum lends the dead man's skin a translucent sheen that leaves no blemish undisguised. Hurried sutures have raised an angry, Y-shaped seam upon the dead man's abdomen.

The young apprentice bows his head and mumbles a brief prayer before unfolding the surgeon's letter with his winter-clumsy fingers.

Amsterdam, 18th Day of January 1632

Dear Sir,

It is with some regret that, after due consultation with my esteemed peers, we have decided that we would prefer to see the torso depicted unopened, as it detracts from the overall composition and may cause consternation among our guests, particularly emissaries of the Church, who might question such a bold display of our enquiry into God's intentions and creative genius. We assure you that our decision has nothing whatsoever to do with the manner in which the organs have been rendered, as this was of the high standard that prompted us to commission you in first instance. Should you feel that our decision has necessitated additional effort on your part, we would like to assure you that we are already considering future commissions that we would almost certainly leave in your good hands.

Sincerely,

Nicolaes Tulp, Praelector Chirurgic et Anatomie

"He makes no mention of the heart, sir!"

"Indeed, Ferdinand, indeed."

"Are these men of science, sir?"

"Among the foremost, Ferdinand, but our friend here evidently confounded their principles."

"This is absurd. First the hand and now this!"

"The client is king, Ferdinand. Let me hear you say it."

"The client is a meddlesome tyrant, sir. Why would they do such a thing?"

"Ours not to reason why, Ferdinand."

"Whatever crimes he may have committed, sir, this man, too, is a creature of God and it is our duty as artists to celebrate the glory of His creation by rendering all of that creation as precisely as we can – alive or dead."

"Of course, Ferdinand, but God does not pay our fee, and the surgeons have every reason to conciliate the emissaries of the Church. To work. We have a great deal to do. And our silent friend will not stay fresh for ever."

"My father shall hear of this. The Guild of Surgeons in Dordrecht would never..."

"That would be imprudent, Ferdinand. Bear in mind that it will be our word, as humble artists, against that of two dozen surgeons, well versed in matters anatomical and very well connected with the city council, before a committee of their peers. And what might we hope to achieve, Ferdinand? Do we wish to cast a shadow of ill repute upon the city's finest surgeon? Will it bring Aris Kindt back to life? A man hanged by the neck is dead, Ferdinand, even if he dies a second time."

"Infuriating!"

"Consider your career, Ferdinand, and at what expense it has been purchased. Your father's investment must be recouped and I have mouths to feed. To work, young man, those details will not draw themselves."

16th Day of January 1632

Master R and I today had the honour of attending the public dissection of Adriaan Adriaanszoon in the Theatrum Anatomicum at De Waag, presided over by Doctor Nicolaes Tulp, praelector of the Amsterdam Guild of Surgeons. It was truly a privilege to sit among the city's most influential councillors and learned men to witness this rare event, which – as you know – takes place only once a year and is subject to the strictest protocol.

We were permitted to sit in the front row in order to make our preliminary sketches, which I did with immense discomfort, knowing that some of the city's mightiest men were looking over my shoulder. This was further compounded by the unnerving butcher-shop scent of the dead man's viscera, deftly laid bare by the Guild's preparator, who stood constantly at Dr Tulp's side, scalpel in hand like a Sword of Damocles. I am not ashamed to admit that I had to make a concerted effort to retain my dejeuner, which rumbled like an angry behemoth in my guts. Fortunately, I did not defile and embarrass myself. Instead, the experience redoubled my respect for surgeons such as yourself and Dr Tulp, who conducted his duties with immense grace and precision under such gruesome circumstances, all the while enlightening the audience with the most fascinating revelations regarding the workings of the human body.

The master and I both made numerous sketches of the proceedings. My hand, however, was seized by an annoying tremor as my body battled with both the winter cold and nausea, and my mind grappled with the knowledge that this poor wretch had been alive at dawn and now found himself the subject of such macabre scrutiny. Hanged for robbery and murder, which seemed all the more pathetic considering the absence of his right hand, hacked off in retribution for a previous offence. A one-armed bandit hardly sounds like a menace at all, but the facts speak for themselves. The court's sentence was clear and, alas, predictable. Every society has a duty to rid itself of such elements, to incarcerate them or excise such tumours from its flesh. Perhaps it is a blessing that, in death, he could contribute to the advancement of knowledge within the community from which he had ostracised himself.

The master and I later spent some time pondering the dead man's unusual moniker, eventually concluding that the simpleton had fallen foul of the commoner's penchant for abbreviation and, when some official had asked him who he was, had replied, "Ik ben Ari's kind," whereupon "Adriaan's son" was duly registered as "Ari's child".

The young apprentice cups his hands and exhales to ease his aching knuckles, stretches and clasps his fingers, then places his hands in the warm cavities of his armpits, staring at his sketch, which will now have to be redone. Without incision. The thought rekindles his ire. "What if the anomaly hints at something other-worldly?"

"Please, Ferdinand."

"What if this man is a fallen angel?"

"A demon seems more likely."

"But surely you agree that it was unusual, sir?"

"It is unlike anything I have ever seen, but does that make it unusual?"

"A dead man's heart was beating, sir! Surely that can be described as unusual?"

"I repeat, Ferdinand, it is unlike anything I have ever laid eyes on. Perhaps our own hearts will continue beating ever more slowly when we too are dead. We cannot be sure unless we dissect every corpse that makes its way from deathbed to crypt."

"True, but Dr Tulp and his brethren surgeons evidently ..."

"Look at him, Ferdinand. I urge you to look carefully and know that it is to your own advantage to conclude and maintain that this man is and was dead. Giving us all the more cause to get back to work. We have wasted enough time on this bandit's damned heart."

17th Day of January 1632

A startling miracle manifest itself today, Father! The dead man's heart beat within his chest! I can now well imagine how bystanders will have witnessed the resurrection of Lazarus – with equal proportions of elation and terror! At first I did not believe my own eyes, and dared not inform Master R for fear that he might brand me a fool unworthy of his attention and tuition. The pulsation displayed itself at unpredictable intervals, as if the organ itself sensed my watchful eye, waiting for me to turn my attention back to my duties, before beating to life once more, presenting as the merest tremor in the corner of my eye. But of course, whenever I turned to look, the heart was still. Infuriated, I vowed to hold my watch without distraction, but the intensity and immobility of my posture drew the attention of Master R, who enquired as to which part of Mr Kindt's anatomy was worthy of such undivided admiration.

Bereft of wit, I stammered my suspicions and endeavoured to attribute that which I had perceived to the shifting clouds and changing light, but at that very moment, as we both looked on, the heart of Aris Kindt pulsated once again, as unambiguously as the twitching fist of a stevedore. Master R's eyes widened in surprise and he bade me hurry downstairs to the quarters of the Surgeons' Guild to summon Dr Tulp or enquire as to his whereabouts, but not before extracting from me the solemn oath that I would not divulge to anyone that which we had both just witnessed.

And so I thundered down the tower's staircase to the Guild's quarters, where I wandered along the murky passage, rapping on several doors before I heard the fall of footsteps approaching. You can well imagine my surprise when the preparator himself opened the door, releasing a pungent draft of camphor and spirits from the room beyond and affording me a glimpse of the macabre specimens that lined the shelves like the pale and misshapen demons of some awful nightmare trapped in glass. Keen to my roving eye, the preparator stepped into the passage and pulled the door closed behind him. He then proceeded to enquire as to the nature of my business, doing so with such a lofty demeanour that I was instantly reduced to a jabbering schoolboy before an irate master. When I haltingly informed him that my master wished to confer with Dr Tulp, the preparator replied that the good doctor was making his rounds and would return only at nightfall. I explained that the matter could not wait that long and almost broke my promise to Master R when the preparator enquired as to the cause of such great urgency. I then bade the preparator accompany me upstairs to the

Theatrum Anatomicum so that we might consult with Master R.

Upon entering the master's realm, the preparator was immediately reduced to an obsequious loon who was only too glad to acquiesce to the master's every wish, whereupon the master bade him ascertain Dr Tulp's itinerary so that the preparator might lead me to him. Once the onerous fellow had departed, Master R immediately sat down to pen a letter to the doctor, urgently entreating me to present it to Dr Tulp and no one else, and insisting that I await the surgeon's reply before returning.

And so it was that the haughty preparator and I set off on foot on our quest through the city's snow-frosted streets, in pursuit of the doctor's horse-drawn carriage. It was an invigorating and not unpleasant ramble, with a low sun peeking out at times, casting long shadows that danced alongside the children playing on the frozen canals. The air was brisk, with the bitter tang of woodstoves burning, the foul stench of the city's waters thankfully contained by a welcome layer of ice.

Having tried two addresses to no avail, we espied Dr Tulp's carriage standing outside the infirmary of the Convent of Our Blessed Lady, whereupon the preparator bade me wait at a nearby tavern, explaining that I was not permitted to accompany him into the infirmary and that he was unsure how long it would take to extract a reply from Dr Tulp. When I informed him that I had been instructed to personally deliver the letter to Dr Tulp, the preparator treated me to a withering glance and boldly snatched the letter from my hand, ignoring my implorations as he strode into the infirmary.

Despondent and deflated, I found myself eating stale bread and rancid stew, washed down with a jug of reasonable wine. Fortunately, I had that very morning purchased the Courante from Amroussi, my preferred bookseller on the Kalverstraat, but I had little opportunity to read, owing to the presence of a company of privateers who were engaged in a relentless battle of one-upmanship, armed with tall tales of hardship at sea, which they thrust upon one another – and all those within earshot – with impressive vigour. Their self-appointed captain, a ruddy giant endowed with a dense shrub of beard, had upon his shoulder a remarkable aepjen that had the look of a wizened great-uncle, but the agility of a child and the wits of a cat. When the men burst into song, the creature bobbed up and down upon the man's shoulder in a delightful manner, causing me to laugh. Seeing my mirth, the captain invited me over to take a closer look, demanding in return that I stand them a round of jevener, a fee so raucously chorused by his companions that I had little choice but to accept.

"Windmills!" roared the captain, whereupon the proprietor began pouring gin into pewter cups resembling little bells, which had, instead of a foot, a tiny windmill with turning sails. As I raised my cup to admire the comically crafted ornament, the captain roared, "Ad fundum!" In an instant, my new companions had drained their cups and placed them upturned on their heads, roaring in chorus: "Wind ho!" They guffawed loudly when they saw my untouched cup and bemused expression. Before I could give cheers and take my first sip, the captain surprised me with a bearlike embrace that lifted me onto my toes, not only causing me to spill my jenever down the fellow's broad back, but also prompting the aepjen to leap upon my head, giving me the full scent of its loathsome groin, as its tail curled about my face seeking purchase.

And of course, at that very disconcerting moment, glancing desperately over the giant's shoulder, wearing a foul helmet of fur, I espied the onerous preparator surveying the premises, letter in hand.

Having extricated myself with some effort, I bade the privateers farewell, gathered my cloak and hurried over to the preparator, pursued by a barrage of well-aimed quips and jeers. My arrogant guide, the pious loon, then had the temerity to lecture me, your virtuous son, on sins of the flesh before handing over the letter, which upon entering my pocket seemed to instantly ignite, speeding my return to De Waag. I had to fight my way through the cacophony of commerce that throngs around the weigh house in the afternoons, clutching the letter in one pocket and my treasured dagger in the other, lest they be picked by one of the sleight-fingered vagabonds who secrete themselves amongst the crowd to rob unsuspecting merchants of their purses. (Guard your pockets, Father, for I am sure this loathsome skill will already have found its way to Dordrecht!)

Having made my way on weary legs up to the Theatrum Anatomicum, I found Master R absent, but noticed that he had worked diligently during my foray. Upon the vellum template lay the exquisitely rendered torso of Aris Kindt, its viscera sketched with immense precision in the cavity beyond the jagged scar, his heart fair leaping from his chest like a cresting whale.

A macabre curiosity drew me to the dead man's side, where I stood hoping that his heart had now finally stopped beating. And again I vowed to wait and watch, but I was foiled by fatigue, and perhaps the wine, which sought refuge in my head, causing my eyelids to grow heavy. So I placed the letter upon the master's easel and lay down on one of the wooden benches that surround the theatrum, wrapping my cloak about me to stave off the cold and welcome sleep, staring up at the vaulted ceiling where the gilded crests of Dr Tulp's predecessors gazed down upon me, sternly announcing their names in turn.

I awoke, startled, to Master R's oaths echoing into the rafters: "Madness! The buffoons!" Stirring from the warm burrow of my cloak, I sought to rise, only to discover that the aching cold had paralysed my legs, causing me to stumble onto hands and knees. As I struggled to my feet, Master R treated me to a summary of Dr Tulp's letter: "The blackguards insist that we depict his severed hand!"

When I enquired as to whether Dr Tulp had made any mention of the palpitating heart, Master R simply crumpled up the letter and cast it aside. He then paced and fumed about the room, muttering barely comprehensible curses, wishing the plague upon our clients. Finally, having circled the recumbent remains of Aris Kindt several times, he began to regain his composure. He stopped, inhaled profoundly, held his breath, eyes closed, and then exhaled at length.

"Remove your cloak," he said, "and roll up your right sleeve, Ferdinand, if you please."

As I did his bidding, he cast a sheet over the dead man's upper body. He then instructed me to stand at the head of the table and lean over the shrouded ghoul, artfully positioning my exposed arm alongside the dead man's waist. And so, in that absurd theatre, I found myself abruptly cast as the right hand of Aris Kindt.

The stench was nigh unbearable and when I informed Master R of my discomfort, he took it upon himself to tie a kerchief laced with several drops of perfume about my face, instantly rendering me a highwayman myself, a role I played with mounting tautness of the back for the better part of an hour, before Master R discharged me from the task, affording me the opportunity to admire my own forearm now attached to the sketched remains of Aris Kindt.

We worked until darkness began to fall, whereupon we hurried to the crackling hearth of the master's house, where dinner and a cosy cot awaited us, restoring our vitality so that we could surmount whatever absurdities and challenges the new dawn might bring.

✣

The young apprentice looks on in bemused exasperation as his master hollows out a loaf and rolls a dough ball, which he uses to gently erase the superbly rendered wound in the dead man's torso.

"A remarkable anatomy lesson this will be with so little of the viscera in plain sight," ventures the young apprentice, approaching Aris Kindt's body, clutching the perfumed kerchief to his nose. The putrid odour of decay hangs like an Ottoman drape about the table, secreting itself in the garments of anyone who dares draw near. Before the next day is out the gravediggers will retrieve the bandit's corpse to bring it to its final resting place. "Perhaps we could incorporate our friend's exposed left arm into the composition, sir?"

"Yes, Ferdinand, I was just contemplating whether I might elevate you from bandit to surgeon in a single day. But first find me that letter I balled and cast aside yesterday, for I fear both shall come in handy before this commission is completed."

Ferdinand scans the floor for the letter and sees it half-hidden under a heavy armoire. He prises open the crumpled ball with care and smoothes out the creases with the side of his palm. Before pressing the two letters under the hefty volume of Vesalius' *De humani corporis fabrica*, which serves to guide the master's hand when rendering anatomy, the young apprentice scans the letter.

Amsterdam, 17th Day of January 1632

Dear Sir,

I write this missive in great haste, beset with duties and patients that screech for my attention. Your letter reminded me that there is a matter of some urgency that I neglected to raise earlier regarding your proposed depiction of this Adriaanse fellow. From your sketches, which I glimpsed only briefly, I surmise that you intend to portray the man true to life, with his severed right hand depicted as a stump. We – my esteemed colleagues and I – feel that this grotesque detail is likely to draw undue attention from the Church and Council, which would be to the detriment of the painting's true subject: the gentlemen of the Guild. We therefore kindly request that you consider restoring the bandit's severed limb, so that the painting is more in keeping with its true purpose.

Sincerely,

Nicolaes Tulp, Praelector Chirurgic et Anatomie

"I am dumbfounded, sir."

"Consider it another hard lesson in the politics of commerce, Ferdinand. Vent your fury behind closed doors, then bite your tongue and give them what they want. You know my adagium."

"The client is king?"

"Indeed, Ferdinand, and this king wields great power and influence. Tulp has political aspirations and, at the risk of being a loathsome pedant, I beg you to remember that whatever matters you are privy to in the course of our negotiations should be viewed as confidential and treated as such."

"But my father..."

"Your father's concern is heart-warming and understandable, as is your devotion to your filial duties, but we cannot risk biting the hand that feeds us – for it is the hand of a giant, which would not only withhold sustenance, but would crush and destroy us in an instant. Is that understood, Ferdinand?"

"It is, sir. I shall censor my reports to Father."

"Thank you, Ferdinand. Now, let us get back to work. Perhaps you will better understand the responsibilities of our honourable client if you are briefly cast in his role. I bid you take those forceps and play the doctor's hand with verve."

Binding the now heavily perfumed kerchief about his face, the young apprentice takes the forceps and, in keeping with the directions of his master, attempts to raise the dissected left arm of Aris Kindt, so that the intricacies of its anatomy may be fully rendered. But the cold has stiffened the dead man's arm, making it easy to imagine he pulling back.

"I see our friend does not wish to cooperate," says the master, rising to fetch a log from the unlit fire and joining his apprentice. Together they wrestle the left arm into an artful pose, propping it up with the log. "Doctor Bol, your forceps. Try not to cast a shadow."

"Thank you, sir. I have already decided that I would rather be a painter than a surgeon. Or a bandit, for that matter."

"A wise choice, Ferdinand. This exercise will do wonders for the dexterity of your brush hand."

"Thank you, sir."

"Can you name the tendons in that arm?"

As the master sketches, the two men discuss the nature and function of extensors, flexors and abductors, revelling in their fascination, forgetting time and the macabre circumstances in which they find themselves, until daylight fades and the master announces that the time has come for them to rest their arms and minds.

As they go about their business, preparing for their final day in the presence of Aris Kindt, they hear footsteps ascending the stairs.

"Dr Tulp perhaps? With some new request," whispers the young apprentice.

"He wishes us to paint the dead man as a lady," says the master, laying a finger on his lips to stifle the guffaws of his apprentice.

Ferdinand coughs his last laughs into his fist as he walks to the door, which groans its welcome as it is opened. Outside, the haughty preparator stands waiting in the shadows.

"Good evening," says the preparator, without any further token of recognition. "Might I speak with your master? It is a matter of the utmost urgency."

"Enter, sir. Please accompany me. We were..."

"I would prefer to confer with your master under four eyes. This matter does not concern you. Please wait downstairs."

Swallowing his indignation, the young apprentice descends the stairs, keenly eyed by the preparator, who only closes the door when he is satisfied that Ferdinand is beyond earshot.

Perched on the staircase, the young apprentice strains to hear. Outside, the hubbub of commerce is dying down, while upstairs a riot is brewing. Thumping footsteps pace the floor, stop and turn, the hushed tones rising in amplification, culminating in a clearly audible roar from the master: "I bid you goodnight, sir!"

Hurried footsteps approach the door and the preparator comes scuttling down the stairs, clearly distraught, ignoring Ferdinand and instinctively ducking his head as the theatre's door slams like a thunderclap.

Unsure what to do next, the young apprentice hovers on the stairway, attempting to divine the magnitude of his master's rage from his footsteps, but his question is swiftly answered from on high with a resounding "Ferdinand!" that sends him racing up the stairs.

"More bad news, sir?"

"This will not stand, Ferdinand! He will not be portrayed, the supercilious buffoon!"

"Did he give a reason, sir? The heart?"

"No, of course not, Ferdinand! The undead heart of Aris Kindt shall be interred with his bones and forgotten. But all that pales into insignificance beside the abhorrent fact that this pious blackguard, this preparator, will not be portrayed. He claims that debts prevent him from contributing his share of the commission, the errant fool! First the hand and then the heart and now this! We have been robbed, Ferdinand, but I shall give them more than they bargained for!"

19th Day of January 1632

O Father, I am exhausted! It is just past noon and we have returned home after working through most of the night and on into the morning. Never before have I seen Master R so impassioned, so incensed! Having obeyed the curious and exasperating dictates of the Guild of Surgeons to the letter, almost without question, for several days, there came a last drop that caused the master's rage to overflow: the withdrawal of one of the clients from the commission.

I am drained, too tired now to divulge all the intricacies, but you can imagine my horror when Master R bade me roll a dough ball of my own, so that I might assist him in obliterating almost the entire sketch, save the recumbent corpse of Aris Kindt.

Having briefly paused to rest our arms, we then worked side by side by candlelight on the vellum template, like scheming villains in the shadows, to contrive a work so full of hidden meaning that only the blindest fool would overlook it.

As we laboured, the master shared his reckless plan with me. I repeatedly implored him not to execute it, convinced as I was that the surgeons of the Guild would take umbrage when they saw through the obvious detractions and would contrive to stymie our careers. But the master was adamant, declaring that he would prove that no surgeon could match the artist's aptitude for transfiguring the truth. "I assure you they will only have eyes for themselves," he said.

He also bade me swear that I would not share the details of our nocturnal exploits with you or anyone else, and so I am torn between two loyalties, Father. Perhaps I shall destroy these pages once I have revisited them, but for now I seek solace in the fact that someday someone with an artist's eye will ponder the gross discrepancies in the dead man's hands; will question the gaping absence that mars the composition on the right; will notice that three of the attendant surgeons (when their portraits are completed) are watching the parting back of the preparator, who casts a dark shadow upon the dead man's feet – sketched by none other than young master Bol! That they will scrutinise the background and realise that this is not the interior of the Theatrum Anatomicum, but that of a nearby brothel. And that their roving eye will ultimately fall upon the master's initial, marking the dead man's navel as if to say: in this world I am both the father and mother of Aris Kindt, I am his Creator.

AN EXPERIMENT IN THE FORMULAE OF THOUGHT

Simon Guerrier

THE TITULAR EXPERIMENT had its origin in a suggestion by Mr Charles Dickens. This fact might well surprise those that know the author's work, for, despite his many qualities, he is not renowned for an interest in science. But yet, the first germ of the idea, that essential seed, had been born from his pen; and later, when – out of courtesy – his opinion was sought on the project, his one recommendation wholly transformed the enterprise.

I learnt this salient detail at the infamous dinner which took place on the last night of the year Eighteen-fifty-three. In all fidelity – and I shall be completely honest in this account, even when the truth comes at my own expense – I had not been sure whether to attend the dinner, for I am but a popular journalist, and hardly a scholar of the latest geologic theory. Besides, the card had arrived mere days before the event, and I already had made tentative plans. All rational thought said *not* to attend; but then that is the moral of this story, for the experiment I describe has taught me one thing: we are *not* a rational species.

So, at a few minutes to five of the clock that cold Saturday evening, my hansom pulled up on a dark street in a south-eastern part of London. I stepped down on to newly lain pavement, hardly impressed by the sight presented to greet me. Plain wooden hoardings lined the street. They concealed the building works beyond, from whence emanated a stink of chalk and new-forged steel. There had surely been some mistake; or I was victim to some prank; for it was not conceivable that I had been invited to dine in the midst of a factory.

I turned to say as much to my driver, sat atop the hansom – and my heart stopped in my throat. Ahead of me, lined right the way down the street, stood a great number more hansoms; the horses with nosebags, the drivers huddled together round mugs of steaming tea.

Some hansoms bore impressive coats of arms. At first I felt relief at this clue to my august company, but then came a sudden, cold horror – for I am not often acquainted with those of nobler blood. Thank Heaven, I thought, that Angus had put out my second-best waistcoat and my best gold chain.

With what courage I could muster, I left my driver to ingratiate himself among his peers, and made my way to the gap between the hoardings that allowed entry inside. Lanterns hung from the sparse, young trees, illuminating a tawdry earthworks. Wooden boards had been arranged as a gangway across the mud. Yet a man stood on duty, for all the world as if he stood on the door of the Savoy, touching his hat as I stepped into view.

"Good evening, Mr Quake, sir," he said with all good cheer – though he had surely never looked on me before. "You're expected in the marquee."

"Thank you, my man," I said, grandly; for though the circumstance was altogether absurd, we are yet creatures of habit, our responses deeply ingrained. I made my way across the boards, and by some miracle did not slip.

I did not see the marquee at first; the boards only directed me toward what appeared to be a barn. Since my only recourse was to turn back – and face, with all embarrassment, the man on duty – I continued my present course. Then I heard laughter from beyond. In short, the barn was not a barn but the studio of Mr Waterhouse Hawkins and the marquee had been erected *inside* the wooden building. I stepped from the darkness of the night into a dazzling space of white drapery, chandeliers burning overhead.

A group of more than a dozen people stood in their finery, sipping Champagne and exchanging pleasantries. I stared in wonder at my fellow guests: the most unlikely admixture of persons. Some of those present were quick to appraise my costume – and clearly drew conclusions as to my position in society, and the impudence of my wearing that gold chain. But one man broke from the other guests and came to greet me warmly.

Benjamin Waterhouse Hawkins I had met before, when he exhibited four sculptures at the Royal Academy. He was a keen-eyed, passionate gentleman, and now thanked me again for a small description of his work that I'd penned for the *Manchester Guardian*. This, of course, had been the motive behind my being invited that night.

"We need good press, Bartholomew," he told me. "Or they'll cut us off. They say we've spent more than the budget already, and I'll warrant that thirty thousand pounds amounts to quite a sum! But there's still so much to do."

"Of course, I'll do whatever I can to assist you," I said, for I had always liked Waterhouse Hawkins. But I could also see the sly smile on his face, and with all the strange business of this dinner in the earthworks, I felt certain he was teasing me. "But come now," I said, playing the good sport. "Thirty thousand pounds on sculptures?"

"Wait and see," he said. "But let me introduce you to your fellow diners."

And so, as the sculptor's favoured guest, I was introduced to some of the leading figures of our age: Forbes the naturalist, Prestwick the geologist, Gould, who was an expert on birds, Armstrong the hydraulic engineer. I was introduced to the managing director and his chief acolytes in the Crystal Palace Company, and other important persons. As we shook hands and exchanged curt pleasantries, I detected their discomfort, and thought it a question of my class. But then one man refused to take my hand, gazing at me with the utmost malevolence.

Sir Richard Owen I knew from his image in the *Illustrated London News* but it was a startling experience to meet him in the flesh. The pronounced cranium gave the strong impression of a head near to bursting with brain; his bulging, staring eyes even served to suggest we were on the brink of an explosion. In short, the famous naturalist was quite a *specimen* of humanity – he seemed like his own caricature. You will intuit that I did not take to him; but he likewise made no secret of *his* disdain for my person.

"Um," said Waterhouse Hawkins, coming to the rescue. "I fear we interrupted Sir Richard in mid-flow. Do forgive us, sir, and continue."

I, of all people, had upstaged the great man! There would be no forgiveness. Sir Richard still fixed me with that glare.

"There are those of our brethren," he said, returning to his point, "who would not know the difference between *Megaloceros* and *Megalosaurus*."

The pun is more apparent written down; spoken, I could not discern any difference between the names, as must have been readily evident from my slack-jawed bafflement – I made the other guests laugh. Owen smiled, cruelly, at my discomfort. "This," he told the group, "is exactly to the heart of it. But let us, pray, not condescend. We must raise up the common man to our own understanding."

Burning hot with shame, I paid studious attention to the debate that followed, the learned men picking over the conclusions to be drawn from the latest fossil discoveries. "I would not speak ill of the dead," said Owen, in a tone that suggested quite the contrary, "but Mantell was completely wrong. The class dinosauria – which I, of course, first named – were quadruped." He smiled again at me. "That is, they went about on all fours."

I could see that some felt sympathy for my position, but none dared rebuke or interrupt the esteemed professor – for fear he would turn his Wit on them. One, a woman – the only woman in the company – tried to change the subject; why, I thought he might even strike her! But he contained his fury, only glaring towards her – while she, to her credit, stood her ground.

She was a fine-looking woman of becoming middle-age, elegant, even dainty, yet with such fire in her eyes. She had us all transfixed as she held Owen's gaze. To whom, I wondered, of the other men in our company did she belong? Not one of them stepped forward to support her – or to stay her hand. Then, with girlish grace, she bowed her head to Owen. "Professor," she said, "you were saying..."

It says much of the professor's character that he thought he had won a victory over her, and continued with his lecture.

At last rescue came and a gong was sounded. We were led into the next section of the marquee for our dinner.

Now, there has been some contention about the practicalities of what followed. The common image of the dinner, a lithograph in the *Illustrated London News*, is, while accurately drawn from the life, framed in such a way as to deceive the eye. We did not all sit *inside* the Iguanodon's belly. Of course not; those readers who have since visited the dinosaur sculptures in the gardens of the Crystal Palace can clearly see there would not have been space for but six of us, let alone twenty. We were not, in fact, inside the beast at all. Rather, there were two tables in a T-arrangement between the two halves of the *mould* from which Iguanodon was cast. The mould was, of necessity, larger than the cast and in sections. Even so, it was still quite a squeeze to fit twenty-one esteemed persons into the enclosure.

We ascended a few steps to a platform constructed round – and between – the two halves of the creature. A chandelier hung overhead and, as we seated, Waterhouse Hawkins drew attention to the names above our heads: Mantell, Cuvier, Conybeare, Buckland – who, said those who had known him, would have delighted in such a feast. We raised a toast to these men who had laid so much of the ground for the current project. I noted that Owen would not be looked down on by these departed giants: his own name appeared among them.

By good fortune, I was placed next to the lady, and away from Owen. He continued to lecture the company as the first course was brought in. I felt a pang of pity for those sitting at that end of the table; those of us at the other end were able to discourse with one another, albeit in hushed tones so as not to disturb the professor.

We ate well – mock turtle soup, then fillets of whiting followed by raised pigeon pie. The food came from the public house some way up the hill, and the lady and I laughed at the imagined scene of servants in tailcoats, scurrying down through the thick mud with each platter so as to serve it still warm.

It is the method of well-schooled women across Europe: make the man talk and say little of yourself. The lady played her part well, with words and inference to suggest that she really did find the life of a middling scrivener of inordinate fascination. It would have been easy to pour out tales of my tawdry existence, and bask in the glow of her interest – and flirtation, for I flatter myself there was that, as well. But I was just as fascinated by her story; more so, for my interest was genuine. Who was she? Who was she with? She surely wasn't a geologist?

"Oh no," she laughed – earning her a stern look from the far end of the table. Suitably cowed, we sat silently until the professor's lecture had resumed.

"Then your husband..." I suggested, glancing round the table. The lady noticeably cooled.

"My husband," she said, "does not accompany me this evening."

"Oh," I said. "Then what on earth are you..." I thought better than to finish "doing here?" But the lady took my question as I'd asked it.

"I don't know what I am," she said. "Only what I would escape. You want to know why I'm here tonight. I have an interest, Mr Quake. You might say I was born to have an interest. For the class dinosauria, the hulking brutes who once walked our Earth... Do they not horrify you? Such power and menace and rage. And yet, in them I see my salvation..."

I confess I did not understand her allusion for I did not know who she was. But I saw the distress I had evidently caused with my question so, over our entrées and game, we spoke of other things: how we'd marked Christmas, and how much the feast day had altered in recent years.

"That too," she said, "is down to Mr Dickens."

"I'm afraid I don't understand you," I said.

She explained without condescension. "His story, with Scrooge and the ghosts."

"No," I said quickly. "I mean, yes: Dickens breathed new life into Christmas. But you said 'that too'. What else is the man to be blamed for?"

"Oh," she said. "All this." She gestured round the room. "Us being here – myself in particular. It all stems from his *Bleak House*; the first chapter – the very first paragraph. Don't you recall? He describes London in November, the awful rain and mud. As if, he says, the waters had but newly retired from the face of the earth. So that you might well imagine a Megalosaurus, climbing Holborn Hill."

The man to the far side of the lady butted in. "But Dickens got it wrong: Megalosaurus never measured forty feet."

The lady only smiled. "It was not his task to be accurate," she told him – and the rest of the table. "It is ours."

The men around us murmured their agreement. Owen, glowering at the end of the table, even conceded the point. Then he got to his feet, pulling a thick sheaf of papers from his inside pocket. His speeches so far that evening had been merely an appetiser for the full ordeal.

"Gentlemen," he said – he did not include the lady. "What might Cuvier have made of our achievements?" I shall spare the reader what followed – a florid account of Owen's own accomplishment in deducing the shape and character of ancient creatures from scant fossil evidence; how he'd led Waterhouse Hawkins and his team to create full-size replicas of the dinosaurs in iron, brick and clay; how these sculptures would transform public understanding of the pre-Adamite age.

Owen talked at considerable length, and continued on as our next course arrived, was consumed and the plates withdrawn. I fortified myself with wine and endeavoured to maintain an expression of keen interest. Yet, no one else round the table seemed the least bit fatigued: indeed, they became increasingly enthralled.

Of course, they did not sit forward in their seats because Owen spoke; rather, it was that the longer he spoke, the nearer he approached his end. They were keen to move on to whatever was the next piece of business. At last the moment came.

"We are explorers in more than the field of geology," he said. "Our efforts open doors on to biology and ancient history, perhaps philosophy, too, in the more modern understanding of that word. But we are also making inroads into mathematics – and more, into the workings of the animal mind. Is that not right, Lady Lovelace?"

I started, as if touched by lightning, while the other guests politely applauded. Owen took his seat, raising his glass to hide the sour look on his face at having to surrender the stage. Only I saw that fact; all other eyes were on the lady beside me.

She got to her feet with that same lightness of movement I had observed before, colouring at the attention, a sweet smile on her face. I could not help gawping at her, for I did not know her as the men around me did. To them, she was a pioneering analyst and metaphysician, with a rare and practical insight into computational method. To me, her name spoke only of scandal, for she was the daughter of the late Lord Byron.

She spoke. For all her nervousness before the crowd, her words were succinct and clear. There were profuse thanks to all of us round the table for our indulgence. Then she began to discuss how she had become involved in the "sculpture project" – as she called it. As Owen and Waterhouse Hawkins had progressed with their great work of deduction in moulding full figures of dinosaurs from scant fossil specimens, they had needed some advice. Mr Dickens, whose latest novel had inspired the work in the first place, had suggested her Ladyship.

"Yet I could hardly see why I should be involved," she admitted to the table. "Oh, I saw a bold enterprise with a welcome, public purpose. But what was I to contribute? Professor Owen and his colleagues had already established a method of comparative anatomy, deducing the shape and size of a dinosaur by comparing the fossils to specimens of known creatures. Thus, famously, the fossilised teeth found in Sussex by Mantell were shown to resemble those of the much smaller iguana, a specimen of which was held in the Royal College of Surgeons. It was a matter of scale, not mathematics. I am afraid to say that at our first interview, I tried to insist they would be mistaken to employ me."

This occasioned some laughter. Professor Owen did not laugh – I doubt he ever did. But even Waterhouse Hawkins sat demurely. He had joked about his own work; he did not joke about whatever it was that the lady had done.

She started to explain: at least that was her intent. But after some initial words on the new, abstract science of operations and how a loom might be instructed through a series of punchcards to weave a complicated pattern in a carpet, I found myself at sea. The lady quoted a considerable number of mathematical formulae, lightly and easily as though they had been favourite verses. The deltas, cosigns and powers of V left me so baffled that I started to wonder if I was the one to have madness in the family. My only solace was that I was clearly not alone in being so lost; and her Ladyship clearly saw that.

"Well, gentleman," she concluded, a teasing look in her eye. "That is all perfectly simple. But how might such expressions be applied?"

She left the question hanging. For a long moment there was silence, just the wail of the wintry breeze outside.

Then something *stirred*.

Behind the bright fabric wall of the marquee, something huge and heavy *sighed*. There came the snort of steam, as if a locomotive had come to a halt just beyond the partition. A shadow, a movement... and then a vast and animal face poked out through the curtain. It blinked at us dolefully. A dinosaur!

It resembled in shape a rhinoceros, without its horn but many times larger, the skin cracked in thick wedges of bottle green. Its snout was as long as a man, the teeth the size of a human head. Thick smoke puffed from its nostrils. The power of it – the awesome power; and yet the thing was *tame*!

At her Ladyship's call, it padded forward, heavy feet making the very ground tremble; our cutlery danced on the table in response to each step.

"The hydraulic workings are thanks to Mr Armstrong," said Lady Lovelace – and Mr Armstrong bowed. The lady continued in the same gentle tone as before, as if this were all an everyday sight. "But the creature's brain is an entirely new sort of engine. We programmed a number of simple operations. It has been a fascinating experiment: what combination of basic responses will create the semblance of autonomous thought. In point of fact, we need very few responses to conjure the illusion. The machinery is housed inside the beast, and there is room to spare. So there is still much that we might explore with the mechanism. This is merely the first stage."

She made her way down the steps to stand with the vast creature, and it backed away to keep a discreet distance, snorting steam. The behaviour seemed completely natural, no different from an elephant who respects his keeper in the hope of earning a bun. The others stared in awe, but my profession demands certain instincts – and besides I was eager to ingratiate myself with the lady now I knew who she was.

"What is the next stage?" I asked.

Lady Lovelace fixed her extraordinary eyes upon me, and, like the beast, I felt an urge to take a step backward.

The manner in which she looked at me was quite brazen. At dinner, I'd mistaken her candour for flirtation, under the influence of wine. But no, she addressed me as a man might; as an equal – no, as my superior.

"We will develop the programme," she said. "Explore more complex operations. Perhaps even shed light on to the formulae involved in human thought."

I might have said something cutting in reply, had I been able to think of it in time, but the Megalosaurus suddenly let out a deep sigh, exhaling a last bloom of smoke. It took a step towards us... and then was perfectly still. Its eyes remained open and staring. There was a soft ticking from within, as of hot machinery cooling, but otherwise the creature did not move. It might have been a statue. Lady Lovelace looked sad but not surprised.

"It is powered by more than steam," she said, "and has an appetite for Daniell-cell batteries. We continue working on that."

She ducked under the creature's belly and, with a quick twist of her hand, opened a hatch which spat steam and oily droplets. Even so, she poked about inside – yes, in all her evening finery. I felt so affronted I turned away, to find Waterhouse Hawkins beside me.

"Well," he said, offering a cigar. "What do you think of that?" I hardly knew where to begin, but fortunately, he did not press for an answer. "You can see why we've been burning up funds. And why we can't halt proceedings here. My dear fellow, this is just the start. Think what we might do!"

"I think," I said, "this is where you tell me what I might do on your behalf."

Waterhouse Hawkins beamed. "We need our funds to continue. We need to improve the mechanics in time for the opening of the park, so our small creation might have an audience with Her Majesty."

It seemed quite absurd; I told him so, but he only continued to beam. "Write that, then. Say it in so many words. Lay down the gauntlet and we shall deliver. If only we have funds!"

I did as he asked; I wrote an article on what I had witnessed that night. When I learned that the *Illustrated London News* had also covered the dinner – and had lithographs showing the table nestled inside the Iguanodon – I felt a low disappointment, for that journal's circulation eclipsed that of my own publication.

Yet their account was – how does one put it? – overly melodramatic.

I pride myself that I describe the world and events as they are; there is no lurid embellishment, only a concise laying out of facts. But such facts! There was no need for added effects. To dine inside a dinosaur! Then to meet one, face to face! And the vast creature, breathing fire and obeying the commands of that madman's daughter!

My account seemed more effective for being understated. It created a sensation. A longer monograph was published. I received a considerable fee, and donated a percentage to Waterhouse Hawkins for his work. He sent a curt reply, thanking me for my efforts if not in fulsome terms. I put that down to his being too caught up in his project.

No, I had little thought of a change in his attitude toward me until the tenth of June, Eighteen-fifty-four – and the official opening of the Crystal Palace Park.

What a transformation had been wrought since the night of the great dinner. That night I had borne witness to a wasteland of mud and earthworks, now there were gardens and vast ornamental lakes. Even more spectacularly, instead of a scant two dozen of us, huddled in a barn, there was now a great multitude of people in those virgin gardens, that Eden: later estimates said some forty-thousand attended. I jostled my way through them up the slope to the wide terraces that led to the bright cathedral of glass and steel, the Crystal Palace itself.

There were soldiers on duty but they knew my name; indeed they had read my articles and welcomed me almost as a friend, so I was passed on through to the royal enclosure. At least, that is what I thought. As I made my way up the last steps to the glass building, a figure hurried down to meet me.

"Benjamin," I said. "I hope the day finds you well."

He regarded me coolly. "You were not sent an invitation," he said.

I brushed the matter aside. "It might have gone to the office in Manchester, or been mislaid while I was out of the country."

"Mr Quake," he said – and just his using my surname served to bring me up short. "You were not sent an invitation; it's ill-mannered to come all the same."

I could hardly believe it; for a moment I simply stared back at him, expecting that he would apologise for a joke in poor taste. But no, he stood quite firm.

"Am I allowed to know the reason for my fall from grace?" I asked him.

"You mean you do not know?"

"Of course not," I said. "I have sought nothing but to champion your work – and you."

"I see," he said. "You have been our friend in the press?"

"Exactly," I said, but the first doubts had crept into my mind. "If some part of what I wrote met with your objection, you have only to say. Whatever it was, I apologise. Come, let us not fall out today of all days. Indeed; allow me to correct any perceived wrong to you in a new piece I'll write. If I spoke to you and Lady Lovelace..."

He regarded me with such disdain the words died in my mouth.

"You have already spoken enough," he said, then turned away and marched up the steps. I started to follow, wanting to beseech him to have some measure of pity, but a soldier nodded his head, directing me back the way I had come.

As I made my way out into the *hoi polloi* crowding the ornamental gardens, I felt desperately sorry; for the truth was I knew what I had done to so offend my friend – and her Ladyship, too. I had known it when I composed my article, but dared believe – or dared fool myself – that it would be overlooked. Oh, the allusion was well drawn, and struck a chord with the reader. For these forty-thousand persons swirling round me had not come solely for the gardens and the glass palace. They were keen to see for themselves the animated dinosaur, the Megalosaurus, which I had dared to name a Frankenstein creation.

The public, of course, knew that book well and took the simile to heart. But they also knew the link between the devising of the story and the late Lord Byron. I had spoken, too, in my articles of Lovelace's passion for her project, and her mannish bearing. In doing so, I had conjured the impression – without ever stating it baldly – that she might carry some of her father's madness.

It had been a calculated risk, I assured myself as I made my way back down the terrace steps. Waterhouse Hawkins had asked me to engage popular support for his project; I had made his work a sensation, stoked a controversy and ensured his funding – for the scientific fraternity could not allow it to be thought that the project had failed due to the pressure of public distaste. Such a conclusion would have damaged investigations of every bent for many years to come.

I told myself that I had done Waterhouse Hawkins a favour, and that this would be acknowledged in time; we would be reconciled. But for the moment, I had been cast adrift. So I made my way down towards the southern corner of the gardens and the three small islands arranged on the tidal lake.

Already, a crowd filled the pathways and spilled over the grassy banks. I tried to get my bearings and establish in my mind where the studio had stood – but all was utterly transformed since the night of the grand dinner. What had been a muddy quagmire had become a vision of an ancient age, complete with concrete vegetation and ferns with iron leaves. There was much made in the official handbook of the way each island matched the conditions of a distinct era, and showed rock types within which fossils had been found. I dare say it was all correctly staged, but the people did not care for the rocks or fauna, only the creatures on display.

The sculptures were extraordinary. I marvelled at three examples of Labyrinthodon, like giant, bloated frogs; the Teleosaurs like modern crocodiles but for their long and slender jaws; the great head of Mosasaurus emerging from the lake; the huge sloth-bear Megatherium, grappling with a tree. And these enthralling monsters were but the curtain-raiser before the main event.

By the appointed hour, I had myself a position in the midst of the crowd on the upper bank at the very border of the park, with a good view of the three islands. There was such a fervour in the air, the whole mass giddy with excitement. I spoke to strangers as if they were old friends.

Then the clamour of voices faded. Word travelled, man to man down the hill from the Crystal Palace itself, that the Queen had begun her speech. We listened in rapt silence – and did not hear a word. For long minutes we strained to pick out any hint of sound.

Then there came a susurration, as if of great bodies of water moving through the pipes that I knew supplied the tidal lake. No; as the noise grew it became more clear: the throng of people ahead of us had erupted in applause. The noise came towards us like a tide and was quite infectious: I cheered and clapped just as keenly as my neighbours. That detail is important – the way each individual will was subsumed into the crowd.

It happened before the applause had died down. There was a commotion from across the park, towards the avenue of new trees. From our vantage point on the bank, my companions and I could make little of the disturbance; though we all felt, distinctly, that something had gone wrong. Then, yes, I detected the telling puffs of steam.

A woman's voice cried out: "Save our unholy souls!" The words cut completely through me.

There were more screams, off towards the trees from whence the steam had its origin. People around me turned to one another. I heard a man tell his wife that perhaps they should make for the exit – and she told him not to be such a coward. But, as with the wave of applause just before, we were soon caught in a tide of fear; washing through us, every one.

Then I saw it: the dark shape lumbering through the mass of people. The same slow, comical gait I had witnessed once before. Smoke billowed from its nostrils as it came. The Megalosaurus striding freely among the people.

There were others, too – I saw more huge and heavy shapes move solidly between the trees, blowing smoke.

Those around me started to jostle and push; some wanting to reach the south-western gate, others just as determined to stand their ground in this crisis. Had they not known, they said, that there would be a parade of mechanised animals? Had they not been thrilled by the thought, as described in that newspaper piece?

I wrestled with my own awful foreboding, telling myself that I felt no urge to flee. With contrived calm, I instead consulted the handbook in my shaking hands.

Megalosaurus, it said, "was decidedly carnivorous, and, probably, waged a deadly war against its less destructively endowed congeners and contemporaries". There were now also two examples of Iguanodon that were roving about – "the character of the scales is conjectural" – and a Hylaeosaurus, with a row of spikes running down its spine. With each description there was a simple, bold sentence: "These mechanised creatures are under our control and will do no harm." That note went entirely ignored.

There are many accounts of what happened next: the stampede of ordinary men and women from all classes, the acts of courage and barbarity, selfishness and self-sacrifice. The truth is, there was little kind of narrative, just an awful mess.

The crowd panicked. Those near the dinosaurs wanted to escape but there were too many people in their way. Instinct took over from reason; wild and animal instinct at that. I see it vividly, still: those trampled underfoot, those doing the trampling, those who fought and kicked their fellow men in their efforts to escape, all to no avail.

I managed to scale the bank and then up into a tree. I had not climbed one since my boyhood but in my terror the method came easily, like a second nature. Others followed, but too many crowded the lower branches, and

I saw more huge and heavy shapes move solidly between the trees.

they snapped – dropping those poor souls back into the mayhem. The few of us remaining clung tight to the higher branches, unable to save anyone else. I saw a child, held aloft above the heads of the crush. Hands reached out, and I saw the desperate effort to pass the small bundle towards the southern gate and safety. If those doomed souls had succeeded, it might have made the tragedy easier. But I saw the hands lose their grip, and the child lost.

Someone, anyone, might have caught the child and raised it up aloft. Someone might have but did not. It was but one example.

It's said the dinosaurs trampled the bodies, that they charged, that they ate from the corpses. I know that isn't true; I could see them plainly from my vantage point high up in the tree. They stood, unable to move in the chaos around them, unable to make sense of it, watching sadly as we murdered ourselves.

Waterhouse Hawkins went to jail for his part in the tragedy, and years later he travelled to New York to build dinosaur sculptures – static ones, of course – for the Central Park. Sadly, that project was never realised.

Richard Owen stood trial and was acquitted, but with his reputation marred. Within four years of the tragedy, it was shown from new fossil evidence that Megalosaurus and other dinosaurs had been bipedal – two-footed, not four. Owen continued to deny the hypothesis, and opposed Mr Darwin's new theories when they were published the following year. It is an irony that the word Owen conjured – *dinosaur* – has taken a new meaning to describe a type of man.

Lady Lovelace was not put on trial: the authorities would not credit that a woman, even one from such a notorious lineage, could have been anything more than an assistant in the scheme. It is said she and Mr Dickens have grown close since his divorce, but I would not wish to intrude into her personal circumstance.

And the dinosaurs? They remain on their islands, for any to behold should they but happen by. The creatures in the south-western part of the Crystal Palace gardens no longer enthral a huge crowd. It is known even by the smallest child that the shape and character of the sculptures is entirely wrong. Indeed, it is not uncommon, should you sit and regard them of an afternoon, to hear passers-by dismiss them as "mistakes".

The word twists a little in my heart, for they only slumber. On a quiet day you can just about hear the slow tick of their mechanical brains. Who knows, with a supply of new batteries and a little water, they might even walk among us once more. In the meantime, as we laugh and wonder at them and then hurry away, they are watching.

CIRCULATION

Roger Luckhurst

8 Nov 1790

I LEFT LONDON EARLY and reached Gravesend at nine in the morning. Weather execrable, the cloud low and that drear reach of the river filled me with melancholy humour. Our departure was delayed by low tides, which exposed the sandbanks, and I filled the time by domesticating myself in a cabin which surprised me with its comforts. The captain is a pleasant enough man, but rude; Forbes is his name. His sailors eye me with the calculation of card sharps. I unpacked my writing desk and wrote letters to my mother and master as the pigs that will feed us were driven up the gangplank, squealing.

I do not wish to go, yet have been obligated and so commanded.

13 Nov 1790

We are out in the open sea, having left Southampton behind. Weather continues intolerable. Everything must be tied down; alas not my stomach, which is bilious. A ship boy, Jem, brings me soup and speaks of fierce storms and schooners dismasted in the blast. He cannot fathom why his excitement turns me green. The first promise of landfall among the Windward Isles seems far distant. The boy, no more than eight or nine, has crossed the ocean many times, thinks nothing of it. I try to read, cannot. A wretched state in which to make preparations.

17 Nov 1790

The gales have gone, succeeded by dead calm. The captain paces fore and aft, waiting for the winds to fill the sails to push us across the ocean; they will come when they will, he says, with curt dismissal. Jem clambered up the mast like a monkey but he could see no clouds.

I was later called to the side of the ship to witness a shoal of flying fish and two dolphins swimming with them. I was struck with beauty of God's creation; the colours are many and glorious, rippling in the glassy water, such as I had never seen. I thought the sailors thus struck, too, only to understand that they were tempting one of the creatures near to harpoon the beast and set supper. Their imprecations shocked me, but I did my best to hide it all. Not well, I think.

The calm ended my sickness, but this means only that I read and re-read my instructions anxiously, and think on the interview with Mr. Craster.

He called me from the clerks' office after the calculation of figures was concluded for the day. The sugar pours in to the wharfs in the Pool of London; I am tasked to concern myself with guaranteeing the payments of those plantations not situated on the main island of Jamaica, but principally in San Domingue. Our trading company is cosmopolitan, mainly dealing with the Dutch, but the French traders in the London market are more numerous since the late events in Paris. Many of the plantation owners long since left the island and returned to count their riches in the wealth of their grand apartments; many are now exiles in London, fleeing the mobs. They keep a concerned eye on their profits.

Craster had a particular ledger in his hand; I rather thought I knew which one it would be. The Cranache Plantation has the greatest acreage on that unhappy part of the island of San Domingue forty miles north of Port-au-Prince. It is a task to load the ships from that remote region, requiring many slaves, but the harvests are plenteous. Profits pour from that whole swathe of the island. Without speaking, Craster tapped at the figures I had calculated in the ledger.

"Are your calculations quite regular, Mr Fotheringham?"

I assented. I had re-calculated the figures several times, burning many a tallow after main business had been concluded, and asked of the warehouse foreman by letter whether mis-attribution of the cargo might be the cause. This was unlikely. The reduction was greater than three-quarters, large enough to cause consternation, affect profits and change the price of sugar on the exchange. Rumours circulated as to cause.

"I am a great respecter of your mathematics." Mr Craster is a stern master, but fair, and thinks only to preserve the wealth and name of the trading company. I could see that he was not intent on blaming me, but was merely worried. "I was concerned enough to send Marshall ten days ago to make inquiries at the dock, speaking with the captain of the *Queen Jane* before she turned around."

Marshall was a gruff brute of a man, Mr Craster's agent in matters amongst the crooks that swarmed around the docks. "There is intelligence to be had, sir?" I asked.

Craster's brow rarely furrowed in these days of wealth and plenty, but he looked vexed. "Nothing that Marshall could venture to understand. Captain Jenner would say nothing openly, but Marshall learned that he was stuck in port because the entire crew had abandoned ship, vanishing into the hovels of Rotherhithe ne'er to be seen again. Jenner was having trouble recruiting from the dock rabble, because rumours were that the ship was cursed."

I was confused. What could curse a sugar ship? Sailors are superstitious clods, heathens to a man, but rarely principled enough to refuse a wage. Coin restores sanguinity, I have found.

"Marshall is a persistent man. He thought one of the mulatto sailors would be easy to track, particularly a huge ex-slave who ventures by the name of Philippe Nègre! Sure enough, he found him rooming behind a gin hovel off Rotherhithe Road. Sadly, he was not coherent. Nègre had drunk himself into a rage when Marshall met him, and was shouting about duppies and unnatural beasts. Later that night, he went to the trouble of filching a pistol – and shooting himself in the heart."

I waited respectfully as Mr Craster ruminated on this matter. "Nothing about this is regular. I need to send you there."

I pointed out that I corresponded with the docks by missive; what good was a book-keeper amongst dock-hands?

"Not the docks. San Domingue."

I was astounded. I had never travelled beyond London in my life. This was a matter for a man of the world, with knowledge of its sinfulness; a man such as Marshall.

"Marshall has left my employ after sixteen years," Craster said. "I sent him back to Rotherhithe to investigate further. He wrote only that Captain Jenner's body had been recovered from the Limehouse Reach, apparently another act of self-destruction. They had dredged the body, much battered in the tides. Just yesterday, I received a letter from Marshall declaring himself done with this work and that he was returning to his family in Newcastle. I am beset with worries. Something is wrong. You must go," he said.

A clock chimed in the back room.

"You *must* go," he repeated, with a stern look.

It was sentence laden like a barque with all the debts my family owe to Mr Craster. I thought of the doors opening on the debtors' gaol, my father emerging, blinking in the light. My labour, his reward. There was no question but that I must go.

21 *Nov* 1790

I was roused in the early hours by the sound of shouts on deck. Jem hammered on my door, and with great excitement pulled me up the ladders. It was remarkable: to see lightning caught in the rigging, pulsing like a spectral creature caught in fishing nets above us, as if the world were turned upside down. The sailors call this Saint Elmo's Fire and are full of omens as to its import. We are not superstitious in our profession. But the sea makes people so. The Lascars and Negroes squabbled and gesticulated. When I stepped forward and touched the mast, I must have disturbed something of the balance of these mysterious forces. The blue flames vanished. Several men stepped back afeared, as if I had offended one of the spirits of these latitudes.

27 *Nov* 1790

Becalmed for two days on a glassy sea. A thrilling azure that could not be conceived in London. The water courses with life, the fish arching high. I sit Mesmerized by them. The sun is larger in the sky, a vast orb in these regions. Seeking breeze, I read my letters of instruction on the deck, worrying if the French-man Devereux would wait in Port-au-Prince for a boat long delayed. I would need a guide for the journey south. I had sought accounts of travellers, but had little time before the boat sailed and the only information I read was complaints of the terrain: the broken wheels and axles and the pressing in of the jungle.

The tedium of that second day was broken by an unnerving sight. The captain was using the cunning of his trade, pushing the stun-sails out to catch the faintest wisp of wind, for we were moving through those waters, though at a laggardly pace. I understood this movement only relatively when I saw that we were gaining on a large cargo ship that loomed on the horizon, growing visibly by the minute. Jem called out and scrambled up the mast to the lookout. He soon called that he could see a British ensign on the ship's rigging and the anxiety amongst the crew dispersed. We are not in piratical waters, but there can be uncomfortable encounters with the French. Once the identity of the ship was secured, our sailors warmed to the prospect of hailing their brothers.

The captain had been assessing the ship, a vast engine of the Atlantic, through his eyeglass. I scanned with bare eyes but could see little movement, glimmers on the poop deck. The rigging was empty of sails; the sun caught it, glinting like restless gossameres. I was standing close to hear the captain swear an oath. He slammed the eyeglass down and began to hurl orders to pull in the sails.

When a sailor began to complain, the captain hurled vitriol at him. "Learn to obey me, you d---d hound! It is the *Brooks*! Understand me, it is the *Brooks*!"

There was a concentration of activity and our boat halted. Still we drifted closer, wood creaking in the swell. No sound came from the cargo boat.

Jem descended the mast with his familiar dexterity, but came with saucer eyes to the captain.

"On the deck," he began, "I see –"

"I don't give a cuss what you see, boy! Shut your d----d mouth! Back below!"

I turned from watching Jem scuttle like a beaten dog, and out of the corner of my eye caught the first signs of activity on the *Brooks*. Two men silhouetted on the deck, looking down at the water, where something heavy splashed.

"Blaggards," one of the London sailors said, who had been watching. "Never would I work on the *Brooks* for all the whores in Rotherhithe."

I saw that some of the Negro sailors turned away or busied themselves on the aft.

"What was that? Man overboard?" I asked. The sailors on the other boat did not express agitation. They did not call or gesticulate, but stood motionless. They seemed to stare into the water for a time, hands on hips, deemed themselves satisfied, and disappeared from our view below. They had ignored our presence.

"See no evil. Speak no evil," the Captain said, with a face of thunder.

I did not understand. Captain Forbes ordered the rudder turned and sails set. We began to pick up a little speed. It was a great oddity to me that there had been no communication between English boats traversing this vastness.

"I thought them becalmed. I wish it so. Rot in hell!" the Captain roared at the ship. They could not have heard.

As we turned, the wind shifted, and we caught the smell that came off the *Brooks*. It was the stench of what they carried that made me sick to the stomach, my body understanding quicker than my reason. The cargo they stow. I stayed below for two solid days, eating nothing, drinking little, and thinking, I confess, greatly ill of my master.

8 *Dec* 1790

After many days we are anchored off Port-au-Prince, waiting for daylight. I have been awake much of the night in dread anticipation, and calm my nerves by scratching a few words.

At length we crawled into the Caribbean Sea. At night, the intense phosphorescence of the weeds in the water is an extraordinary thing, and seems to light our way. Our wake churns the glow. The sun is an immense globe that burns the air, plummeting at dusk with the speed of damning Judgment, awful in its majesty. The dolphins that hail the boat cry up at us with plaintive human voices, quite like the sirens of the Greeks I realise, and the night waters are alive with invisible things that break the surface and menace the fancy.

The impressions of those landings on Antigua and Barbados overwhelm my capacity for adequate description. We offloaded goods and took on water at docks that teemed with thousands of people of every imaginable hue, from jet black through walnut to a reddish hue of skin I had never encountered. There are men the colour of the lightest molasses. The sailors welcomed the women as old friends on the dockside; there was some change of crew amidst the sailors, including a pilot for the treacherous tides to come. Forbes welcomed him with a stream of invective, which I gathered was a mark of admiration.

I walked on the dockside on Barbados, too timid to venture further. There were signs of a town edged around the dock, little more than tumbledown shacks, rather picturesque. I do not think I have ever been an object of the intense scrutiny such as I was subjected to by these harbour boys. They were as astonished with my pale English hue as much as I with their rainbow skins. They gibbered in a language of which I could glean nothing, except the occasional ghost of an English word, mixed with French or Spanish. I fear it will only be worse in San Domingue, where the French have allowed a bastard tongue to flourish.

These islands are mere dots of land on the Captain's charts, yet still crammed with more souls than could ever be possible to count. Yet the people seem happy, laughing like children in paradise.

It was only once we set sail that I thought of the ledgers resting on the shelves of Craster's office so many leagues away in Cheapside, the regular columns of figures that derive from these smudges in the ocean.

Forbes steered the boat towards Jamaica, and, when we arrived at the port of Kingston, I could discern that the British have made a start on a proper town, with wide boulevards and stone buildings and attempts to hack back the foliage that seems to burst unrestrained from every part of these islands. There is an air of purpose. I found my way to Craster's agent's office without difficulty as the business quarter nestles closely to the dock. Negroes thronged the street, in rags, shoeless: I envied them their artless dispositions since I was much discomfited in the heat. The office boy, a young Negro in proper dress and an excellent delivery of English, look consternated upon my explanation of my business, as if London were nothing other than a phantasm conjured by his master. The boy scrambled off to find Mr. Canevin.

This gentleman appeared to share his boy's disconcertion, and arrived ten minutes later, disarranged in his habiliments, unshaven and barely decent. He was a fat man and his belly protruded above his breeches. I was three days late arriving, but he seemed amazed that I had made an appearance at all. It was rare, he said, for men of distinction to travel to these far-flung lands unless there was direct involvement in the estates, or on a matter of inheritance. His method of flattery was rusty. His olivaster skin, darkened and weathered by the sun, gave him an air of flummery and I did not trust him entirely.

However, when we spoke of the Jamaican concerns, it became clear that everything was kept with scrupulous regularity. I spent a day and evening there, with the books, using for my guide the annotated list of queries that Mr Craster had provided. The moths flapped around my candle as I bent over ledgers. Mr Canevin was willing to conduct me personally to the Mansfield plantation, should I wish to witness the latest methods for processing cane. It was true that this nearby plantation produced the most regular crop, the highest yields of sugar at a lower ratio of labour, for an impressive rate of return for its owners. I declined, confessing that I had merely a book-keeping interest. He looked at me oddly.

At dinner, over which Mr. Canevin exerted himself greatly, ordering his cooks to deliver a feast far beyond our capacities to imbibe even a quarter of, I revealed that the main purpose of this lengthy journey was less concerned with matters of Jamaica and more to travel on to Port-au-Prince in order to discover the problem at the Cranache Plantation.

At this, Canevin almost choked on the chicken bone upon which he was gnawing.

"You go to Cranache?" His mouth stood open.

I observed drily that he had heard of the place.

"Its fame fans across the waters. *Mon Dieu!*" He feigned distraction, very badly, and rang the bell for his house-boy.

"I would appreciate any intelligence, as I am there for your master and mine: Mr Craster," I said.

He waved this away, his bluff manner quickly returning, as his house-boy pushed through the door. "The reports are contradictory, and the stories muddled."

He ordered the boy to take away the plates and bring more rum. After the servant retreated, Canevin whispered melodramatically: "I would appreciate it if you did not speak that name in the hearing of my servants. Whatever the intelligence, it is much confused with impossible rumour."

He spoke normally as the boy tiptoed in with a decanter: "One must be careful. These blacks have a want of development in organs of reason and truth."

The following morning, Mr Canevin had left a note detailing an emergency over the Blue Mountains in Buff Bay, and regretted his departure before dawn.

As the houseboy served me tea, he hesitated at the door, plucked up his courage and please-begged me a question: "Is it true, Sir, that you visit the Wizard Sangatte?"

I smiled encouragement, but said I had never heard the name.

"The white *bokor*," he added. It was evident I did not understand. "Who rules Cranache? They say he is very powerful."

"The Cranache Plantation is still in the hands of the family, I understand. That is all I know."

Dawn is breaking, and I hear the pilot calling instructions. We are to be landed at the dock of Port au Prince within the hour.

Who is Sangatte? The name is nowhere in my papers.

10 *December* 1790

Port-au-Prince is a tumble-down, riotous, Godless place, where the streets are cracked in two, running with torrents of people, beasts and effluent. The great houses are ruins choked by weeds. They lie empty, the old families abandoning them. The atmosphere is solely composed of violence and intrigue. You hear mutters at *les blancs* when you pass groups of men in the street; the natives stare in open defiance. Everyone – the mulattos too! – carries a cutlass at their waist. The French army do not have control of the capital. They have not cauterised the wound of this Parisian intoxication.

We landed with sunlight lancing off the waves and, as I had long feared, my man Devereux was nowhere to be found. Forbes vanished into the offices to make his arrival known to the harbour master and to receive instructions for the return voyage; the sailors disappeared into the crowds swirling about the harbour. Even Jem was gone, leaving me alone to wait for the agent who would conduct me.

There were many boats, so low in the water one fancied the weight of the sugar might capsize them. One of the things that I spied were rows of Negroes. They were difficult to make out in the shadows, as they sought respite from the sun under a narrow awning, hundreds it seemed, lying or seated in manacles, their bodies listless and defeated.

"You are here to make trade, Englishman?"

A greasy Frenchman, much pocked by a tropical affliction, had seen the direction of my gaze and sidled up. He was small, unshaven, and one of his arms was horribly withered.

"The boat, it arrived from the Niger delta this morning. The strong, they survive, yes?" He gestured with his good arm. "They are to be sold this afternoon, monsieur. You require service?"

I thought of spurning him, but instead asked him if he knew Devereux.

A sly grin spread across his face, the blisters along his jaw tightening. "*Mon ami,* Devereux is indisposed. They say it is from the same poison that took the Marquis de Rabinard and his Marquise Isabella."

"Poison?"

He looked surprised. His grin widened: a new man, easily gulled.

"The weapon of choice amongst the insurrectionists, monsieur. It is invisible, *hein*? And the blame? It scatters to the wind." He made a gesture as if broadcasting seeds. "*Les blancs*, they drop like flies. Faster than our friends resting over there. I am Jules de Grandin," he said, offering his good hand. "I will take you to Devereux."

We walked into town, Grandin offering scurrilous commentary in crude English on the sights and sounds of the capital. The chaos of the streets, the stench of blood and effluent, the riot of races all appalled me, and made me long for Kingston and the English temper.

Devereux lived in the lower rooms of a large house that seemed on the brink of returning to the forest, so entangled was it by creeping plants. The man was propped on a banquette and deathly pale and it was evident he was not fit for travel. He tamped his bluish lips with a square of white linen, and drank some medicinal concoction that swirled chalky white. Grandin scurried away from the death-bed.

"You find me at a disadvantage," Devereux said in educated tones that relieved me. "I could not trust my servant to find you on the docks; accept my humble apologies. Is Mr Craster well? I have fond memories of your City. I did not expect to die here, in a hovel on the edge of the world."

I did not have the courage to ask what ailed him. He had arranged for Jericho, a trusted overseer from Cranache, to take me by curricle the forty miles. He had been waiting for several days, and was anxious to set out.

"Is all in order there?" I asked, simply. "Mr. Craster fears some irregularities."

"There are... complications," Devereux laboured to say. He waved vaguely with his hand.

"And Sangatte? Will I meet him too?"

He was too weak or indifferent to register surprise. It was as if I had merely resumed an imaginary conversation that had much absorbed his reveries amongst the clutter of this stifling slum of a room.

"Sangatte," he said, struggling to light a candle in the gloom, "is a man of great wisdom. All Europe contributed to the making of Sangatte. He is a great *philosophe*, perhaps the greatest France ever produced. At least, he was, before his... nerves went wrong. He was great; immense, *vraiment*. Yet none will know what he achieved here."

"And what is that?" I asked.

"Circulation, monsieur: Circulation. He will be the envy of every man of Science."

13 *December* 1790

Wearisome journey over the jungle paths completed. Jericho is a garrulous mountain of a man, who chattered merrily the entire distance, but in a language of which I understood less than one eighth. I am too wearied to document that execrable road, the villages of a hundred staring eyes, silent and sullen people holding clubs and machetes, the hexes and marks that litter the roadside, the pathetic signs of vaudoux. The terrible roar and chatter of the forest: will I ever get it out of my memory? I must sleep.

14 *December* 1790

The Cranache plantation. We arrived in the jet black of night after a long day under the sun. I am a long way from home in a savage place.

We entered the gates of the plantation, tall solid doors with the family arms mounted in relief. The doors are heavy and designed as defences, but they stood open, one with sunken hinges so that it had cut into the soft ground. The large house was on a rise, where the front windows had a magnificent view out towards the coast. Most of the blinds were drawn and there was an air of abandonment. I assumed that the bulk of sugar cane fields were hidden behind, and the prevailing wind at first concealed the smell.

In the morning, there was consternation amongst the house servants, who had not been expecting visitors. Black faces peered from the door to the kitchen as I interrogated the senior household servants, Jericho at my side. One or two had a vestige of English. When I asked for the master of the estate, I was given a brutal answer that even I could understand: "Mr Cranache – he dead."

I was thunderstruck; this had been several months ago, but no report had reached Mr. Craster. I asked what had happened to his wife and children, but there was much averting of eyes and Jericho was unwilling or unable to translate the mutterings around me. Later, I spied the melancholy spot of a row of graves with Christian markers under a large tree not far from the front verandah. If they are not in France, the family is dead. I wonder if it was from poison.

After the initial confusion, it transpired that Cranache's elderly mother was still alive and resided in a suite of rooms above. I was relieved to find some proper order preserved, and requested urgent counsel. There were more pained looks and evasive machinations. My insistence was such that one of the head servants, a man named Trac, took command of that rabble and led me upstairs to an elegant reception room with French furniture in the modern Louis style. With a mix of French, English and mime, I gathered I was to wait.

I spent the morning there, arranging my papers, wondering how best to impart the concerns of Mr. Craster and the London market about the state of the plantation to an august lady of the clan. My experience of the French was limited to the men of the Royal Exchange. I was weary and must have fallen asleep; I awoke to find afternoon had arrived and yet still the maid-servants offered continual excuses. I had wasted much of the day in formal expressions of conduct that I realised would not be returned: she would not receive me, or was unable to do so. There was something in the air that I distrusted, whispering and stifled laughter in the corridors, that signalled a breakdown in the regular order. I resolved myself, went downstairs and demanded to see Trac.

Eventually the servant acknowledged that Madame Cranache was old and confined to her bed where she took vapours to ease her breathing; she had entirely ceded the running of the plantation to the overseers. The task then was to find an overseer who might converse with me.

Trac bowed and asked me to follow him. We went through a series of interconnecting rooms, the last doors opening on to the back verandah of the house.

The stench of rotting cane caught me at once and near caused me to vomit.

Stretching beyond limit were fields that had not been cleared of a crop perhaps several months old. The tall canes may have been cut, but the harvest never occurred, and the rot had set in. The fields contained not a single worker and the place seemed abandoned.

"Have you come to rescue us?" a voice asked in a cynical snarl. It came from a degenerate blanc in an accent I could recognise came from Louisiana. The man identified himself as Vincent. He was dressed in patchwork clothes and rested on the smashed remains of a chair below the verandah, in the midst of cleaning his whip. There were rags stained with blood at his feet.

"I have come to see Sangatte," I replied with as much authority as I could muster.

It had the desired effect; I had the advantage of intelligence.

"He is at the factory, *la bas*," he pointed at the horizon. "He won't come back to the house now, not whilst he is so close."

"Close? To what?"

The man smiled broadly through a ruin of teeth, rotted by cane. So I did not know, after all. He looked up at the sun, calculating the time.

"It is too late today, Monsieur Englishman. We can visit tomorrow, if Sangatte is in the mood for receiving guests." He laughed bitterly, looked me up and down. "What are you: a lawyer? A bookman? Yes? You want to know where the sugar has gone, yes? Your money, yes? But soon Sangatte will give you all the money in the world."

Vincent offered me liquor from a bottle, shrugged when I refused. He warned me to be careful of the food and drink I took; the hills beyond the plantation were teeming with freed or absconded slaves, massing for Revolution, poisoning the old masters. Although I ventured to steer the conversation, I received only snippets of knowledge.

"Sangatte", he said, "is one of the godless ones. He made a great name for himself at the Academie Francaise, in Paris." About what, Vincent could only say it had to do with blood and circulation. "He will tell you tomorrow. The maestro: he will explain."

I have resolved to venture to Sangatte's "factory" tonight without my disgusting chaperone.

15 *December* 1790

Who can speak of San Domingue, the black night, the drums in the *honforts* scattered through the mountains?

I waited until after midnight, when a sliver of moon rose above the horizon. That glint of light was enough to guide me. I navigated as silently as I could to the labyrinth of doors on the back verandah and stood adjusting to the darkness. Infernal insects screeched their songs and attacked my eyes.

The first fields behind the plantation house carried the worst of the rot. The smell of decay forced me to hold a kerchief over my mouth. I thought this would be just the beginning of a very bad story, but oddly the plots further on revealed a fresh crop of noble canes rising in regular rows, bulbous beets glinting in the moon. These were ordered and well-tended fields.

I had only the memory of Vincent's vaguest gestures to guide me, but soon I found the first huts of the plantation workers, all quiet, and I steered a path to avoid alarms. I followed the line of the canes, jet shadows with leaves blinking moonlight.

There was a faint depression in the landscape; presently I was following the path into a hollow, the horizon of cane rising above me. Things crashed and jabbered in the trees; I stilled to adjust my eyes.

Up ahead was a clearing and three huts, placed in a triangular pattern. Weak candlelight came from the window of the furthest hut, and stopping to listen, I heard the thrum of some mechanical device. The clearing was otherwise empty. It was not a factory that one might see in London, but I thought this must be where Sangatte worked.

As I ventured down a rough path, I came across a gully bridged by logs. It was only as I took my crossing that the stench below assaulted my nose. I reeled. It was animal matter, something unburied. I beetled to the other side and peered into the hollow, but without artificial light saw only slicks of shadow below. I thought it might be where the beasts of burden had been hurled once they died.

I need to be steady with my quill to reconstruct the sequence of what happened when I entered that clearing. The moon had waxed a little; light was better. As I passed near the first hut, I noticed the ground beneath my feet had a scorched quality, the dust coating my tongue with a cloying tang. Nothing grew there. The strangeness of the scene was heightened by the silence of the insects and susurrus creatures, as if they had all sensed my transgression and held their breath.

The cadence of the device was low and peculiar; not the grinding of metal parts; nor something worked with screws. I crouched at the corner of the first hut, a mean thing with an unravelling thatch. It was good fortune that I stopped. Something grunted and lurched out of a door, scraping feet across the powdered earth before fading into silence. A beast of burden, perhaps? I couldn't imagine what the dark held. I looked hard, and saw then that the whole clearing was criss-crossed by threads or filigrees of thick wire, pulled taut a yard or two off the ground. There was an immense network of these cords that seemed to run back and forth between the huts. I glanced up and saw that I was near one connected to my hut. I reached up to touch it, but was repulsed by its oddly warm and sticky feel. It glistened with black grease and it *thrummed* with the regular rhythm of the mechanism from the far hut, where the candlelight glistened.

I shifted my course, walking the perimeter of that blasted land towards the furthest hut.

Candlelight is magic. It colours the night where moonlight gives a world of stark black and white.

There, in the flicker cast beyond the window, I saw that the ground of the whole clearing was stained a dull ochre. The cords that stretched from the window were livid blue, slopped with the red of human oil. They did not *thrum*; they *pulsed*.

I was standing among the warp strings of Sangatte's vast machine.

I very much desired not to see what lay beyond the window. I did not wish to disturb Sangatte in his night studies.

I moved with caution towards the edge of the hollow, thinking I might find pick my way back through the canes back to the house. I felt I had sufficient an answer to Mr. Craster's inquiries to leave at once, willing to walk the further miles to Cap-Haitien if necessary.

It was my position and the angle of the moonlight that revealed the stacked bodies. There were the slaves of the Cranache plantation, limbless and staring, the bodies ripped open for their sinews in this experiment in efficiency, in circulation. The slops trailed to the choked gully.

19 *December* 1790

I barely recall the last days, but I must have walked and scrambled back along the road to Port-au-Prince without rest, night and day. The last miles I was near delirious, carried on a cart pulled by a man with the smile of a smashed cemetery.

I wait for an English boat to take me home, resting here under a narrow awning.

This climate does not suit me. I feel feverish and distempered. My thirst rages. In the cheval glass, my features seem pallid, my lips blue.

I wait for an English boat.

THE DARKNESS

M. Suddain

From the Diary of Samuel Pepys

Thursday 30 *August* 1666

OUT EARLY, and met Greatorex along the way. At an alehouse he showed me his new Armillary Sphere, and spoke eagerly of his plans to construct one 35 feet high for display at Greenwich. Spoke, too, of his calculations for shooting a rocket up towards the heavens, powerful enough that it could take a steele chamber into orbit around us, and look down upon the Earth from the sky. He says the chamber could be built large enough to carry a monkey, or a bear. When I asked why the craft should carry a monkey, or a bear, he became agitated and said, "Well it could be a dog!"

Then to Westminster by Tunnelcar, and to my barber's, overtaking Captain Okeshott in his silk cloak, whose sword got hold of many people in walking. Then to the Swan to see Herbert's girl, and lost time a little with her.

So to my Lord Crew's and dined with him. Then to the Beare-garden, where I have not been for many years, and saw some good sport of the bulls tossing of the dogs: not quite into orbit, but one into the very boxes. But it is a rude and nasty pleasure. Then about nine o'clock to Mrs. Mercer's gate, where her son and some other young sparks had gathered with an abundance of serpents and rockets; and there got mighty merry till about twelve at night, flinging our fireworks, and burning one another and the people over the way. A little fire is a restorative thing.

Friday 31 *August* 1666

Up at six to go by appointment to my Lord Bellasses, but he out of town, which vexed me. So I to Greenwich, where Doctor Pett's brother shewed a draught of the new ship which they intend to build for the King, and which can take him to near the same great heights as our spy ships. It has its own pleasure garden, with fountains, a pianoforte, even cages for lions and bears. Seems no one any more can take to the skies without at least one bear for company.

Thence by Skycar to Gresham where I had been by Mr. Povy proposed to be made a member of the Virtuosi. Was this day admitted by signing a book, and being taken by the hand by the President, my Lord Brunkard. It is a most acceptable thing to hear their discourse, and see their experiments. This day there were talks upon the nature of fire, and particularly of the new Plasmatic Fire, which can be concentrated in spheres, and to near the heat of the sun. There were proposals for a "waste-disposing sepulcher" which could turn corpses to powder, and also a kind of weapon, which could do the same to French and Dutch sailors. All were impressed, but for our young Mr. Fernod, who has recently returned from school in France, and has learned much, the French being eager to intimidate Englishmen with their advancements. He claims they have already made weapons with Plasmatic Light: such that they successfully destroyed, from 1500 feet away, a small boat containing a bear. There are already, he said – somewhat smugly –plasmatic privies in Versailles. But more critically, he said, the French have begun experiments with Darke Materials. In attempting to describe the nature of these materials he explained how there is far more material "not" in the universe than there "is", and so managed to confuse even the formidable brains of his assembled elders, and took some pleasure in it, I think. He told how a physicist called Le Fougue had demonstrated at their school a vortex which, though open for a blink, took a mouse away, apparently for ever. Our assembled were unimpressed, with Boyle saying he saw a man make a mouse vanish at Bartholomew Fair the previous week, and Hooke saying that it wasn't the first time the French had gotten excited over discovering nothing. Young Fernod became flustered at our laughter, and seemed to wish a hole to vanish into. Here excellent discourse till ten at night, and then home to bed.

Saturday 1 September 1666

Up and at the office all the morning, and then dined at home. Got my new closet made mighty clean against tomorrow.

Sunday 2 September 1666
(Lord's Day.)

Some of our maids sitting up late last night to get things ready for the feast today. Call up from Jane at three in the morning to tell us of a strange disturbance in the City. I rose and slipped on my nightgown, and went to her window, but saw only darkness, as all the lights in the City were out. Jane said, "But listen, the church bells are running backwards." It was very black, even under moonlight, but no flames. Thought I could see a glow around Fish-streete, as of lamps crowding in, and leaning out we could hear the bells, and the cries of many people. Told her it was no fire, just an outage, that people were panicked to stop their goods from being looted. Stayed to soothe Jane for as long as she needed, and her I, then back to sleep.

About seven woken by still more bells, and rising cries of panicke from the city. Rose to dress myself, and there looked out the window, and saw fireships floating above the place around Fish-streete. But still no flames, and not even the smell of smoke, though saw now that St. Magnus' steeple was vanished.

Could make no sense of it, so to my closet to set things to rights after yesterday's cleaning. By and by Jane comes and tells me that there is a fire gone out of control, but it is a black fire, burning without smoke or heat, and it is beyond London Bridge already, as high as Cannon Street, as low as the river, almost, and has taken St. Magnus away. She hears that beyond 300 houses have been eaten by black fire, and that this inferno grows bigger by the hour.

Made myself ready presently, and to the Tower, and got up on one of the high places, Sir J. Robinson's little son going with me, and there I did see the terrible sight for the first time: not an inferno as we would know, but a ragged circle of darkness stretching from the waterside as high as Grace-church Streete. Inside it was a very pure kind of black, and only at the edges did it seem to have substance: where it moved and sparkled like a pale gas flame. I could see houses at this end of the bridge half eaten by the Black Fire; not charred or smoking, but simply vanished; and this troubled me. Robinson's son, too, was very troubled. Many fire ships floated above, and dropped great scoops of water from the Thames, but these deluges simply vanished into the breach; and where pumps were used by men upon the ground, their streams finished abruptly where the Darkness began. We saw that the Darkness had eaten away the supports of the bridge, and it was near collapse, with many people still fleeing over it to safety. Nothing was immune; the very stones of churches vanished before our eyes. I wondered how the simple people would react to this menace: those who start at comets or eclipses, or think the barking dog nearby portends their death, and who have now to contend with a black shadow devouring their City.

So down again, with my heart full of trouble, to the Lieutenant of the Tower, who tells me that it began this morning as a small vortex contained in the storeroom of a baker's house in Pudding-lane. The baker said he thought it was some kind of new mould. The family retreated upstairs, and were trapped, but managed to climb from a window to the house next door, except for a maidservant who was too frightened to try, and became the first victim of the Darkness, having fallen into the hole and vanished with not even a scream.

So I down to the water-side, and there got a boat, and on the water saw a lamentable sight: houses as far as the Old Swan already taken, and the Abyss running on, that in very little time it got as far as the Steeleyard. Along the banks an army of people trying to save their goods. Some flung them into the river, others brought them into lighters that lay off on the Thames. Poor people stayed with their houses till the very darkness licked the walls away, and it was like magic: timber, brick, even steel melting like mounds of sugar in the rain, vanishing with no dust, noise or heat. Still the airships hovered above, their hoses and scoops hanging useless, and like me helpless to do anything but observe.

Having stayed, and in an hour's time seen too many dreadful things, I to White Hall, and there up to the Kings closet in the Chappell, where I did tell the King and Duke of Yorke what I saw: how the Black Fire rages calmly every way, senseless to our hysteria, and nobody, to my sight, has a mind of how to quench it, but only to save their goods, and leave the rest to the Darkness. The King said it seems on the face the Devil's work; I said more likely it is the work of some black science, and said so without mentioning young Fernod, or the French experiments in Darke Materials, as did not wish to fan the flames of rumour. Could offer nothing more, but told how the Darkness appeared to go more slowly where it was not fed, and how it had stalled at the Thames, sated by the volume of water pouring in. The King commanded me to go to my Lord Mayor and tell him to spare no houses, but to pull them down before the darkness every way.

So to Paul's, and there walked along Watling-streete, as well as I could, every creature there coming away loaden with goods to save, and here and there sicke people carried off in beds. In places people tried to save their possessions, while in others, for no obvious reason, they hurled things into the Abyss. People had stormed the churches to seize relics, and they ran back to fling them in the pit, crying, "Take mercy on us, Darke One!" and such. I saw one woman, stricken with madness, hurl a baby in, crying as she did: "Only pure souls can fill his hunger!" It was a mania such as you would never see from fire, which more often in Londoners inspires a kind of secret worship. Some thought to try to burn the black material away, and in doing so started a number of fires which quickly spread, and woke the fireships from their gloomy slumbers. But they were not as effective in battling the flames as the Darkness: which, where it touched the fire, vanquished it. I saw a boy who had reached out to touch the glowing hem of the pit, while his Mother was turned to their belongings, and his arm was eaten clean away to just above the elbow, and the mysterious fire had sealed off the wound so there was no bloode, but much screaming from the boy. There were a number like this I saw. A woman set on fire fainted and was eaten by the creeping Chasm, and her husband was heard to say it was a mercy. A large fire soon was up in the east, but the wind shifted, and pushed the flames back against the hungry Darkness. Soon the black circle was ringed in smoking red.

At last met my Lord Mayor in Canning-streete, looking like a man spent, with a handkerchief about his neck. He had not come when called about the small hole in the baker's house, as he had thought the man drunk.

To the King's message he cried, like a fainting woman, "Lord! What can I do? I have been pulling down houses; but the darkness overtakes us faster than we can do it!" So he left me, and I him, and I walked home, seeing people fleeing still, and not looking where they were running, some stumbling blindly into pits where the Darkness had come around in silent rivers and overtaken them. The houses, too, so very thick thereabouts, and full of matter for eating, were as pitch and tar to a fire.

I to Paul's Wharf, where I had appointed an airship to attend me, and took in Mr. Carcasse and his brother, whom I met in the streets, and carried them above to see the Darkness, which had now got rapidly further. The sky over London was filled with clouds of spectator ships, and it was chaos, with many terrible collisions. A considerable fleet of navy ships had been assembled to destroy the buildings around the Darkness with explosives, but the great unknown was hungrily eating the debris left behind, and there looked from here to be no likelihood of stopping it expanding. Below, a mob found themselves trapped against the Wall with the Darkness coming at them. Several grabbed ropes which dangled from a fireship, and made to climb up, but seeing this more people came, and the mob succeeded only in pulling the ship to earth, and all were swallowed by the Darkness. Carcasse wept. We saw how the Darkness had eaten right to the edge of the river, but there it stopped, unable to move across the water. The water from the Thames flowed into the blackness in an unending torrent. "Will it eat the whole river!" cried Carcasse. Could not take his mania, so went down, and to an alehouse where I met my wife, and we watched the river full of lighters and boats taking in goods, and goods swimming in the water, and being taken slowly into the unnatural Darkness. It having grown naturally dark while we watched, we all departed for home, and I to bed after a small supper alone.

Monday 3 September 1666

About four o'clock in the morning, my Lady Batten sent me a cart to carry away all my money, and plate, and best things, to Sir W. Rider's at Bednall-greene. Did this by moonshine. Then rode in my nightgown in the cart. And Lord! To see how the streets and the highways are crowded with people running and riding, and getting carts at any rate to fetch away things. I found Rider tired with being called up all night to receive things from friends. Then home, with much ado to get away the rest of our things, and little rest to be had.

Then to my tailor, Mr. Langford, who has made me a new black cloth suit and cloake lined with silk moyre, and it is so black: as black, almost, as this Darke Material. Then away to meet with the King, Duke of York, and Hooke, Boyle and others, to go up in the King's ship, to talk among us about the nature of the Darkness, and how it might be stopped. All climbed in with great passion, but few did so from sound knowledge, young Fernod being the only one who might offer anything substantial, and he not here in substance. I sensed in Hooke and the other Virtuosi no desire to tell of Fernod and the French. They are most likely afraid the King and others will come to see our whole group as a menace. Sightings of Fernod in the City, Hooke whispered, though unconfirmed.

We agreed to some sensible ideas, such as testing various substances against the Darkness in the hopes of finding some resistant material. The King suggested dropping many gallons of holy water from fire ships; this was politely acknowledged. I suggested extending the Thames around the Abyss in a series of canals, and this idea was well received, though there were doubts about how much water would be needed to sate the Abyss from all sides, the Thames not being an infinite resource, and the tidal flow from the sea being inconsistent. But it was agreed that something would need to be done, with the Chasm at its rate and course now threatening to engulf the City, St. Paul's, the electrical factories beyond Moorgate, even our antenna array near Aldgate, which would make us vulnerable to French attack by air.

We moved across to see the Darkness take St. Paul's. Watched in silence as the shadow slithered under the grand structure, melting away the land beneath the temple first, so that the choir began by degrees to cleave away into the hole, like slices carved from a magnificent cake. With this taste of Heaven the devouring blackness seemed to gather strength, and in mere minutes the choir was gone, the portico had fallen silently away, and then the spire bowed to us and vanished. The whole sad banquet took less than one hour, and someone was heard to say that Wren had gotten his wish: the old monstrosity had been demolished, but now he had no ground to build upon.

Having seen as much as we could now, the King away, and we to a little ale-house on the Bankside, over against the Three Cranes, and there staid till it was dark almost, and saw the fires the people had lit flare high along the edges of the Darkness, pushed against it by the wind from the East, and as it grew dark again that luminous glow appeared around the edge of the Abyss, which by now had swallowed a great piece of our beloved city, and looked so ominous that by comparison the fire at its edge looked merry and familiar. We stayed till, it being full dark, we saw only the fires.

Tuesday 4 September 1666

Up by break of day to get away the remainder of my things; which I did by a lighter at the Iron Gate. In the evening Sir W. Pen and I did dig a pit, and put our wine in it, and I my Parmazan cheese. Pen said that the talk has already turned to the French, and that the sensible amongst them have already fled home. Many rumours about the Abyss, and fancy is plentiful: that it reached out an arm to grab a baby from his mother's arms; that it speaks in whispers – but only so you'll lean close enough that it can eat you; that it is God's punishment for our persecution of Catholics, or for our general sinfulness, or even for the approval by Church leaders, just a week ago, for the building of Wren's pagan dome on Paul's Church.

If this is all the work of the French, Pen said, then it gives us an enemy to vent our fury against. I said that it also reveals how advanced their weaponry is. An army that employs pure Darkness as a weapon need not fear our Plasmatic Light. Yet I see nothing of the French in this attack, which has targeted so far our slum houses, our ale houses, our churches, yet not one of our strategic assets. Nor has it been followed up with an air assault, and our decryption stations have uncovered nothing indicating an impending invasion amongst the French or Dutch communiqués.

So to Hooke's, where I meant to convince him that we should tell the King about Fernod and the French experiments, but found him gone to help friends, his wife remaining there with servants to remove their things. She told me how young Fernod had shown up in the night, scared and babbling, with his eyes wide and weeping floods, and talking, too, of the French, but not in any way that made sense to them. They had been alarmed, and she had taken up a fire poker, and Hooke had said that he should tell these things to the King, and at that the boy cried "What authority does the King have over this Oblivion! The King of Nothing! The King of Nothing!" and ran off. She seemed upset by the recounting, so stayed a while to comfort her.

This night Mrs. Turner and her husband supped with us upon a shoulder of mutton, without any napkins, in a sad manner, but were merry. I after supper walked in the dark down to Tower-streete, and saw the black eye across the whole City, surrounded by the ring of fire. Who knows how big it will be tomorrow. It has slowed a little, but has gotten to the Old Bayly, and is running down to Fleete-streete, and Paul's is gone of course, and all Cheapside. I wrote to my father this night, then walked all the way to the wire-house, but it being burned, my tele-message could not fire.

Wednesday 5 September 1666

I lay down in the office again upon W. Hewer's quilt, being mighty weary. About two in the morning my wife calls up and tells me the Darkness has reached Barkeing Church, which is at the bottom of our lane. I up, and finding it so, resolved presently to take her away, and did, and took my gold, also, and W. Hewer, and Jane, down by Proundy's boat to Woolwich. But, Lord! What a sad sight it was by moonlight to see the City vanished, that you might observe the hole from the moon if you were on it. On arriving, I found the gates shut, but no guard kept at all, which troubled me, because of discourse now begun that there is a French plot in it. I got the gates open, and to Mr. Shelden's, where I locked up my gold, and charged my wife and Hewer never to leave the room without one of them in it, night, or day. So back again, and whereas I expected to have seen our Seething Lane devoured, it was not. But

Fanchurch-streete, Gracious-streete; and Lumbard-streete are all vanished. Walked into Moorefields and found a mass of poor wretches living in a vast encampment there, like the saddest army, and everybody keeping his goods together by themselves (and a great blessing it is to them that it is fair weather.) Never have I seen such misery assembled as I have from these souls who've lost not just their homes, but the very land beneath it.

Thence homeward, in poor spirits, and lay down and slept about midnight, though when I rose I heard that there had been a great alarm of the French being risen, which proved nothing. The talk of plots has spread like the Darkness, devouring reason. A number of French people had been found hiding in a market cellar, and had been taken directly to the Abyss and thrown in. Still no sound theories about how this could all begin in a baker's house; though there is a convenient rumour that the man brings in and stores some special butters from France.

Thursday 6 September 1666

To the King at White Hall. He spoke boldly of the plans to rebuild the City. But how can it be rebuilt, I wonder. There are no ruins to haul down. There are no ashes to sweep away. How deep would piles have to go to build a church upon this Darkness? Then told him all about the business with Fernod, and the Darke Materials, and he was not upset, saying he had already heard the stories through his spies, who have told him that Fernod plans to escape the City. He says there is no cause for fear amongst the Virtuosi, who are sensible men, or from Fernod, who needs only present himself and state his case. He was so calm at the news that I wondered if he knows more than I do. The fleets, he tells me, have been in sight of one of another, and most unhappily by foul weather were parted, to our great loss, as the Dutch came out only to make a shew, and please their people, but were in bad order. There is no sign of the French fleet.

To Sir R. Ford's, and there dined in on a fried breast of mutton; a great many of us, but very merry, and indeed as good a meal, though as ugly a one, as ever I had in my life.

Friday 7 *September* 1666

Up and to Bednall Green. No Skycar, no Tunnelcar, so by humble coach, my brother with me, and saw all well there, and fetched away my journal book to enter for five days past, and then back to the office where I now find the silence overwhelming. It is strange how long this time did look since Sunday, having been so full of actions, and so little of sleep, that it seemed like a month or more, and I had forgot almost the day of the week.

Saturday 8 *September* 1666

Up and with Sir W. Batten and Sir W. Pen by water to White Hall. The Fleet is above Portsmouth, there seeking a wind to carry them to the Downes, or towards Bullen, where they say the Dutch fleet stays. News that Fernod was caught by militia on the road to Dover, hiding in an empty grainstore on its way to Calais Tunnel. He is being brought back to the Tower. He will be interrogated, but his story will be uninteresting, I think. If he was a "mule" for this French weapon, then why would he have declared his knowledge of the Darke Materials so openly to our group; and why would he have put it in a baker's house? Admit his attempted flight to Calais doesn't put him on firm ground. But nothing now is on firm ground. Bought two eeles upon the Thames, cost me six shillings.

I was much frighted and kept awake in my bed, alone, by some noise I heard a great while below stairs; and the boys not coming up to me when I knocked. But soon to sleep; and all well all night.

Sunday 9 September 1666
(Lords Day).

Up and was trimmed. Has been a week since the Darkness came to take our City. I to church, where our parson made a melancholy sermon about the Great Flood, and its purpose in cleansing humanity of its sins, and most in the church wept floods, specially the women. The church on the edge of the Abyss was greatly full; but few of fashion, and most were strangers. Walked to Bednall Green, and had a bad venison pasty at Sir W. Rider's. But good people they are, and good discourse; and his daughter, Middleton, a fine woman. Discreet.

Our surveyors estimate the growth of the breach across London has slowed, but still expands by a few dozen feet per day. It goes west as far as Temple Church, near Holborn Skybridge; to the north as far as Moorgate; in the east it approaches Aldgate, and ends just short of Tower Docks. It has taken many homes, but thankfully not ours, and equally it has not yet reached the electrical factories, the radio stations, the armament stores, the airfields. If this is a French weapon, then it is one designed to bring terror, not tactical advantage. It is a cruel one, too: one which leaves no corpses here to mourn, no loot to plunder, no maides to violate, not even a scarred and smoking landscape to plant a tattered flag in. If this weapon was made by man it is a work of madness; by God, an act consuming meaning, or sense.

They say Fernod will do nothing in his cell but pray. He will not eat, or take water, and when asked any question he replies only with the Lord's Prayer. They say, too, that a French ship has arrived in the City; and under heavy guard, including from our own soldiers, the delegation has been brought to Whitehall. It is hard to know what to infer from this. To Whitehall, but found the King was indisposed and would not see me.

With nothing to do, went back to the City. Went to brave the edge of the Abyss, as close as any man would dare. How strange it is, this thing which is no thing, and yet by its very absence amounts to something. It is blacker than my cloak, even than a night with no moon or lamps, since there's no sense of anything lurking in the shadows. Just an unfathomable nothingness. But a nothing does not become a nothing until illuminated by a something; and by then, of course, it is something too. Perhaps this nothingness is God's answer to the sins and disorders of our City. Once the Great Flood had covered the entire Earth; and the Earth sat suspended at the very centre of the nothingness, which God had created out of nothingness. And so perhaps one day the universe will return to nothing. Here, foolhardy urchins were teasing the edge of the Abyss. One showed me a wound on his arm where the Black Fire had grazed him. It was white and puckered and painless, he said. Then he ran off again into the growing darkness of the evening, and played at pushing his friend at the Abyss, catching him by his skinny shoulders as he tipped towards his death, and making the boy scream with terror and delight.

Our surveyors are already proposing a grand new London; a City in the South. This new City will be guarded by our river, and its Governors will gather in Greenwich. It would take a dozen years, the engineers say, for this hole to drain the Thames entirely, and by then our best minds will certainly have found a remedy for the invading Darkness. Water flows in, too, from the sea, where it covers most of the Earth. Meanwhile the nothingness remains. Nothingness cannot be vanquished like an ordinary enemy. The shape of our fear is a rough circle, crawling slowly west and north, and by the east in quiet inches towards my place in Seething Lane.

Monday 10 *September,* 1666

Up at seven with a fright. To Woolwich with much haste, to retrieve my wife, who was extremely vexed at me.

A WOMAN OUT OF TIME

Kim Curran

"...why for so many centuries, not one good tragedy, one good poem, one esteemed history, one beautiful painting, one good book of physics, has come from the hands of women. Why do these creatures whose understanding appears in all things equal to that of men, seem, for all that, to be stopped by an invincible force?"

Emilie Du Chatelet
Translator's Preface for The Fable of the Bees
1735

Paris, May, 1716.

Or is it June, 1717?

ONE CERTAINTY: we have found him. Our man of his time. He has the potential to become the voice of his age. With the right influence, the subtle exertion of force, we will make that potential manifest.

The heat in the salon is equally as unbearable as the noise to our delicate ears. The intellectual élite – those who claim fine titles for themselves: *mathematician, poet, philosopher* – have gathered here to trade ideas. Yet, all they deal in is gossip.

Their chatter rises above the sounds of the harpsichord and we see him, walking among the crowd. François Marie Arouet. Although history will remember him by a different name. One he will give to himself.

Voltaire.

Light radiates from him. A soft, soothing glow like the faint rings around a moon. It is how we know him. How we have known those like him before and how we will know those to come. It is what draws us to them – like moths to a flame. It is our duty to ensure that their gentle, guiding light continues to shine.

He is short, unimpressive physically: pallid and frail, recently returned from exile. He makes a joke out of his punishment, but we were with him in the darkness when his God abandoned him. His pleasure with himself outstrips his talent, for now. Men and women stop him to talk, to compliment his first publication. They believe him to be a radical thinker. He believes it too, which amuses us. There is nothing radical about him.

If there were...

As he passes, we whisper ideas into his heart. Liberty. Divinity. The nature of the soul. Fertile seeds that will find their ground.

It is time for humanity to take a step closer to the final echelon of complexity and consciousness towards which the universe is evolving. Or will evolve. As long as we are able to do our work.

It is a subtle game. A push too far and their feeble minds will retreat. Not enough and they will stagnate, their minds becoming dull and indolent.

Voltaire's wit will make the ideas easier for them to accept. He will challenge church, state, the universe itself and they will laugh. And in laughing, they will think. But not too much. Not too far.

We have done our work. We fade back into the shadows, unseen and unseeable once more. Darkness is our habitat. And yet, without light, we cease to be. It is a delicate balance. A balance we exist to maintain.

As the salon – with its golden façade in imitation of golden times gone by and its stink of musk and jasmine and humanity – begins to diminish a new light appears. It grows till we are blinded. This ray, and the person from which it radiates, is an irregularity. It is dangerous. It threatens to destroy us. A shadow can be both created and banished by light.

We materialise once more, bewildered and blinking, seeking out the source. We consult our records but find nothing. Have we failed to notice another great mind? Another man of his time?

The light appears to be coming from a man named Nicolas le Tonnelier de Breteuil. He owns this salon, is a favourite of the king. And yet, he has remained unnoticed by us. How have we missed this? His light should have been contained, focused and directed, years before. It is unharnessed energy.

The man raises his arms, addressing the crowd, and introduces the next speaker.

We are wrong. The light is not coming from within him but from behind him. From a child.

A hush passes over the gathering as they indulge this creature. Even our man watches as the child lifts its head, square chin tilted upward, strong hands clasped before it. It begins to recite:

Alors levez vos yeux et de recherche, et une fois que vous le trouverez.
Retirez les branche. Il viendra volontiers,
Facilement, si vous êtes appelé par le destin.
Sinon, de toute ta force que vous ne pouvez pas vaincre,
Impossible de lop-le avec le bord de l'épée .

We recognise the words. We were there when they were written in their original tongue centuries before, bending over the man who wrote them, guiding his hand. What is this child doing with them?

The audience applaud, delighted by the child's precociousness: its talent for translation. We are not delighted. We are *disturbed.*

The child takes a bow, the embarrassment of the attention dimming their light slightly. It is then we see that the child is a girl.

Just a girl.

The relief is shared among us all. Rippling from one agent to the next across time and space. A female. We will not need to intercede. Society will do our duty for us.

And yet... we have to know where the spark began and where it will lead.

Paris, 1710

A girl – plain and already too tall for her young age – reaches up to take hold of a wooden doll that has been made for her. We breathed the idea of the toy's creation into the mind of one of her father's servants.

Please the girl, we whispered into his ear, *please your master.*

She is only a child and yet must be taught to receive all of her satisfaction and contentment from the bearing of children. We must ensure that her nature is contained by the expectations of her time. This is how we will distract her from the other path. The path that leads to our undoing.

We can apply only the faintest pressure to change the course of a life. Like a breeze catching the sails of a ship. There are laws. Principles. The forces that control the movements of the spheres control us too. It is how we have always, will always, operate.

The child looks at the doll, strokes the pale blue cotton of its dress, picks at the white ribbon of the cloth gathered around its wooden legs in lieu of slippers. She peers under the skirts, more fascinated by what lies beneath than the surface of the thing. In a single swoop she pulls the dress off – sending the doll's roughly painted face crashing to the ground – to reveal the structure over which this toy was built: the closed V of a mathematician's dividers. The servant must have taken this tool from her father's study.

She opens and closes the wooden arms of the device, presses the fleshy pad of her little finger against the pointed end, attempting to divine its true purpose. She runs, giggling, to find a scrap of drawing paper and uses the dividers to scratch a circle into the parchment. Uneven and imperfect. But a circle none the less. She hugs the instrument to her chest, rocking it like a baby.

She begins to glow.

There is still time, we think, time yet to extinguish this light.

Versailles, 1731

The glowing child is now a woman and, we are relieved to see, wife and mother. She adores writing her new name in full: Gabrielle Émilie Le Tonnelier de Breteuil, marquise du Châtelet. She elongates the ascenders, indulges the descending Q in marquis.

It is a good marriage. The husband: a sturdy, predictable man with many titles and much land spends most of his time away fighting wars. The wife: daughter of finance and influence. In the trade of bloodlines this has been a good bargain.

She strides through the scented gardens, a bright yellow domino mask hiding her unexpected beauty from the world, arm in arm with friends. Her only delicacy is in her wit. She is a colossus – with terrible feet and formidable limbs. And yet, despite her lack of grace she has embraced and restricted herself to the feminine world. She has put aside her studies or any attempt to unravel the mysteries of that which is hidden from her. She laughs with her friends about her latest delicate purchase from *L'Empereur*, directs her intellect towards the winning of card games.

Her life and the life of our man, Voltaire, run in parallel. Overlapping briefly but impacting little on each other. We have mapped the consequences of what would happen should they intersect and we will, we must, keep them apart.

The time will come when women will contribute to the progress of history, to the cultivation of ideas. When their light will shine as brightly as that of men. But that time is not now. We are here to ensure that.

We follow her up the steps and through the glowing corridors. As her laughter drifts through the windows to the gardens below we fade into the shadows almost certain that things are as they should be. Chaos has been bridled.

And yet: almost certain? We work in light and darkness, absolutes.

Lunéville, Summer, 1749

She sits, bent over a parchment, leather apron over a green silk dress, black India ink freckling her face. The candles are stumps, but we do not need their flickering flame to see her. The light within her glows once more. And it has found its focus.

We watch as she bites down on her lip, trying to find the right word to convey a subtlety of meaning. We approach as her quill skips across the page, leaving a spider's web of marks in its wake.

Ours are not the only eyes watching. A large portrait of her and her husband peers down from the wall. In the painting, in her left hand, there is a small book. A delicate finger holds her place. We look closer. The Bible? A moral text?

We should have known she would never have acquiesced to such conformity. Not for her. Not for this woman out of time. She has chosen to immortalise herself in pigment and oil holding a treaty on geometry.

Her library is chaotic: books and papers piled high and close to toppling. How does she ever find anything in this farrago? We blow open a blue folio of pages, using the breeze from an unlocked window, and see an essay.

Dissertation sur la nature et la propagation du feu by Émilie du Châtelet.

She has made her study the nature of fire. Of energy. The irony is too much.

We lean in to see what she is working on, our presence causing a curl of her dark hair to tickle her cheek. She brushes it away.

"Impressed force is the action exerted on a body to change its state either of resting or of moving uniformly straight forward."

No. It cannot be. We loom over and watch as she works from his original Latin, translating the works of another of our men.

She dares not only to translate Newton but to correct him! We read her messy, untamed handwriting. She has examined his assumption on the homogeneity of the universe and found it erroneous. The cosmological principle – a principle we ensured was in place – cannot be questioned, not for generations upon generations.

And more! She has turned her unique, anomalous intellect on the nature of light and found it to be without substance. Without mass. She scratches letters onto a page – the sound of her quill claws into our very substance – *MV*2. Before it, she places a single letter and symbol. *E =*.

She is so close. Too close. To an idea that will not, *should* not, exist for over one hundred and fifty years. That idea belongs in a time and place far from here. June, 1905, Vienna. It is a fixed point.

How did she come to this? Fearing for our very existence, we must understand her transformation from the laughing fool at the palace, to this dazzling, dangerous mind, in eighteen short years.

Semur, Spring, 1732

She is with child again. She has turned away from the excitements and heady liberty of Paris and seconded herself in her husband's family home. The very model of the dutiful wife. All should be well.

And yet, her light still burns.

As the life within her grows, so does an idea. She is a thinking creature. Blessed by nature with a hot, *male* temperament, which permits her, she believes, to pursue a life beyond that of wife and mother. She knows, now, what she wants to do. Not for her a life of foolish things, swimming in the sea of uncertainty. She has direction. She has focus.

She surrounds herself with men of geometry. Reacquaints herself with philosophers. She drinks ideas as other women drink wine. She is aglow with knowledge.

She must be stopped.

Paris, Winter, 1733

She is attending the opera, adorned in her yellow domino once more. She is impatient to hear the music, has missed these entertainments during her confinement at Semur. Perhaps the attractions of Parisian life have taken hold again? Perhaps indulging in the frivolousness of culture and art will satisfy her hunger for knowledge and her ember passion for geometry was nothing but a passing whim?

And yet, the light glows still.

Worse, our man is here.

We whisper in the ear of her companion.

They should leave now, during the interval, and go on to the Villars-Brancas' for supper, cards and conversation.

She cannot meet him. Not now. Not as the spark of her fire threatens to catch.

But it is too late. He enters the box.

They exchange a few words about the performance. We try and distract him. Other women. Other men. We almost succeed and then, without warning, she begins to talk about her lessons in mathematics. They share a tutor. They share ideas. She quizzes him on his interpretation of Locke.

In desperation, we see to it that the opera resumes ahead of schedule.

It is too late. Voltaire is bewitched by her.

Cirey, Autumn, 1737

She sits in the window, picking at a golden croissant as Voltaire, our man and her man too now, reads his latest essay aloud. It is his study into the nature of fire. His attempt to reveal its mystery. He intends to enter it to the French Academy of Science, assured that it will win the prize set by them.

She interrupts him at times to challenge an assumption he has made, correct an erroneous calculation. He bears the interruptions well, knowing that her grasp of mathematics is superior to his. And all the time she smiles. She has been working in secret on the same topic. Forbidding the servants to tell him. She wants it to be a surprise.

We know him better than her it seems. When her essay is chosen alongside his, his damaged pride will douse his passion for her. It is a risk, allowing her work to receive even momentary acclaim. And yet it will divide them.

It is a risk we will take.

Cirey, Summer, 1788

She lies, covered in a peacock-blue silk quilt, her black hair now grey. And yet, she still glows.

Light streams in from the open window, a gentle wind causing the curtains to dance. She knows death is on its way and welcomes it. She mutters to herself as she drifts in and out of wakefulness, believing herself to be in conversation with our man once more. But we took him over a decade ago.

They remained close till the last, our attempts to divide them foiled by the bonds of friendship. We quenched their lust, but their respect for each other was not so easily unpicked.

Visitors have been coming and going all afternoon: friends who have known her; admirers who wanted to see her before it was too late. The greatest mind of her generation. They talk of her great legacy, of how she has pushed forward the frontiers of science beyond anything thought possible. They call her the female Newton.

She is loved. She is respected. She will never be forgotten.

This cannot be allowed to happen.

Lunéville, Late summer, 1749

She is still at work. As if the weeks between our last visit to this place and this time have not happened.

She leans back in her chair stretching out her neck and we have to scuttle out of the way or risk intersection. She has been at her work for fourteen hours straight, with nothing but her dark syrup to nourish her. Why the urgency, we wonder. Then we see, the swell of her belly. She is with child again. Her fourth. At such an advanced age? It is madness. It could be our chance.

She looks around, as if suddenly aware of our presence, and stares into the shadows. She is a creature who is unafraid to look into the dark to seek answers. This is why she is so perilous to us.

It is nothing, Émilie, she says aloud. *Just your mind once again.*

Satisfied that she is alone, she pushes aside the essay she has been working on and finds a sheet of pale cream writing paper, with a delicate hand-painted border. On it, she begins a letter.

She writes of the blackness she sees, of the presentiments of death that cloud her walks in the gardens. She begins to write in smaller letters, in tighter lines, so that she may finish her last thought before the page runs out. Her last sentence, in smaller script, runs along the pale-green border.

I finish because I can write no more.

How does she know we have come for her? Perhaps now is not the right time?

We play out the consequences once more, map the choices. We are at a junction and only one path may be taken. She is on the cusp of shifting the course of ideas. A few more years and she will have the breakthrough that could undo everything. All our work. We cannot permit her those years.

But she senses us. She fights to hold on. For now, we must retreat.

We will allow her to finish her work, we will allow this one indulgence. The birth of her child too, we will sanction. Her writings, in the right hands, will prove useful. We will see to that.

We will return.

September 10th, 1749.

Time has found its grip once more.

We took her in the early hours of the morning. They will say it was sudden but it was thirty-nine years in the coming. She looked straight at us, unafraid to the last. Daring us to come. In her last moments, she turned not to God, but to her idea of multiple universes. The notion that somewhere a different version of herself continued to live and to work gave her comfort. And yet, in every possible universe, we are there, an invincible force ensuring there is only one possible path.

Her grand project is completed. In time, we will permit it to be seen. The work she began will inspire other men – our men. But we must wait till her light has faded from memory.

We will see that her brilliance is framed solely by her relationship to our man. It is *his* name that will, that *must*, echo through out the ages. Sharp-tongued gossips will disparage her work. She will become nothing more than Voltaire's mistress. A parrot of great men. A curiosity and nothing more.

She was a woman out of time.

We do not, cannot, think on the morality of our actions. Only that they are necessary.

Our work is done.

We fade into darkness once more.

FAIRCHILD'S FOLLY

Tiffani Angus

1736

MY DEAR MR. FAIRCHILD,

He held the quill, waiting for a way in. Carl Linnaeus corresponded with learned men across Europe, all interested in the natural world and his bold idea of ordering the creatures found upon it, yet none of them, alas, *amort*. It was no surprise that he found himself ignorant of the agreed upon courtesies required when corresponding with the dead.

Pinks, he wrote and then stroked his chin with the feather, hoping to tease out the next word.

Pinks are... what? Thomas Fairchild had known everything there was to know about pinks.

Carl crossed it out and began again.

The genus Dianthus has, for me, a bittersweet connection.

It still wasn't right. A drop of ink marred the line. No matter.

He waited, determined to find the correct voice. Mannered? Humble? Cordial with a tint of solemn? Making the acquaintance of the nephew had given him the idea, but he resisted the urge to begin a list of moods and their matching facial expressions, each of which affected a voice's timbre and delivery. It would be a game for another time.

East of the City of London I found your Hoxton awash in Pinks, defiant against hard Stone, soft'ning Man's Creations with the rose colour of a Child's cheek, the ruddiness of a Nipple viewed through gauze. The picot edges of each bloom saw at the sky, unconcern'd that rather than Meadow they grow against Brick and Iron, risking hooves and carriage wheels. They are a hardy Plant, and even blanket'd the dead lying beneath their stones in the Churchyard. Which brings me to this letter.

You may think me ridiculous to admit that it was a Pilgrimage of sorts. I allow myself to believe that you would not, for I know you to be—to have been—a man of God. We know God's Message by studying his Creations.

In the Ground at St Leonard's where the Poor are laid to rest, you lie alongside Men who—in spite of their station—had what you had not: Children to continue their Name, a Wife for their Comfort. Yet those same souls sleep eternally near Thomas Fairchild, a Man who left what they did not: a Legacy....

1716

His face flushed, Thomas Fairchild trembled as he pulled at his neckcloth, but the thin puff of air that slid down beneath the fabric of his shirt did little to alleviate the heat that built in his chest. For a moment, he even considered undressing and going as Adam into his Eden, but his workers were nearby, pushing barrows of dirt, tending to the trees and plants in his nursery. Already the thought of them – of anyone – watching what he was about to do both terrified and excited him. Not that anyone – except, of course, the educated crowd at the Royal Society, and only then if it worked – would know what he was about to do. Except, of course, God.

It was so unnatural as to be invisible.

He picked at his shirt front again, the limpness of the fabric reminding him of the crush during the dance a week before, and breathed her name.

Miss Rebecca Wade. The hard consonants of her given name tapped at Thomas's sensibilities, waking him up, holding him there until letting him loose with the descent of her surname, the final *d* bringing to an end the sigh of the *a* following the lip-pursing *w*. He'd taken to repeating her name under his breath, a tiny prayer among all of the others.

Each repetition, each meeting of his lips on *m* and *b*, was a kiss on the lace that finished the hem of her mantua.

She was a walking exotik, a living advertisement of her father's Spitalfields weaving house, the bizarre silk design of her dress by turns spiky and soft. Thomas, apprenticed to a clothmaker in his youth, wanted to study her, to find where she ended and the fronds, leaves, pistils, stamens, petals, seeds, and roots of her dress began. Thomas had never travelled, his plants shipped to him across the seas, but with Rebecca he imagined he could conquer a foreign land. And now in his shed he stood at the edge of one discovery, a culmination of his lust for recognition, from the society and from Rebecca. To create something that no one had seen before: an exotik not imported but bred on home soil.

This, then, had sent him to his gardens to find the right shade, shape, ruffle to capture her attention.

Outside, his men called goodnight to one another as they stored their tools and hung up their aprons. Thomas returned their goodbyes to keep them away and was soon alone.

He returned to his task.

He was a man, wasn't he? With all his faculties? He wondered whether he was the first person ever to think of it. Or just the first to brave the Almighty's wrath.

Adam and Eve did what they were destined to do in their garden. Thomas Fairchild would take the steps necessary to claim his own destiny in his garden.

It would make his name.

On the table, he placed the female to his right, the male to his left. The arrangement was important. Fertilisation should happen from left to right, in the same order as one would read.

He considered his personal potting shed – the smallest in his nursery, its few windows covered in condensation, every cubby full to bursting with papers and catalogues, pots and tools – as a glowing cocoon, a hen's egg held up to a candle, a bright womb.

"Enough," he said to himself. "Philosophy is made confused with such poetry."

Before him lay the materials necessary for new life, each party in the transaction displaying a deep blush, their essential parts open and ready. The humid room filled with the mingled scent of the happy couple. Thomas said a little prayer to himself, a sort of nuptial service, uniting the two in a matrimony before consummation.

He had assigned the Sweet William the role of patriarch on account of its name. With a brush of Thomas's feather, it gave up some of its essence. He turned to the bloom chosen as his heroine, her frills reminiscent of Miss Wade's. With a flick of his wrist, the carnation, its scent so reminiscent of sugar pastries and cloves that Thomas's mouth watered, was fertilised. He twisted the feather between his fingers, tempted to force nature's hand even further.

A goat bleated nearby. A carriage rolled down the lane. A sprinkle of rain fell on the roof above Thomas's head. He laid down the feather, the end piece of a broken pen, nothing decorative or regal about it, just a practical item given one final chore before being crushed into the ground with the table scraps. There was nothing to do now but wait.

That evening, as he wrote orders at his desk, answered correspondence, and recorded the newest shipments from the Netherlands, he couldn't help but return again and again in his memory to the afternoon in the shed. The moment with the feather. The late afternoon light. The closeness, the heat, the condensation on the glass panes. "You act like a man half your age, walleyed with lust," he said to himself.

He resisted the urge to return to the nursery. He resisted the urge to tell his brother-in-law. He resisted the urge to call on Mr. Wade.

Rebecca.

Would that he could recollect a tryst with her. But it hadn't yet happened. Nor had any nights with Miss Mary Buelton, her cousin Henrietta, or the Misses Cavendish. He had loved none of them, but had lusted after all of them. Did lust mellow to love, or was a man who married in haste forever sorry for it? Thomas didn't know. He had never made it past the first flush of physical yearning. The more he aged, the sillier it all seemed.

What had he done?

1729

Dear Sir,

Mr. C—n, a Gentleman of your Acquaintance, inform'd me of your Great Idea last evening over a delightful Lamb pie. By Divine Providence or plain Luck I recently receiv'd word of your Thesis on the Sexual Reproduction of Plants, a topick with which I am very familiar. Perhaps you have heard of me? Or are aware of my Presentation to the Royal Society on my Experiment on that very Subject?

I was informed that you are considering the devising of an ambitious Strategy to create a System by which to organise every Animal and Insect, Fish and Flower. I inquir'd over Pudding, curious in the extreme to know how one Man could take upon himself such a Task, for aren't there more Lands upon the Earth than we have seen, leading one to assume that there are divers more Creatures upon it than those with which we are familiar. Will the discovery of a never before seen Plant or Butterfly undo the ranking, bringing it crashing down higgledy-piggledy as surely as a young Child playing with his Blocks? Not that I equate You, sir, with a Child. On the contrary. I am but a curious Botanist.

Please excuse my Ignorance. I am, with all Humility, Your faithful Servant,
Thos Fairchild

1736

It was several minutes before a man clad in a dirt-smeared apron over simple clothes met him at the gate.

"Mr. Linnaeus, sir, I am John Bacon." The young man held out his hand. "You are welcome to my nursery." His tone indicated a certain weariness, leaving Carl to assume he said the lines by rote. How many voices were there, Carl wondered, and how might they be ordered? By tenor or by purpose? Commands, exclamations, manipulation.... The number of voices was as endless as the assortment of faces, yet did not all faces contain two eyes, a nose, a mouth, etc., each component flexible into only a limited number of variations?

"Sir?" The young man directed Carl's attention back to the moment.

"I have come to inquire after Mr. Thomas Fairchild," Carl explained. "We corresponded many years ago, but I have been travelling." He patted his satchel, feeling the familiar bump of letters. "Is he about?"

The young man nodded. "I'm his nephew—"

Carl mentally aged young John, giving him reddened cheeks and a bulbous nose, a paunch that strained the buttons of his waistcoat, and lines at the edges of his eyes.

"—but he has been dead these six years," John continued, and the image of the uncle disappeared inside of the slim young man.

"Six years?" Carl tried to control his shock. Another voice to add.

"Mayhap seven," John said.

"That explains the lack of response." He trailed off, only brought back to the present by the smell of manure carried on a shifting breeze. "Please excuse my manners. My condolences, sir," he said and bowed his head. "I truly regret that I never was able to know your uncle. In person."

John nodded. "My uncle was proud of his wide correspondence. He never travelled. He loved London and its gardens, kept a greenhouse for his own projects."

Carl thought for a moment. "May I see it? I wrote a thesis on plant reproduction. To observe the mule's birthplace...."

As John led the way, he described the new greenhouses being built with bigger windows and better ovens, and he proudly listed which new plants had arrived and from where. Carl nodded but barely listened.

"Here it is," John said and opened the door to the smallest greenhouse.

"And the mule?" Carl asked.

"At the Royal Society, pressed on paper, I believe."

"Seeds–?"

"–No seeds, of course."

Carl realised his mistake. "Of course."

"I've no need of this shed," John explained. "Too cramped for more than one man at a time, and the windows too small. I'm thinking of tearing it down."

"It's rather well kept," Carl said. The building's floor was free of muddy footprints, its shelves dustless, the pots stacked in a corner without cobwebs or moss.

John Bacon grunted. "'Twas a squirrel's nest when Uncle was alive. I loved it as a child. If I didn't know any better it wouldn't be a stretch to think that a shelf snapped with the weight and the plants fell upon one another in their passion."

Carl kept his disappointment to himself. He had hoped, standing in the man's private shed, for a feeling of connection to Thomas Fairchild, but the longing disappeared in a breath. There was no life in the little building: no papers or a forgotten cap, no boots by the door or an old glove, its thumb worn from use. Thomas's business legacy, the nursery, had been left open and his nephew had stepped in seamlessly, as Carl could see by the number of workmen tending to the plants and trees. His other legacy lay in a dark drawer in a stone building in London.

"My search for your uncle is destined to be unsuccessful," Carl said and stepped backward out the door to allow John to return to his work.

"He's buried near to here," John said as they returned to the gate. He explained his uncle's endowment and the annual sermon that Thomas had felt was necessary for forgiveness. "You've missed the Whitsun sermon by a fortnight, I'm afraid."

Carl rested a hand on his satchel before asking whether Thomas had ever married.

John shook his head. "There was some talk, when I was younger, about a betrothal. My own parents are gone now, and no one to ask." Carl noted a tone of resignation, another voice to add to the growing list.

"The letters?" the man asked. Carl pulled his hand away from his satchel and wondered whether the man had any claim on the packet. "May I ask how you were acquainted?" John then asked and Carl relaxed.

Thomas's letters had followed Carl from post to post, their author already dead by the time Carl had opened them. While he sat at his breakfast and read Fairchild's questions, he had been conversing with a ghost, though one with a kind temperament and a keen mind. It was the order of things, of course, to grow and then wither and die.

"I wonder," Carl asked the nephew, "whether you took possession of a letter that arrived after your uncle's death?"

The young man's eyes lifted as if the answer were flying above; he cocked an eyebrow and stuck out his lips, and Carl Linnaeus saw Thomas Fairchild in his nephew's face. He clapped his hands together, eager to receive what he had sent.

Later, as Carl said his goodbyes, he asked one last question. "Where do you rank love, sir?"

John leaned on a shovel and studied the ground, his demeanour not one of a man trying to remember a past event but one attempting to consider the impossible or even unworthy. "I've never thought on it. The seasons turn quick. Not much time for contemplation–"

"–of something so abstract?"

"Of something so important."

"Your uncle loved you. He said it in a letter."

John raised his head and nodded. "He said so when he trained me and left his nursery in my care. He gave me the one thing he ranked above all others."

Carl turned away soon after and made his way toward St Leonard's.

1729

Dear Sir,

I do hope that the lack of a Response to my Initial Letter is not indicative of Irritation on your part. I will, until I hear otherwise, assume that it is your Study of the Natural World that hinders your Correspondence and not a humble Gardener's inquiries.

It is your Study itself that brings me to write to you again. I have found myself, at my age—I am two and sixty, and I understand you aren't half that!—wondering more Things than I can write in a simple letter, unless that letter were to grow to the length of one of Defoe's Novels. It is a Conversation to be had over a Dinner—a Feast even, with many Courses, one for each Topick. It would last into next week! Please excuse my wandering. I shall blame that upon Age as well, and be forgiven for it by someone such as Yourself.

What about Love, sir?

That is the centre of it. Love. I find Myself, at my advanc'd Age, taking stock—both literally as I inventory my Possessions and Business and figuratively as I collect my Memories. I have had some small Success, a Trifling thing when compar'd to that which you are sure to have for your great Projeckt. Here I finally come to the Point. Where is Man in your order'd List? We, as one of God's Creatures, are sure to be part of your Great Order. Yet are we not different? We Love, and in divers Manners.

I have a young Nephew John, not yet grown, and I Love him, an Uncle's love for his Nephew. He is now my only Family, for his Parents, my dear Sister and her Husband, are both gone. Is the Love I have for the Boy the same as a Man has for his own Son? Can one be set higher than another, when it is All that I have? Were I to marry soon, would the Love I have for my Wife be different than if I had marry'd young? Is Love of God the only Love that matters?

I ask too many Questions.

If you see fit to humour and old Man and his Curiosity, you are truly a generous Soul.

Yours, etc.,
Thos Fairchild

1736

Inside the church, Carl found little beyond Fairchild's name on the list of sermons, as John Bacon had described.

Outside, among the flowers that he had loved, was a stone dedicated to Fairchild.

There being no bench, Carl made a seat for himself on the grass. He took the pack of letters out of his bag, keeping the newest and replacing the rest. He cracked the seal and unfolded it, enjoying and fearing the feeling of reading his own letter, as if it were he who had died.

1732

Dear Sir,

I look forward to making your Acquaintance and to the Feast you describe.

Your letter has found me, after many Travels, Home again after an expedition to study the Flora of Lapland. Yet it has shot straight to my Heart and Soul. For while it is a Prodigious Thing, begging your pardon to speak about my Projekt in such a manner, it is an even Greater Thing to understand the will of God as it relates to Man, and, especially, as it has to do with that great Thing Love.

I had not consider'd the Question until I receiv'd your Correspondence. I believe that a Man may write on Paper what he cannot utter in the hearing of another. A Confessional of the Soul, from one to another, with God listening in, of course. Is it not God who creat'd us all? And so to order God's creations is to understand the Creator. It is clear, then, that to examine Love is to understand Man and, above all, God, as well.

I am thinking on it.

Yours,

CL

1717

The carnation wilted. Its petals withered and dropped, indicating that it was time.

Thomas harvested the seeds and placed some into a paper twist that he labelled clearly. The others he planted. And then he waited some more.

Thomas took possession of a new *Primula auricula*, a striking specimen with a golden centre, with plans to pass it on to Mr. Wade, who would appreciate its addition to the small theatre at the side of his house.

At a fete, Thomas danced with Rebecca Wade. She danced with every available young man, her mother at her heels.

The seeds sent up their first green tendrils.

At a coffee house, Thomas met with Mr. Wade and discussed future designs for the weaver's new silks.

Soon, the little tendrils thickened and grew, and buds appeared at the tips.

Thomas hired an illustrator to begin a set of drawings of the carnations and Sweet Williams. But they could not be completed until the new plant flowered. Rebecca would wear her father's silks, designed by her greatest admirer.

The little plant bloomed. Its flowers were a deep colour, nearly red, with petal edges that mimicked the trimmings of a lady's gown, inviting admirers.

It had no smell.

When the new drawings were finished, Thomas sent them to Mr. Wade, but by that time the fashion for bizarre silks had waned.

The new flowers wilted and died.

And left behind no seeds.

The plant was sterile.

Meanwhile, Rebecca Wade's father announced her betrothal.

Thomas wrote up his findings and took them along with a pressing of the plant to a meeting with his fellow gardeners. From there he went to the Royal Society.

They named the plant Fairchild's Mule.
Some called it his greatest creation.
He called it his greatest folly.

1736

...I understand from your Nephew that you came to regret the Mule, in particular your role in its Creation, believing that you had defy'd God's Law.

The Housekeeper has set out my Supper. Unaware of our Friendship, she is under the Impression that I dine alone. I call you Friend I spite of the Situation that separates us, and this simple Lamb pie, like that you ate when you first heard my Name, shall be our Feast.

After long consideration, I conclude that it cannot be list'd, rank'd, or organis'd in any manner. We may do so to those things that do not change from one to the next. A Deer now is the same as a Deer in my Grandsire's time, as are your Pinks, simple Sparrows, and Oak Trees. But Love–

One can only order those Things which One can see, touch, smell, taste. We may trust our Senses.

Ah, but is Love not a Sense, you ask?

No, I answer.

But, you argue, what of the various Types of Love? A Man's love for his fellows, for his Wife, for his God. Are they not different?

I will shake my head. They may be different. No, listen to my point. They may be different, yet they are all One Thing. They are all a Deer or a Pink, a Sparrow, an Oak.

Yes, you say loudly and bang your fist on the table. Do not upset the Wine, I will say and laugh. It is rather Good and I would enjoy it all this Night.

Yes, you say, they are all One Thing, but there are Deer here in our Land that are different to those in other Lands. The same with Love.

Can you see the Deer? I ask, and you nod. Can you see the Love? I ask. And you stop, gesticulate, sip from your glass. And, finally, shake your head.

I win the Point. Now let me win the Battle:

As a Natural Philosopher, I must only trust that which is observable, which does not alter. Turmoil alters Harmony, if I may be poetic. And Love is, if nothing else, Disorder. Chaos of the heart, the senses, your very Being, whether it is the Love you had for young John, or that, I suspect, you had for a Woman you did not marry, or even the Love I am feeling for this Wine. Ah, would that you were here. The Housekeeper would be jealous of the debate, for it would be as delicious as this meal.

So, sir, Thomas, my Friend, do not regret the Mule. The Materials for its Creation—and your idea to cross those two humble Blooms—are traceable to God. But let us leave some Mystery. Let us understand what is possible to understand, but not fight to know all of it. Let us leave something of Chaos so that we may stay Men of the Earth and not become like God. To do so would be the true Folly.

Your most humble Servant who wishes you were here, etc.,

CL

AFTERWORD

CRUDELY SPEAKING, science is about describing and defining the universe, finding nature's laws and setting them down. But what happens when it fails? What if nature resists and won't be constrained? What about the things that won't fit? These are questions *Irregularity* raises, challenging today's authors to create stories inspired by people's systematic, and not so systematic, attempts to classify, understand and impose order on the world.

Irregularity has been published to coincide with a major exhibition, *Ships, Clocks & Stars: The Quest for Longitude* at the National Maritime Museum, Greenwich. It's a good match, since the age-old challenge of finding longitude (east-west position) at sea was all about finding regularity and the frustrations of nature's evident irregularities. Like this book, *Ships, Clocks & Stars* tells a story that spans the globe, taking visitors from the coffee-houses of London to the shores of the Pacific.

For many, the quest for longitude was itself the stuff of fiction, and the imagination that inspires *Irregularity* echoes that of the men (and sometimes women) who pursued that quest. In the popular mind, it became a fool's errand, like the search for eternal life or perpetual motion. The Longitude Act of 1714 sought to change the game, however, by offering life-changing rewards for solutions that worked. Yet, after twenty years, one author found that although the Act had encouraged many to bend their thoughts to the problem, nothing worthwhile had come from it, just ideas like Mr Jackson's "monstrous Machine" and John Bates's "Chimaera's in his Brain". When solutions did emerge in the 1750s, they were all about regularity. Carpenter-turned-clock-maker John Harrison created a sea-watch that could keep regular time on a pitching and rolling ship. And the Moon's motion – that most irregular of phenomena – was pinned down in the service of a complementary astronomical method.

For this volume, authors were asked for stories inspired by the history of science from the seventeenth to the mid-nineteenth centuries. This encompassed the Longitude Act and the events that followed, with the longer timeframe taking in everything from the foundation of the Royal Society in 1660, through the Enlightenment and Industrial Revolution, to the publication of Charles Darwin's *On the Origin of Species* (1859). It was an extraordinary period that saw important institutions created, amazing inventions, the harnessing of new power sources, countless discoveries and a tireless drive to classify almost everything.

But there is a danger in hindsight. Science does not progress through a simple succession of ideas and inventions. False leads abound, and the theories and inventions that now look to have been the clear winners were not so obvious at the time, when alternative lines of attack showed equal promise. This is certainly true of the longitude story. Had many of the archives not survived, the successes of the 1760s would have concealed the failures, dead ends and might-have-beens along the way. These provide their own fascinating tales. As Nick Harkaway's framing story to this volume says, "It did not matter to me if each and every one was full of provable falsehoods and stupidities: any text is an image of the mind, and any mind is worthy of attention." Nor should we forget that the greatest minds could also make mistakes, reach an impasse. The precocious polymath and Secretary of the Board of Longitude, Thomas Young, noted that even Isaac Newton "was liable to err". Indeed, one of those failures concerned longitude. Trying to model the Moon's motions caused Newton's head to ache, he said. The solution fell to his successors, including Tobias Mayer, a German astronomer who had never seen the sea.

The history of science clearly offers rich territory for the imagination. In *Irregularity* it has inspired stories about people's efforts, successful and unsuccessful, to know the world better and make it comprehensible, for tales about the things that prove unknowable, and the tension between order and chaos. The result is a wonderfully eclectic mix that asks questions about the boundaries of science and what we can know. But it is more than just entertainment; writing and reading fiction can help us interpret the past and come closer to it. Like all writers, historians need imagination to draw together the papers in archives and objects in museums to tell their stories. Without it, history would be little more than lists of dates and facts. It was in the imagination too that longitude solutions and other schemes came into being. Some got no further than that; others became theories and technologies that still define our understanding of nature, and survive in laboratories and museums as evidence of the past.

So *Irregularity*'s stories can help us think about humanity's desire to describe the universe, and the ways in which nature complies with, and resists, that ambition. Some of them offer a glimpse of the past as we think it was, others bend time and space to create worlds that can only be imagined. Not bound by strict historical or scientific realism, they conjure up dinosaur automata, Restoration-era black holes, uncatchable chimera and prophetic spiders. Yet when compared to the quest for longitude, in which impossible schemes were discussed in all seriousness and the line between madness and genius felt precariously narrow, even these fictions can seem remarkably close to reality.

Many of *Irregularity*'s tales dwell on the urge to classify the world, to name and describe its parts, exemplified by the Swedish botanist, Carl Linnaeus, whose *Systema Naturae* (1735) set out his famous taxonomic system. But what of its limitations? "Let us understand what is possible to understand, but not fight to know all of it", Linnaeus himself is moved to write in Tiffani Angus's tale, "Fairchild's Folly", which asks whether science can understand love. Henrietta Rose-Innes's "Animalia Paradoxa" presents a creature that cannot be captured, whether by classifier or hunter. And classification becomes a terrible power in E. J. Swift's "The Spiders of Stockholm", where the knowledge of true names can suck mystery and power from the world.

Manipulating nature, making it regular and exploiting its power also runs throughout. Claire North's "The Voyage of the *Basset*" has Charles Darwin sent to change the climate for imperial ends, while the secrets of the winds are mapped and tamed by William Dampier in Rose Biggin's "A Game Proposition". Yet to meddle in this way is to court disaster; experiments can go wrong and overwhelm their creators. M. Suddain morphs the Great Fire of London into a consuming vortex in "The Darkness", as Restoration natural philosophers treat nature as a toy and lose control. Roger Luckhurst offers something much more unsettling in "Circulation" – sinister powers unlocked by an infernal machine. Drawing on the longitude story, James Smythe's "The Last Escapement" has one of John Harrison's rivals literally give his all for his invention in a tale that echoes eighteenth-century debates about the fine line between genius and madness.

Smythe's clock-maker is pursuing tantalising financial rewards. In a similar vein, Simon Guerrier's "An Experiment in the Formulae Thought" has a Victorian scientist cry, "Lay down the gauntlet and we shall deliver.

If only we have the funds!" It's a call that could equally have come from Charles Babbage or any number of longitude projectors, although the results might have been less catastrophic than Guerrier's account of a misfiring initiative in the public understanding of science.

These concerns about science's impact seem perfectly in tune with the Romantic sensibilities of the period in which many of *Irregularity*'s stories are set. From the late eighteenth century onwards, writers like William Blake and William Wordsworth professed an ambivalence towards science and poked at its limitations. By then there was already a long literary tradition that made fun of foolish truth-seekers, found in satirical plays like Thomas Shadwell's *The Virtuoso* (1676). Romantic authors took the critique further, worrying that science's mechanistic explanations constrained the universe, denying individuality and the possibility of coming to a deeper understanding of the world through imagination and emotional experience. Some foresaw great danger, as was famously explored in Mary Shelley's *Frankenstein, or The Modern Prometheus* (1818). Shelley's has become a defining image: the man of science who over-reaches and leads to his own and others' destruction, yet who is to be admired for his tireless quest to understand the absolutes of life and death. It's an image that courses through *Irregularity*'s veins.

There are other influences too. Guerrier's tale of dinosaurs on the loose in England's capital has an echo of Charles Dickens' opening to *Bleak House* (1852-53), which evokes a London so bogged down in mud that one can imagine a Megalosaurus, "waddling like an elephantine lizard up Holborn-Hill". Dickens created other creatures out of time for Ebenezer Scrooge's life-changing journeys in *A Christmas Carol* (1843). Time travel gained a technological medium in Edward Page Mitchell's *The Clock That Went Backwards* (1881) and H. G. Wells' *The Time Machine* (1895). Theirs is a rich legacy. In this volume, Kim Curran speculates on what might have been if Emilie du Châtelet, "A Woman out of Time", had lived in an age that did not constrain women of scientific persuasion. The story also brings to life the forces that kept her imagination in check. In a very different tale, Adam Roberts conjures up a murderous meeting between Isaac Newton and a time-travelling Robert Boyle, struck by Newton's resemblance to Brian May.

A more recent legacy comes through the literature of steampunk, which explores the possibility of technology rather than people out of time. One of that genre's seminal works, Bruce Sterling and William Gibson's *The Difference Engine* (1990), describes a world in which Charles Babbage's calculating engines have propelled Victorian society into a pre-electrical information age. In *Irregularity*, steam- and coal-powered automata designed by Ada Lovelace and Restoration sky ships draw freely on this rich genre.

Above all, people are the heart of *Irregularity*, with all their ambitions, fears and failings. When primal fears are awakened, Archie Black's "Footprint" reveals, even the most regular of minds can act irregularly. All too human traits – vanity, jealousy, curiosity, morality – infuse the practice of science in *Irregularity*'s tales just as they do in reality. As Richard de Nooy reminds us in "The Heart of Aris Kindt", for example, it is all too easy to turn a blind eye to the unexpected or the inexplicable, weaving a tale in which the pomposity of the scientific elite is punctured.

By setting human stories against the vast scope of scientific thought and technological progress, *Irregularity* helps us remember the countless people caught up in the quest for longitude and other great scientific challenges.

Their personalities can be lost in the archives, but can be re-found by applying imagination to history. As Mary Shelley wrote in the introduction to a new edition of *Frankenstein* in 1831, "Invention consists in the capacity of seizing on the capabilities of a subject, and in the power of moulding and fashioning ideas suggested to it." Her words fit this volume perfectly.

Richard Dunn and Sophie Waring
May 2014

CONTRIBUTORS

TIFFANI ANGUS is an ex-pat PhD Creative Writing student in Cambridge, finishing up her dissertation and an historic fantasy novel set over 400 years in an English country-house garden. She is a graduate of Clarion 2009 and has published fantasy, horror and erotica stories. When not languishing under fluorescent lights writing or teaching writing, she can be found geeking out in gardens that other people have planted.

ROSE BIGGIN writes plays, stories, and lists. She has a PhD in Drama from the University of Exeter, and lives on the same street as a wild peacock who sometimes eats out of her hand. Her short fiction has appeared in *Pandemonium: The Rite of Spring* (Jurassic London) and *The Colour of Life and Other Stories* (Retreat West); her plays include *Sour Nothings* (Tommyfield, London Kennington), *Victor Frankenstein* (King's Arms Theatre, Salford) and *The Very Thought*, a one-woman show about loneliness, love and pole dancing (Bike Shed Theatre, Exeter). Once at the Edinburgh Fringe she won a poetry slam by accident, with a retelling of the Iliad she'll do on request.

ARCHIE BLACK lives and works in London. Her published fiction includes stories about pigeons, bugs, fearsome maiden aunts, secret agents, Lovecraftian monsters and serial killers.

KIM CURRAN is the award-nominated author of books for young adults, including *Shift, Control, Delete* and *Glaze*. She studied Philosophy & Literature at university with the plan of being paid big bucks to think deep thoughts. While that never quite worked out, she *did* land a job as a junior copywriter. She's worked in advertising ever since. She is a mentor at the Ministry of Stories and for the WoMentoring Project. And lives in London with her husband and too many books.

RICHARD DE NOOY grew up in Johannesburg, but has lived in Amsterdam for more than 25 years. He worked as a crockery salesman, data typist, lab assistant, bouncer, cartoonist and translator, all of which prepared him for his career as a novelist. He writes in both English and Dutch. His first novel, *Six Fang Marks and a Tetanus Shot*, won the University of Johannesburg Prize for Best First Book in 2008. He has published two further acclaimed novels (in English and Dutch) since then: *The Big Stick* (2012) and *The Unsaid* (2014).

RICHARD DUNN is Senior Curator and Head of Science and Technology at Royal Museums Greenwich. He is currently engaged on a research project, "The Board of Longitude 1714-1828: Science, Innovation and Empire in the Georgian World", a collaboration between Royal Museums Greenwich and the Department of History and Philosophy of Science, University of Cambridge, funded by the Arts and Humanities Research Council. His publications include *The Telescope: A Short History* (2009) and *Finding Longitude* (2014, with Rebekah Higgitt).

SIMON GUERRIER created and wrote the science-fiction series *Graceless*, broadcast on Radio 4 Extra. He's also written *Blake's 7* (again forRadio 4 Extra) and over 40 audio plays for Big Finish Productions, including *Doctor Who*. He's currently producing a documentary for Radio 3 about Oliver Cromwell's wife and writing poo jokes for *Horrible Histories* magazine.

HOWARD HARDIMAN is the creator of the comics *Badger* and *The Lengths*. He has recently completed a year-long artist residency which culminated in his first major exhibition, *Line & Shade*. He has a studio on the Isle of Wight where he draws, makes oil paintings and vector images for exhibitions, commissions and books.

NICK HARKAWAY won the Oxfam Emerging Writers Prize at the Hay Festival in 2012. He was also awarded The Kitschies' Red Tentacle (for the year's most intelligent, interesting and progressive novel with speculative elements). He is the author of three novels – *Tigerman*, *Angelmaker* and *The Gone-Away World* – and a non-fiction book about technology and human social and political agency called *The Blind Giant*. Before he began writing novels he was a notably unsuccessful screenwriter and a truly hopeless martial artist. He likes red wine, deckled edges and most of Italy, and lives in London with his wife and two children.

ROGER LUCKHURST usually writes cultural histories of supernatural things, such as *The Invention of Telepathy* and *The Mummy's Curse: A True History of a Dark Fantasy*. His history of the zombie appears from Reaktion Press in 2015. He comes out at night, mostly, to teach Gothic literature at Birkbeck College, University of London.

CLAIRE NORTH is a pseudonym for Kate Griffin, who is actually Catherine Webb. All of these people are a London-based, fantasy and science fiction writer with a fondness for urban wonders and Thai food, who also works as a theatre lighting designer.

GARY NORTHFIELD has been writing and drawing childrens comics for over ten years. Famous for his crazy (and creator-owned!) *Beano* character, Derek the Sheep, Gary has also worked for *The Dandy, Horrible Histories Magazine, Horrible Science Magazine* and *The Magical World of Roald Dahl.* He currently beavers away on strips for *The Phoenix* and *National Geographic Kids.* His first graphic novel, *Teenytinysaurs* is available from Walker Children's Books and his next, *Julius Zebra*, will be published in 2015.

ADAM ROBERTS was born two-thirds of the way through the last century. He is a writer of science fiction, and a professor of nineteenth-century literature, and he lives a little way west of London. His most recent novels are *Jack Glass (2013)*, *Twenty Trillion Leagues Under the Sea* (2014, with Mahendra Singh) and *Bête* (2014).

HENRIETTA ROSE-INNES is a writer based in Cape Town. Her most recent novel, *Nineveh*, was published in South Africa in 2011, following a short-story collection, *Homing* (2010), and two earlier novels: *Shark's Egg* (2000) and *The Rock Alphabet* (2004). A new novel, *Green Lion*, which deals partially with species loss, will be published in early2015. Henrietta's is the recipient of the Caine Prize for African Writing and the South African PEN Literary Award, and in 2012, her short story 'Sanctuary' took second place in the BBC International Short Story Competition.

JAMES SMYTHE is the author of *The Testimony, The Explorer, The Echo, No Harm Can Come to a Good Man* and *The Machine. The Testimony* was the winner of the Wales Book of the Year Fiction Award and *The Machine* was a finalist for both the Arthur C. Clarke Award and The Kitschies. He has written narratives for video games and teaches Creative Writing.

MATT SUDDAIN is a journalist and author who has written for *Sunday, The Guardian, McSweeney's, Vice, Five Dials, Opium, BBQ Aficionado, Popular Tree, The Singular Gentleman, Caravan & UFO, Fancier Financier* and *The Onion*. Several of these publications do not exist. His first novel, *Theatre of the Gods*, was published by Jonathan Cape in June 2013.

E.J. SWIFT is the author of The Osiris Project trilogy: *Osiris, Cataveiro*, and *Tamaruq*. Her short fiction has been published in *Interzone* magazine and appears in anthologies from Salt Publishing, Jurassic London and NewCon Press. She was shortlisted for a 2013 BSFA Award in the short fiction category for her story "Saga's Children", from *The Lowest Heaven*.

SOPHIE WARING is completing a PhD on the Board of Longitude, focusing on its role in the transformation of the organisation of science in the early nineteenth century, at the Department of History and Philosophy of Science, Cambridge and Royal Museums

Greenwich, as part of the research project, "The Board of Longitude 1714-1828: Science, Innovation and Empire in the Georgian World".

JARED SHURIN is a trained BBQ judge.

All the images within this book are by Gary Northfield, and are reinterpretations of original art from the collection of the National Maritime Museum, part of Royal Museums Greenwich:

The typefaces used in this book are Igino Marini's careful reproductions of the seventeenth century Fell Types. The body is English Roman and the titles are in French Canon.

I would like to thank the cast of irregulars who made this book possible: David Bailey, Robin Hermann, Rebecca Nuotio, Andrew Mills, Sara Wajid, Sophie Waring and Anne C. Perry. It helps having the world's best editor available for advice.

Irregularity is Jurassic London's third collaboration with the generous team at Royal Museums Greenwich, and I am especially grateful to Richard Dunn and Marek Kukula for their vision, imagination and patience. As Nevil Maskelyne, the fifth Astronomer Royal and Fellow of the Royal Society, famously described his lunar distance method, "it helps to have friends in high places".

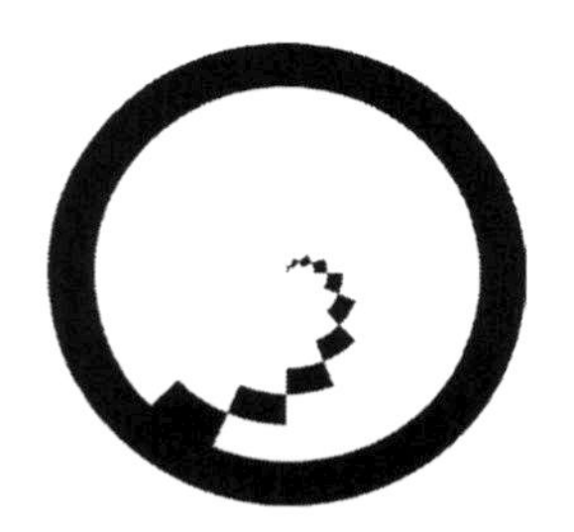

From: root@podolsky.ch
To: Shurin, Jared
Re: Noel "diary" comment

Dear Jared,

I see why you have to give space to this document, of course. The merest sniff of time travel, and the inevitable piffle about a grandfather paradox (in this case, the book that exists in a loop) is always going to be news. Does that culture of infotainment really have to be the driver for a reputable journal these days? I suppose perhaps it does.

What I find difficult, as you no doubt you anticipated, is the way in which this particular hoax seems to be targeted at me personally. I am the custodian of the Noel papers and it's a matter of public record that I derive my genetic map from a historical sample thought to have come from Augusta Noel. And I do also, for completeness, hold the title of librarian here at the Podolsky Energy Institute – though the actual custodianship is handled by trained people while I get on with the physics. I won't belabour the obvious, I'll just note that since the espionage investigation in the 1960s and Podolsky's subsequent exoneration, people here have a profound loathing for sensation. I do, of course, look after an eclectic collection that is organised on an intuitive, non-linear basis according to the wishes of the original collector, so I can not only do duty as the end product of the events in this little fiction, I may even be intended to be its instigator as well - though by what ridiculous sequence of inversions I am supposed to end up as the mother of my own Victorian progenitor, married to some radical libertine blowhard, I cannot begin to imagine. I take offense at the idea! But that's a side issue. The point is that the whole thing is so wrong-headed! Yes, yes, I know, the theory must yield to the empirical evidence, but this isn't evidence - it's baloney. Let me count the ways:

1. Physical time travel is impossible. There is no way to send a macro-scale object back in time. Information, maybe, but a book? No. It's not just difficult, it's bad physics.
2. Similarly, there can never be a grandfather paradox. It is mechanically prohibited. If you alter the past, the timeline branches and never leads to your version of events. You come by definition from a different Universe where you didn't tinker. If we're talking about silly ideas, incidentally, that always gives me the heebie jeebies because it makes me imagine that Parallel-Me is watching and has tinkered with my timeline in preparation for coming here and taking my place. Although what Parallel-Me could hope to gain

from that I have no idea. Perhaps tomorrow I'm going to win the lottery.

3. If I am being cast in the role of "mother", I'm supposedly going to go back to the Victorian period and have a child who is genetically identical to myself. How am I going to achieve that? Am I taking a PCR machine? Perhaps an entire lab and some biomedical specialists? If I do that, chances are the changes I'll inflict on the timeline are going to be a bit more notable than a book and a proto-feminist daughter.
4. WHY? What could possibly motivate me to do any of this? A desire for a simpler life of vaccinated pseudo-transtemporal transuniversal meddling? Some sort of High Science concept pop art? Or maybe a religious obedience to the document itself, if you like predestination cheap and dirty?

I looked it up. There is not, and never was, a book called "Irregularity". No such project has, in so far as anyone in the publishing world can tell me, ever been contemplated. Half the writers listed are characters in novels, from those endlessly annoying books about books. The name of the man who is supposed to have found this new journal of Noel's, "Nicholas Harkaway" is listed twice on Google, and both men are deceased. Neither of them was ever a novelist. I don't like Occam's Razor very much – I think it's lazy to imagine the world as tending to the simple – but honestly: either this is an eruption into our Universe from another one with the aim of creating an apparently impossible situation to ends which must be at best obscure, or the whole thing is a fiction of the most incomplete sort. I think if you're going to go ahead with the publication, you should allow me the right of reply. Print this email in its entirety, if you like, or I'll send you something more fit-for-purpose tomorrow. I'd do it now, but I'm already late for the thing at CERN and I really need a shower before I go. I'm getting a tour of the ring – they have a monorail, apparently – and I'm told it's sensible shoes because afterwards we're going to get plastered on white sangria and dance on the accelerator housing.

I won't ask you to put this aside. Just think, please, about whether it's really a story.

Yours in science and in an absolutely towering rage – but not with you, obviously -

Izzy Millbank

Printed in Great Britain
by Amazon.co.uk, Ltd.,
Marston Gate.